Fall

Fall

The Return to the Temple, Book Two

Grady L. Owens

Library of Congress Control Number:		2021906654
ISBN:	Hardcover	978-1-6641-6635-6
	Softcover	978-1-6641-6634-9
	eBook	978-1-6641-6633-2

Print information available on the last page.

Rev. date: 03/31/2021

To order additional copies of this book, contact:

Xlibris

844-714-8691

www.Xlibris.com

Orders@Xlibris.com

778820

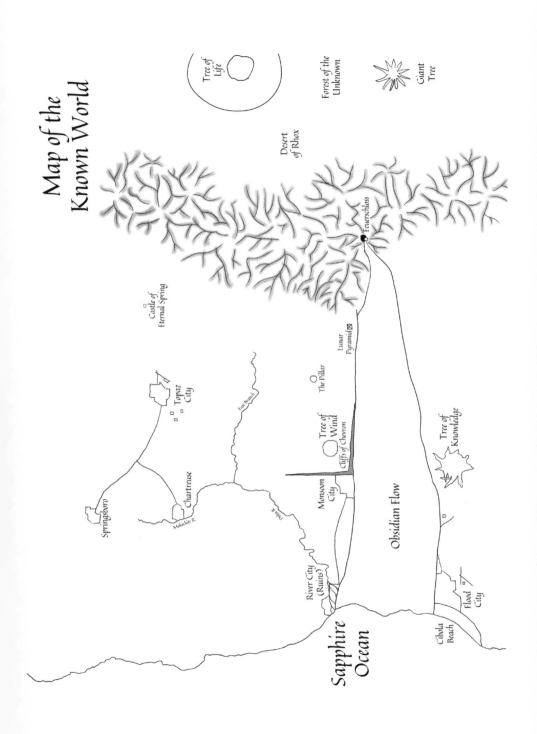

Map of the
Known World

Tree of
Life

Forest of the
Unknown

Giant
Tree

Desert
of Rhox

Feuerschloss

Castle of
Eternal Spring

Lunar Pyramid ⊠

The Pillar

Topaz
City

East Branch

Tree of
Wind

Cliffs of Chevron

Springsboro

Chartreuse

Malachite R.

India R.

Monsoon
City

Obsidian Flow

Tree of
Knowledge

River City
(Ruins)

Sapphire
Ocean

Cibola
Beach

Flood
City

Contents

PROLOGUE

FIVE YEARS HAD passed since that awful day. For Carlos, it was simultaneously the farthest and most dear thought in this moment. He had seen the glow he presently witnessed only once before, after all. His smile belied his past experience; truly, in this moment, he could share in his wife's joy at the successful birth of her first son. The babe, worn out by its earlier screaming, now rested against her breast, hiding his face from the light.

The new mother turned her attention from her son to face him. "Thank you, Carlos, thank you for . . . for everything. For staying with me, for loving me, and now—"

He wiped the developing tear from her eye. "Daelia darling, you know I love you more than the summer rain upon an undisturbed meadow. We both wanted this. I'm just so happy it worked out."

The elven woman returned her gaze to the child cradled in her arms, swallowing down a soft sob. "This time, you mean."

Carlos averted his eyes, the words seeming to cut into his very soul. "Daelia, you know— That's past. Can't we forget about it, please? Especially on this wonderful occasion." A shrill cry returned his attention to his family; the baby had awoken and was hungry. The mother carefully maneuvered around her gown, bringing the child to suckle.

"I know, dear. I'm sorry. You know I only want the very best for all of us. I speak out of worry."

The cloud cover outside parted for a brief instant, the sun casting shadows of wind-blown trees upon the tiny room's yellowing window curtain. Carlos sniffed, returning his finger to his wife's cheek, tenderly stroking the soft flesh. "I know you didn't mean anything by it, honey. And don't worry, I will ensure that we will live happily from now on. We'll raise him together into a strong, strapping, confident lad, I'm sure."

She nodded, sniffling a little herself. "Well, such a strong lad should have a strong name, don't you agree?" The elf winked at her husband, who seemed a little taken aback.

"Wait, you mean . . . are you sure? Will you be happy with that?"

"Absolutely, dear. We have to raise him together, after all. What good would it be if we couldn't compromise with a smile for each other every once in a while?"

"I just don't want it to be a smile holding back sadness, Daelia." He grasped her lesser-supporting hand. "Are you sure?"

She simply nodded. "I know how much he meant to you, how much she meant to you. I only hope we can all live together as you would have."

Carlos trembled visibly, his hand releasing hers to caress his newborn son's scalp. "Son, I want to be the best father I can be for you. I failed my firstborn, but I shall not with you. This in mind, I bestow upon you the name he had, the name we chose for him out of hope. May it protect you when we no longer can, my sweet Angelo."

1

Stripped

THE ROAD'S END Casino had not seen such patronage in some time; a body at most every slot, all tables occupied by some game or other, the main room was quite a sea of persons to try and sort through. Alas, unfortunately for Justin, that is precisely what he was attempting. The member of the clan of Bailey stood in the doorway to one of the many stairwells in the building, gaze wandering in awe over the crowd displayed before him. He knew his half-elf companion's favored dealer, but that only made the odds of finding him minimally better. "I need to put a bell on the boy, I swear ..." The wizard was well aware that the base noise level was far too high to be able to hear something as subtle as a bell under normal circumstances, but at least he could attempt to augment his hearing to the necessary frequency.

"Justin!" A familiar voice rang over the crowd from a less familiar blackjack table; the mage never would have guessed the swordsman might have chosen the location this time.

"Angelo, I thought you didn't enjoy blackjack." Justin managed to part the crowd with some ease; carrying a large implement that could easily be used to beat a body to within an inch of life generally made it easier to pass through even dense groups.

"You know I like to change it up every once in a while." Angelo looked at his hand and knocked on the table. "Besides, does it matter? So long as I provide a show, Mr. Kane doesn't care."

"That's Don Kane." Justin continued pushing his way through the thrall around the half-elf. "Don't let him hear you call him that." He sniffed the air above his companion. "Dammit, Angelo, have you been drinking again?"

The gambler turned to the elf, an astonished look on his face. "And what makes you think the stench of alcohol is on *my* breath? There are plenty of other patrons around. Any of them could have easily had a few drinks."

"I'm sorry," Justin stated as he scanned the table for glassware, "I just worry, you know that."

"Your cards, gentlemen."

Angelo turned back to his cards, waiting for the other players to show. His visible cards, a jack of clubs and the ace of diamonds he'd just been dealt, would otherwise indicate an unlucky hand for the half-elf, but the crowd knew better. One by one, the hands were revealed: a nineteen, an eighteen, and a twenty. Angelo exchanged a glance with the dealer, who simply nodded once. The young swordsman picked up his final card toward himself, laying it down smoothly—a king of hearts. The crowd surrounding the table erupted in applause, not even waiting for the dealer to show his own eighteen. "Well I'm clean now, Justin. You don't have to worry about anything. Besides, you're beginning to sound like my lover."

"Now, Angelo, there's no need for that kind of talk. I said I was sorry, okay?" The mage sighed. "Look, I'm going to step outside, get some air now that I know where you are. Don't wait up."

"Now you're fucking with me."

"You know it." The two exchanged a smile. "I'll see you in a bit, I'm sure."

Angelo waited until the mage's back was lost in the swarm of people, then called over a server who had been paying particular attention to the table. Whispering in the man's ear, he handed him a hip flask that had been hidden in his cloak. "Whiskey, if you would please."

Justin pushed open the gilded double doors at the front of the casino and took a deep breath, savoring the cool night air. Taking a few steps into what remained of the strip, he surveyed the damage as he always did. He knew witnessing such a disaster firsthand was rare enough but being something of the direct cause was always a supremely sobering realization.

There was a reason Road's End was seeing so much patronage— much of the rest of the main strip had been decimated by the igneous flow Asmodeious unleashed upon the earth in an attempt to kill him and Angelo. All that remained of Monsoon City south of a point was a sheet of obsidian, a glassy sheen of black against the deep navy of the evening sky. The skyline of Flood City, a small line of light in the distance, was nevertheless visible now, something that had been impossible with the jungle that had inhabited the locale previously.

This did not make the course between the two cities easier to traverse in the slightest; conversely, the route was now quite perilous, with the threats of scorching heat, broken shards of glass-like material scattered across the otherwise open field, and an obscene lack of water making travel nigh impossible.

Justin sighed, leaning his back against the tectonic mass. The dikes that had previously held back at least this side of the flow had all but eroded away at this point; the mage could tell the Revered had been in full damage control mode since the incident, the near constant storms' resultant gray slab of sky often painting the landscape a monochromatic dreary, a somber reminder in its own way of the many who lost their lives in the eruption. They were truly lucky to have survived, he knew; if there had not been someone watching out for them, they would have been toasted.

* * *

"Angelo!" Justin shouted up the hill toward his sudden companion. "Can you not run any faster!?"

The half-elf yelled back down at the mage. "I'd love to, but I'm not used to running through this dense an undergrowth!"

"Angelo, for fuck's sake, the damn lava flow is going to fry us if you don't hurry up!"

"Do you honestly think I don't know that!? Here, let me—" Angelo, still running, reached down and undid his belt, letting the leather strap fall to the ground, complete with his longsword. "Oh, that's much better."

"Angelo!"

"Keep your pants on, wizard! I'm going as—" He paused to catch his breath. "Look, can we just shut up and run?"

"Capital idea."

The pair sprinted down the overgrown hill away from the deep red glow that relentlessly pursued them. Having lost its cohesive form as Pyror, the flow was nothing more than an immense wall of molten rock with a hefty helping of momentum behind it. The waves of heat radiating from the thing scorched trees many feet in front of it, rendering them dry and lifeless seconds before they were consumed by the flow anyway.

Justin and Angelo both knew it was barreling toward them much faster than either of them were capable of running even if they hadn't been encumbered by the forest's lack of exploration; this was little consolation, and the snags and tears the various thorns and thistles rendered through their clothing only served to compound a mild frustration upon that mortal anxiety. Angelo had already broken into a hearty sweat, and Justin was definitely feeling the heat as well.

As they had begun running away from Feuerschloss, Justin could make out the cliff that lined the Enchanted Rainforest in the distance. At first, the elf reasoned they might be safe if they could manage to get on top of it; however, as they continued to run and their view of the outcrop became obstructed by the thickening trees, it became increasingly obvious that seeking it out would prove to be a valueless venture. Besides, with as fast as the lava was moving toward them, they didn't stand a chance of even getting close to approaching that precipice before the stuff would cook them alive.

Angelo's lungs began to burn with more than just the intense stench of brimstone, inhaling bitter iron with each ragged breath. Justin wasn't in much better shape, his legs stabbed with the daggers of overexertion. Neither was in a position to complain about their physical trivialities, and their sharp wheezing trying to pump oxygen through their weakening extremities made attempting such impossible anyway.

So it was that when they both slammed headlong into a wall that had not been there a second before, their bodies flipped the breaker and both passed out.

2

Catastrophe

*W*HAM! *THUD.* "SHIT."
Luna glanced over the duo now crumpled on the floor in the corner. It had been her intention to teleport them to her palace; however, she did not realize just how close to the wall she had set the arrival port. Mildly concerned, she stuck a pair of fingers beneath the half-elf's nose; sure enough, he was still breathing. They were merely unconscious and would probably walk away from this with a mild concussion at worst. Nothing too serious to worry about aside from perhaps the state of their clothing.

Taking advantage of the pair's passed-out state, Luna turned back to the monitor on which she had been tracking their progress; she'd chosen, along with Dryad, to not interfere with their quest but to watch from a distance should their intentions be what Salamandro warned. Dryad had long since left, but the elf had kept watch through the night; it had been a long twenty-four hours for her, but in spite of her mildly sleep-deprived state, she knew something was wrong when she saw the two blips haul ass away from Feuerschloss. Either they had succeeded in their purported mission, the Revered of Fire was dead and they were hoping to escape retribution, or something else had gone hideously wrong. She looked back over at the pair; certainly, the half-elf had been brazen and naïve, but neither seemed stupid enough to think they could just run away from the Revered.

And what of the others? There had been four originally; two humans had been accompanying these two. One of their blips disappeared very shortly before the other, and it wasn't long after that when these two apparently decided they needed to get out. They had to have died, she reasoned, there was no other way to destroy her tracking spell. So what killed them then? Certainly, Salamandro seemed like the kind who could be counted on to stop a threat on his life by any means necessary, but this still didn't seem right; something wasn't adding up here.

"Salamandro! Can you hear me? Salamandro, please respond." Luna attempted to call her new compatriot.

"Luna!" The elf sighed in relief; he was alive, at least. "What, uh, what makes you call?"

"Salamandro, what happened there? Are you alright?"

"Oh, uh, yeah! I'm fine! Nothing to see here!"

Nothing to see here? And what's with the sudden panic in his voice? Luna could understand if he might be winded, but that was not the sound behind his words. She checked that Justin and Angelo were still out cold, then ran to the far corner of the chamber and teleported herself to the Floating Edifice.

Emerging in her familiar meditation chamber, she walked forward across what seemed to be absolutely nothing; this room was cloaked in an elaborate illusion, the walls and floor completely invisible. To anyone stepping in for the first time, there might be an immediate sense of vertigo—the chamber appeared to be floating at a random point in a massive star field. Luna, however, having created the illusion, knew its secrets and capabilities. She moved straight for where she knew the door was in the wall and promptly exited.

The elf practically ran to the edge of the path outside the room, lying flat on her stomach and looking down through the clouds for any sign of where the building might be at that moment. To both the north and south, she could see a giant tree, which told her she was in one of two places; the steep cliffs around the northern one dictated that she was indeed hovering just south of Monsoon City. Miranda or Chevron had likely been the last ones in the Edifice; this was a great spot for either of them. Luckily, it proved to be an advantageous spot for Luna as well.

As the building was oriented, she could run down to the end of the hall opposite the rotunda and see out through the gap to where Feuerschloss was borne upon its volcano. What she beheld when she got there, however, was a sight the like of which few had witnessed in a long time and never to the extent that she experienced.

The sun, only just past midday, kept the glow to a minimum; the smoke threatening to blot out the star's light, however, was undeniable, thick and potent. She could make out a streak of red-orange flowing toward her, passing her palace even now, beginning to blacken toward the top of the mountain, smoke and flames clearly originating at its edges. She had some difficulty discerning what exactly was happening at first, and when she had finally stumbled upon the truth, she had a hard time accepting it; such a large volume of active volcanism could not possibly be spewing from the mountain, she reasoned—at least, not without some serious assistance. A dark suspicion crept into the back of her mind. As the flow continued to overtake the forest, however, she knew this was no time for throwing blame—something desperately needed to be done to stop this eruption before anyone or anything else was damaged.

"Revered! Every member of the Revered! Rhox, Miranda, Dryad, Chevron, Manas . . ." She hesitated for a second. "Salamandro! This is Luna. I am demanding an emergency meeting right now. Please meet me in the Floating Edifice immediately!"

*   *   *

It was an anxious half hour before an assembly was gathered. Dryad, anticipating such an event after the Inquisition, emerged almost immediately from his meditation chamber. Rhox and Chevron were close behind. As each arrived, Luna could do little but point as the swath cutting through the forests below grew, showing no sign of slowing. Once he recognized what exactly was going on, Rhox was particularly dumbfounded.

"By Her ghost . . ." The great half-orc shook his head in astonishment at the sheer magnitude of the eruption; however, as he realized what was happening to its source, that astonishment quickly melted into a panic. "No . . . No, no! Chevron! Quickly, we must douse the flow before it gets any farther!"

The dwarf turned in confusion to his companion. "Certainly this is bad, but what makes it so catastrophic that you feel you must order me around?"

Rhox grasped his friend by the shoulders, hefted him from the ground, and slammed his back into a nearby pillar in one swift motion, the normally stable column rocking from the impact. Chevron could only muster a surprised squeal. "Because, you great incorrigible ass, that flow is comprised primarily of silica. Given its obvious viscosity and temperature—or had you not noticed those?—it's going to solidify into obsidian!"

Chevron had clearly suffered a concussion from the sudden and intense impact, his head swaying about on his neck as though attached by a spring. "I-I don't understand . . ."

Dryad moved in to separate the two, the grateful dwarf taking a few very deep breaths as the diminutive creature, no more than half the height of the half-orc and a quarter his mass, tried to calm Rhox's rage. "Indeed, I don't believe any of us has the slightest clue what you're talking about. Would you care to explain?"

Miranda emerged from her chamber as Rhox took a deep breath, his sense of urgency not dulled in the slightest by his apparent relaxation. "You know glass, the stuff people have been using for a little while now to allow light into buildings?" The small gathering nodded collectively, Chevron rubbing the back of his head as his faculties returned to him. "Glass is made of melted-down sand, as you may or may not know. Sand has a high silica content but has a few other molecules in there that make cohesive crystallization rather difficult. What we are looking at here is a very hot, very quickly moving batch of nearly chemically pure glass."

"And it's headed for the alluvial fan between Monsoon City and Flood City!" Now it was the water elf's turn to panic. "Water flow will be disrupted! Trade and travel will be nearly impossible!"

Dryad nodded solemnly as he saw the elements of Rhox's concern come together. "And there's little chance vegetation will grow in such conditions. We have to stop this thing."

Rhox turned to the dwarf he'd physically assaulted moments before, extending a hand. "Look, I'm sorry, but could we please deal with this crisis?"

Chevron nodded, albeit a little slowly, and took his companion's offer, shaking his hand in agreement. "What do you need me to do?"

"We need to slow down its rate of flow. If—no, it's too late to stop it before it hits Monsoon City at this point. We must reduce the number of civilian casualties and try to save the land before it is overwhelmed."

The dwarf looked over his shoulder toward the red glow in the distance. "And you want me to . . . blow over it?"

Miranda nodded as she began to understand what the half-orc was demanding. "We need to cool the rock down. The quickest way to do that is to dissipate the heat by bringing in cooler air and allow the heat to evaporate through an additional medium." Even as she spoke, the elf was composing herself, preparing a storm to assist in the effort.

Rhox's face cracked in the slightest smile as obvious understandings facilitated his concern. "Luna, Dryad. Ah, and Manas, you can help with this too."

The gnome, just emerging from his own meditation chamber, rubbed an eye and held back a yawn. "What in blue blazes is going on up here?"

"Eruption, lots of lava, very bad." Manas was suddenly wide awake. "You three, I need you to facilitate the evacuation of Flood City."

The addressed trio nodded together, and Luna motioned them into a small circle. They sat on the cool marble floor, all three entering a deep meditative trance as they began reaching out to points of communication below.

While their presence was not widely known among the general populace, a group does not win the name of the Revered in a card game. Within the circles of wizards and their brethren, the lot was venerated. A multitude of stone figures in semi-public places of magical gathering, carved by the master hand of Rhox himself, stood by as a sort of avatar for the represented members, something of a regular reminder of those who keep the world in balance. A charm placed on the very rock by Chevron allowed the statues to "speak" on behalf of their subject. While this present use was not necessarily their intended one, it was certainly necessary.

One by one the statues within the city called out to any who might be in hearing range. "Get to higher ground. Gather as many other lives as you can safely. Do not waste time gathering possessions or artifacts of livelihood. A disaster is approaching and all who remain in the city risk death. We repeat: a disaster is approaching. Grab as many lives as possible and flee the city. Head north. Do not worry about possessions."

In Monsoon City, the heat was already palpable, the ground rumbling with aftershocks of the eruption. The flow had reached the cliffs and was following them west, straight toward the center of population. To the south, without such a well-defined boundary to rein in the liquid rock, the results were already devastating. So it was that, while panicked commands were being flung left and right, the Revered with the title of Salamandro emerged in the great hall.

"What's all this about an emergency meeting?"

"You!" Rhox pivoted and charged toward the tardy Diablo, his face a mask of pure rage. "The fuck did you do!?"

Miranda and Chevron broke their spells to grab the livid half-orc, barely stopping him in his tracks. Rhox easily managed to lift Miranda and moved as though he might fling her across the room but quickly came to his senses.

Diablo cowered. "What do you mean? What did I do?"

Rhox visibly calmed a bit, prompting Chevron and Miranda to let go and return to their previous post. The half-orc reached out and grabbed Diablo by his hair, dragging him to the eastern edge. "You got something to say about this?"

Manas, taking a momentary break to refocus himself for further evacuation alerts to Flood City, turned to his argumentative companion. "Rhox, now is not the time for this. The cities are fleeing and we need to try and minimize damage immediately. It would be super helpful if you could throw up some makeshift levees instead of threatening physical violence on our newest member."

Threatening? Diablo directed his hazy gaze at the other half-orc in the room.

Rhox glowered at the gnome, but he knew what he said was true; the sooner such embankments were put up, the less risk to life and livelihood there would be to those in the immediate path of the flow. He flung Diablo to the relative safety of the Edifice floor. "You will answer for this." Rhox ran to the southern edge of the room, leaping from the building.

Diablo shivered against the cool stone floor mostly out of fear. They were cleaning up Asmodeious' handiwork and every one of them blamed him for it. Asmodeious, Diablo knew what he was capable of; these magic-users he had no clue. Rhox had taken him by surprise to be sure, but honestly he'd grown used to that kind of treatment; no, what truly frightened him was that at that moment every single person in the room had reason to want him dead, and the only thing stopping them from attempting murder against their newest recruit was damage control on the mess below.

"Miranda, do you think there's anything I could do to help?"

The elf, mind clearly hundreds of miles away as she continued bringing water to the storm above the flow, shook her head. "Salamandro, I think it would be best if you sit this one out for right now. Your abilities cannot assist us in slowing or stopping this lava flow at this point, and unfortunately you're too new to have any of the means by which the others are communicating an evac plan to the cities." She shook her head again and peered down. "I'd prefer it if you kept out of our way for this."

"If that's what you think is best . . ." Diablo scooted himself over to a pillar and sat with his back to it, watching as the others endeavored to save as many lives as they could. Luna, Dryad, and Manas were now delegating evacuation orders to intermediaries in Flood City. Miranda and Chevron struggled to slow the rampaging lava and had by that point succeeded in cooling the easternmost portions to a crackling deep-black glass.

Rhox, meanwhile, was on the ground below, beading sweat threatening to pierce his vision as he repeatedly slammed his fists into the ground. With each pounding, the very earth beneath gave way; hammering at it from an angle, the half-orc was easily able to form a dike of several feet in height. Of course, "easily" was a relative term; as Rhox peered off toward the west, he knew he'd have to continue this for some time and again on the other side. Not one to waste time thinking, especially with a crisis of this scale near literally on his hands, he got right back to pummeling the land into shape. The heat of the lava wasn't making it any easier, and as the flow threatened to catch up with him, he paused. "Luna?"

The elf's concentration broken by the sudden call, she turned away from the circle. "Yes, Rhox? What is it?"

"Luna, do you have a moment? I could use an assist in getting to the other side of this thing. I could try myself but don't imagine I'd last very long."

"I can put you in the center of Monsoon City if you'd like. Unfortunately, it's dangerously close to the trajectory of the flow, but it's the best I can do with limited focus."

"That's fine, just please hurry. I'd rather get there before the flow crosses past the cliffs. The more of the city I can save, the better."

Luna didn't respond; instead, Rhox felt a slight tingle on his skin as his surroundings changed from the jungles east of Flood City to the main strip of Monsoon City. From the stench of burning leaves, he could tell the flow was practically at the city limits. Paying no mind to the throngs of people pouring past him in panicked attempts to get to higher ground, the half-orc rushed toward the towering Cliffs of Chevron, readying his fists once again.

The mage knew it would be to his advantage to leave as many existing stone structures as he could; many buildings in this section of the city were made of brick and thus could potentially slow the advance of the flow that much more. As such, he strove to work around buildings, throwing up makeshift walls in the streets and alleyways. The sheer heat of the approaching flow was beginning to singe his red eyebrows, but knowing where the heat was coming from, he could not back down now.

"I am literally roasting down here. Could we please cool this place down any faster? Any closer and some of these wooden structures are going to start smoldering."

"Would you quit it with the sass?" It was Chevron. "We're giving it all we've got, okay? Here."

Rhox suddenly found himself struggling to remain upright, a microburst with hurricane-strength winds forcing him to the ground. The mage was soaked through in an instant, and while the heat did seem to be slightly dissipated, he could still feel it approaching. "Gee, thanks, now I'll just steam-fry to death . . ."

Without wasting another breath, the half-orc returned to creating a dike to hold back the igneous flow. Streets upended, walls were reshaped; people continued to stream past Rhox in droves, most too panicked themselves to notice his handiwork or else assumed it was part of the disaster.

The next several hours progressed in this manner: Rhox building up flood breaks north and south where he could, Luna teleporting him back and forth as necessary; Miranda and Chevron doing everything in their ability to cool the lava as rapidly as possible; and Luna, Manas, and Dryad facilitating evacuation of populated areas. Luna excused herself once, not explaining to the others that she presently had the two individuals most likely at least semi-responsible for the volcanism unconscious on the floor of her palace.

3

Windfall

"*THE EDGE OF the flow along the Cliffs of Chevron will be cool enough to traverse. Make haste, and do not turn back.*"

The final words Luna had spoken to the pair echoed in Justin's mind. She hadn't even paused long enough to allow them a chance to object before they found themselves in the very location indicated. Her assertion was correct, but the scene had left a sour taste in his mouth. No deliberation, no explanation. Surely the Revered considered the remaining two dangerous hostiles after this fiasco, so why did Luna let them escape? Was it a second chance?

But they didn't need a second chance! Their first chance wasn't tainted by their actions! It was that dragon who had summoned the firebird Pyror and the same being's direct deeds that cost them the lives of two of their own!

Justin bit his lip, eyes surveying the scene laid before him. Luna had done well to place the pair far away from the smoldering sides of Fire Mountain, but there was still a bit of a hike before they'd reach the first semblances of civilization in Monsoon City he knew. This flow, this gargantuan sheet of black molten glass, stretched clear to the ocean; from their present distance, it was difficult to tell exactly where the two met, but Justin knew they had. Countless lives in the way snuffed out with literally nary a thought, the eruption merely spilling forth in whatever direction gravity pulled it. The jungles between Monsoon and Flood cities, the farmland in the fluvial plain, the high-rises within each city, he knew them all to be beneath the new rock still warm beneath his feet. The losses he and Angelo had suffered at Feuerschloss were nothing compared to the losses felt afterward.

He looked over to his new traveling companion, the half-elf slumped forward and trudging on almost as though he weren't looking where he was going, just walking because it was the only thing left for him. Justin knew the loss of Stephen wasn't a thing to take lightly with Angelo; just a few short days before, he'd already lost the people who raised him. This must have felt like a final blow, the cold-blooded murder of what was essentially the only family the young half-elf had left. To Angelo, Justin suspected, the loss of Stephen *was* the loss of the world.

Justin gasped in surprise as the obsidian before them ruptured, an ear-splitting crack shattering the uncomfortable silence as the material began to settle; steam rushed up from the new fissure, water formerly trapped beneath escaping into the fresh air. Whether it was a bubble in the glass with water from Miranda's rains or simply groundwater forcing its way up after being super-heated by the molten rock, it was impossible to tell; any structural instability seemed to force its way through the full thickness of the black sheet, forming jagged edges, sharp ridges, and scalloped fractures. If it weren't responsible for the destruction of a multitude of environments and peoples, it would have been almost beautiful to the introspective elf.

The hike back to civilization continued on like this. Justin wasn't sure what to say to Angelo to break the tense stillness on the sharp boundary of the barren rock and the Enchanted Rainforest. Angelo, meanwhile, flat out didn't want to talk; to be perfectly honest, he didn't want to return to Monsoon City either, least of all with this useless wizard he still didn't trust, but it seemed to him to be the only way forward. As such, he trudged on alongside the still strange, forced companion.

Reaching the Cliffs of Chevron, Justin paused momentarily, taking in the results of the eruption here as well; the sheer granite face of the original rock had been scorched pretty badly toward the base, but aside from this and the occasional piece of debris having fallen against the rapidly cooling glass below, the land had weathered it surprisingly well. Justin knew granite itself was volcanic, which he reasoned must have been the cause of any apparent lack of scarring.

The sound of sliding rubble and a sickening thud brought Justin out of his contemplation. He looked over to find Angelo lying on his side, left leg wedged in a crevice.

"SHIT!" The wizard ran over to help his fallen companion, wrapping his arms around the half-elf's torso and lifting the prone figure with all his strength. Angelo didn't move a muscle, deadweight in Justin's grasp. "Angelo, buddy, talk to me! You okay?" A sudden resistance brought his attention back to the ground; Justin practically yowled with surprise when he realized Angelo's left leg had been sliced open, the white of his tibia nauseatingly obvious beneath the flow of deep red blood. "Shit, shit, shit! Come on, Angelo, work with me here, buddy. You're gonna bleed out if you don't help . . ."

Justin managed to heft his companion out of the crevice, laying him flat on his back on the toasty rock. He removed his shirt and wrapped it around Angelo's lower leg, tightening it down in an attempt to stop the bleeding. *This isn't going to work,* Justin found himself thinking. *The leg will need sutures, and it's likely the bone is fractured the way it wedged into that crack.* He lifted Angelo's leg up, changing the direction the half-elf's blood was flowing in an attempt to slow the bleeding. Angelo winced as his leg was hefted but showed precious little else in the way of emotion.

The elf wasn't sure what else to do. His magic—or what little he could begin to claim to have—wasn't specialized enough for this much healing. He needed help. In a panic, still on his knees, he browsed the barren landscape, hoping to find someone—anyone—who might be able to assist.

"Why?"

Justin's ears perked. "Angelo? Angelo!" He grabbed the half-elf's hand. "You're okay! Don't move, I'm—"

"Why?"

"What?" Justin's eyebrows furrowed. "What do you mean why?"

"Why . . . bother? Why try? Why help me? Just . . . why?"

Justin, taken aback by the questions, paused for a moment, almost forgetting Angelo's still open leg wound. "Why? I don't . . . I want to get back, I guess. Return to the life I had. And you, you're . . . perhaps not a friend just yet but we've been through a lot together. I wouldn't be able to live with myself if you died after all that."

Angelo's eyes developed an ever-so-slight wetness before he closed them. Stephen. Stephen had died. And yet here he was, alive, getting help for a stupid accident instead of dead alongside his lifelong friend, the only person in the world who knew him anymore. Justin's words had opened that fresh wound and it hurt far worse than the gash in his shin. "Don't . . ."

"Hmm?"

Angelo swallowed. "Don't worry about my leg."

"What? What are you talking about? You've lost a lot of blood, you're not thinking!"

"It's a shin wound. It probably looks bad, but-but I don't think I'm going to die from it. Maybe bleed out . . . I am a bit woozy. Tighten the knot against the wound."

"Angelo . . ."

"Don't get me wrong here, I just need your help to get back to civilization."

"But the bone! It's—"

"Twisted, not broken. Doesn't hurt enough to be broken. Probably sprained the knee though. I can barely bend it." Justin watched as Angelo attempted to flex his left leg, the half-elf inhaling sharply through his teeth. "Yeah, it's damaged."

"Stop trying to move it!"

Angelo sighed, his breath nowhere near as shaky as before. "We're close to Monsoon City, right?"

"Yeah, I can see the end of the cliffs up ahead."

"Think you can support half my weight until we get back to your place?"

"My place?" Justin's eyebrows furrowed again. "I doubt my place survived. But you! We need to get you to a clinic! That cut may not be fatal but it won't heal right without medicine magic."

"And you can't do that."

Justin's cheeks flushed. "You know I-I'm not—"

"Even though you healed your own broken jaw before."

"Medical magic is very specialized! It's easy to perform on yourself, you can immediately feel if you've done anything wrong. It's a totally different animal to perform it on someone else!"

"Compromise: See if your place survived, then go to a clinic?"

"Fine. Just . . . give me your arm." Justin hoisted Angelo's left arm over his shoulder. "Now on the count of three we lift, okay?"

The pair hobbled slowly down the rest of the flow, making sure with each step that their foot was secure before lifting the other. Justin's right leg did most of the work, supporting himself and Angelo. The half-elf occasionally tried to put some weight on his damaged leg, but every time he did he shrieked. Justin insisted he stop trying lest he damage it more, or arguably worse, cause his still fresh gash to bleed harder.

Upon arriving at the end of the Cliffs of Chevron, Justin almost dropped Angelo in his haste to get back to the city; it was land he knew, land he, albeit barely, recognized. Maybe his domicile hadn't been destroyed after all!

But as they shambled into the outskirts of town along the muddy levee that now bounded the igneous glass, that optimism swiftly faded. Precious little was left of the once sprawling city, and even outside the flow most buildings within several hundred feet of it were at least singed, if not outright incinerated. Angelo just stared at each building as they passed it, tears in his eyes, dumbstruck, trying not to recall a similar scene in his own recent memory, failing miserably.

Justin recognized these streets, and he knew before they'd gotten there that his home hadn't survived; even so, some faint glimmer of hope made him trudge on, dragging his acquaintance in tow. Sure enough, as they approached the neighborhood, the alley where Justin's place had been was deep within the rock, only tangential streets of tangential streets visible anymore.

"I thought I might find you here."

It was a familiar voice for the elf. He ducked his head into his shoulders, not terribly wanting to turn around and face the man behind him. "Mickey?"

Angelo glanced over his hoisted shoulder, not needing to look too far back or down. "Yeah, it's Mickey."

"The Don was sure you'd died in the eruption. I tried to tell him I'd seen you four head out the morning after I stopped—Wait, where'd the other two go?"

Justin paced himself around, being sure to continue supporting Angelo's left side. "We . . . um . . . We encountered some . . . trouble."

Mickey's eyes had fallen to Angelo's swollen, bloodied, barely bandaged leg. "Is he gonna be okay? The hell happened?"

Justin let out a sharp sigh. "It's been a long week, okay? We need to get to a clinic. I assume you're here to tell me Don Kane's lost his patience with me. Believe me, I get it."

Mickey blinked at the elf's sudden mood swing; he'd never talked back like that before. It took him a moment to recompose himself. "No, look. I already says the Don thought youse was dead. He's lost a lot himself." Mickey looked briefly in the direction where Justin's place had been. "Maybe not as much as you. But he had assets all over town. And he'd understand your losing . . . you know, everything. Besides, it's not like you've got a place to pay rent for at this point anyway."

Justin lifted a finger to rub his temple. "Look, why were you looking for me if not to shake me down?"

Mickey lifted his hands up, almost as if to defend himself. "All's I'm wantin' is for you to take an audience with Don Kane. You may be delinquent, but . . . you know, you lost everything. And in spite of it, you *were* one of Don's more regular clients."

Justin paused, eyes peering down, not focused on any one thing as he thought. "Tell you what: If you can help me get him," he shrugged his shoulder to indicate Angelo, who gave a weak wave with his right hand, "to the nearest medic, we'll go once he's been healed up. Deal?"

"Oh what, just because I'm hired muscle nows I gots muscles?" Mickey cracked a grin, turning to Angelo. "Kid, your arms ain't gonna fall off if I carry you like a backpack, is they?"

Angelo was pretty woozy from the regular loss of blood but he managed to shake his head. "I don't . . . uh . . . I don't think so? It's really just the leg . . ."

Mickey turned around and took a knee. "Alright, Justin, just lay him on me. Kid, put your arms over my shoulders."

"M' name's Angelo."

"Yer name's gonna be 'Worm Food' if we don't hurry up."

*   *   *

The heavy metal door from the stairwell opened into a large brightly lit hallway; a thick, plush red carpet lined with golden accents inviting those approaching to enter. It was mostly for show. This floor of the Road's End Casino, Justin well knew, was occupied exclusively by Don Kane's office. Doors inset in the intricate wooden framework on either side of the hall either opened into an immediate wall or else were locked down tight, no one save for Don Kane himself knowing what lay behind them. They were part of the ambiance, the atmosphere the Don desired to present to anyone approaching him. The only other function the long hallway served was to accommodate long waiting lines in the event he might have had an excess of appointments on any given day.

With the recent ruin of Monsoon City, this particular afternoon happened to be one of his busiest. Justin sighed in mild frustration as he lay his back against an oaken wall, closing his eyes and lowering his head. Angelo remained standing, though he did brace himself against the same wall with a hand, his leg still shaky even after being healed; it had been open for so long and sliced so perfectly, the medic said it would be some time before the muscle would heal well enough that he could put his full weight on it for any time again.

Mickey, who'd left the two shortly after dropping Angelo off at the clinic, stood beside the immense doors at the other end of the hall, himself almost looking of reasonable proportion beside them; his eyes scanned the hall, keeping watch for any troublemakers as his ears were trained on what was happening behind him through the wall. He heard his name and knew that was his cue, pulling the door open with one hand to let the last person out and the next one in.

Justin lifted his head and looked down the hall as he heard the door open. "Wait, is that . . . McKearney? Todd McKearney? Wow, what's *he* doing here?"

Angelo perked up a bit. "Who's Todd McKearney?"

"He's the head of the McKearney clan, another of the major families in Monsoon City." He paused as he watched the withered older gentleman walk by, eyes cast to the carpet, little tufts of curly red hair bouncing with each step, the only part of him to seem capable of bouncing. "He looks *awful.*" He paused again, turning his head in a direction. "Yeah, I guess their homestead was right in the way of the flow. The Revered must've been evacuating the cities or he'd be dead. Man."

Angelo looked down the hallway at the line of people waiting for an audience. "You think everyone here's looking for the same sort of help?"

Justin lowered his head back down. "It wouldn't surprise me. Don Kane's a well-connected man and he's not stupid with his money. Even so, there's no way he can rebuild all of Monsoon City after that. Doesn't look good for us."

"What about your family? The Baileys or whatever. Didn't you say they were a well-respected family of wizards?"

Justin exhaled. "Yeah, well, they don't tend to help those outside the family. They barely help those *inside* the family." His fingers clenched. Angelo turned away to face the opposite wall, eventually slumping down to sit on the floor.

Minutes passed. Quarter hour. Half hour. Then an hour. The pair didn't speak, merely shuffling down the wall each time the door opened. Angelo watched each new figure trudge by, faces turned down, weakly pushing the door open into the stairwell before disappearing.

By the time the two of them had made it to the other end of the hall, the sun shone through the door every time Mickey opened it. Justin began biting his lip.

"What am I gonna say? What should I even *ask* him?"

"Why not ask Mickey? He invited you here, right?"

"He's working. It's poor manners to distract him."

"So? You two seem to get along."

Justin turned to the half-elf. "That's a joke, right?"

Angelo pursed his lips.

Several more minutes passed before the two could barely make out a shouted "Mickey!" from behind the door. On cue, Mickey reached over and pulled the door open; it almost seemed effortless when he did it, but every time it closed it swung so hard the two were blasted by air. There was no way either of them could move it.

Mickey stepped out of the way of the door, motioning toward it with his opposite arm at the pair. Justin gave the slightest of nods as he pushed himself off the wall, Angelo giving the gigantic man a small salute as he walked past him into the waiting office.

"Justin! What a surprise!" The figure behind the desk straight back from the door stood, holding his arms outstretched. He too was a large man, though more so in girth than anything else; his short black hair, combed back, reflected the golden light filtering through the windows behind him. "Mickey told me he'd found you but I didn't believe it!"

Justin bowed his head to the older gentleman. "Yes, sir, reports of my death have been greatly exaggerated."

The man—Angelo could only assume him to be Don Kane—let out a hearty boffola. "So what can I do for you? I'm assuming you're not here to pay what you owe in rent."

Justin's muscles visibly tensed. "Err, no, Don Kane. You see—"

"Is your friend there gonna be alright?"

Justin turned his head to see Angelo biting his lip, neck strained upward, chin out. "Err, sir—" He turned back and gave the Don another short bow. "Might Angelo be permitted to sit? His left leg was badly injured earlier today and he really *shouldn't be putting all his weight on it.*" He slowly turned his head to the half-elf as he spoke the last bit, as though that much were more intended for him.

"Oh, you're the boy Mickey helped to the clinic." The Don waved with his hand. "Yes, please, help yourself to the chair in the corner." Angelo sighed, turning and shambling his way over to the plush-looking lounge chair Don Kane had indicated.

"Thank you, sir." Justin turned back to the man behind the desk once again. "Now, you see—"

"Justin, I know you lost everything in the eruption." Don Kane placed his arms on his desk, fingertips touching fingertips, forming a pyramid in front of himself. His expression had turned far more serious. "I'm aware you can't pay me what you owe right now, and that's acceptable, considering the circumstances. But I also know you need help."

"Err . . ." Justin again bowed his head, much more quickly this time. "Yessir. I—We," he motioned back to Angelo, "have nothing left, sir. Anything you could do—"

Don Kane lifted a hand up. "I'm gonna stop you right there, Justin." He sighed, turning his chair around to look out the window behind him, pausing as he looked down at what remained of the city. "It was devastating. If you'd've been here, you would have witnessed it firsthand. Hell, you probably would've died. I'd assumed you had."

Justin took a step forward, lifting an arm out to the man behind the desk. "Don Kane, I—"

"I can't help everyone, Justin." He turned back around to face the elf. "I want to. I *desperately* want to. This is my city, these are my people." He lowered his head. "But I just can't. And you . . ." He lifted his head again. "I like you, Justin. I've been lenient with you. But you're just one person—well, I guess two people now."

"It's not—"

Don Kane lifted his hand again. "At-at-at, I know. But I assume you're going to be taking care of this man, at least until he's—you'll pardon the expression—back on his feet, yes?"

"I'm . . .," Justin turned back to Angelo, who nonchalantly waved at his companion from the corner, "not sure, sir."

"Justin, you can barely take care of yourself. And I'd love to help, really I would, but I just—I can't. You know that."

Justin hung his head. "Yeah. It wasn't even really my idea to come here."

"And yet, here you are."

"Right. Come on, Angelo."

"Mickey!"

*   *   *

Rhox emerged from his meditation chamber into the Floating Edifice, the structure more or less stationed in the same position it had been in when the eruption began. He wiped the sweat from his brow, the heat from the still cooling rock causing the clouds concealing the structure to swirl and dance. It would be more beautiful if it wasn't a symptom of such destruction.

He strode down the marble hallway to the central rotunda, all five other extant thrones already occupied by their respective owners. "Oh good, everyone's here."

"Are . . . Are we not waiting for Salamandro?" Manas cocked an inquisitive eyebrow.

Rhox couldn't stop his grimace. "I did not want to… involve him in our discussions."

"Was that wise? He *is* the one we chose to deal with . . . you know, fire."

Rhox ignored the question. "Circle up. I wanted us to talk about how we're going to deal with this . . . situation."

It was Chevron's turn to interject. "Why are you pausing to think of euphemisms? This is a *disaster*. Salamandro *caused* it. I say we *deal with it* by dealing with *him*."

Dryad nodded. "I hate to agree with something so . . . violent—"

Chevron bristled. "Stop that."

The halfling continued. "But he's absolutely right. This eruption has *destroyed* the balance we regularly fight so hard to maintain! Do you have any idea how many different forests were lost?" He immediately threw up his hands as others began opening their mouths. "AND waterways AND convection currents! Lives, people! *Lives!* Because he wanted to . . ." Dryad paused again, much to Chevron's chagrin; however, he wasn't trying to walk on eggshells here. He'd been on the Inquisition. He shot a quick look at Luna. "Whatever his motives, this was unacceptable."

"Now wait just a minute!" Miranda stood deliberately as Rhox sighed, slumping into his chair. No one had bothered to circle up. "Yes, what has happened here is a disaster, and I can't deny I'm probably every bit as pissed at Salamandro as everyone else is. The flow system between Monsoon and Flood cities was *vital* to the survival of *each*. But we *know* there was a plot to attack us! What ever happened with that, anyway? Luna, Dryad?"

Dryad shrank into his chair. "It . . . was inconclusive."

"Oh, well, isn't *that* convenient!" Miranda flourished her hand at the diminutive man. "*We don't know!* So for all we know he was trying to defend himself!"

"Defend himself by causing the most destructive eruption in the known history of the world?" Rhox stood back up. "You don't think that's just slightly overkill?"

Manas stood next, throwing his hands in the air, palms out at Rhox and Miranda. "Guys, guys! This is no time to be fighting!" Rhox and Miranda both shot side glances at the gnome. "I mean yes, this is a problem, and eventually we'll have to confront Salamandro about it, no matter how little you might want to, Rhox. But *right now* we need to know how to deal with . . ." He motioned wildly toward the floor. "This! All this!"

Rhox looked back to Miranda, heaving another sigh. "The little man's right. We need to start working on this right now, the sooner the better." He slumped back into his chair. "*That's* the real reason

I called this little meeting." He looked back over to Manas. "I'm not sure what you think my motivations are, but I *absolutely* want to confront Salamandro about this. I didn't want him here *now* because if he had been I likely would've thrown him over the edge."

Manas gave a little nod. "Look, we don't know his reasons. Maybe we need a tribunal in the near future once everyone's cooled down at least a bit?"

"I don't care. We need to discuss this lava flow now though."

Miranda sat back in her seat, giving a sweep of her hand. "Well? Rhox, this is your bailiwick. What should we be discussing?"

Rhox rested his head in his hand. "This is different. I don't— We're talking about literal glass here. We need to get rid of it as soon as we can but . . . It's not like this stuff just weathers away."

"*Can* it weather away?" Miranda leaned toward the half-orc.

"I mean, eventually. *Everything* erodes with enough time."

"So what we need is an accelerated schedule is what I'm hearing."

Rhox winced, rolling his head to look down. "I don't—I'm not sure it's that simple. I mean, yes, that will eventually work, but . . ."— he gripped the skin between his eyebrows—"there are so many other problems. How do we deal with the shards of silicate? How will people travel across? Hell, how will *water* travel across? You said it yourself, that flow was essential. Monsoon City will simply flood, and Flood City . . . well, it won't."

Miranda nodded. "But we can try to get particulates washed out to sea, and the water flow . . . I mean, it'll take some time and engineering, but I might be able to set something up that'll allow both cities to thrive again."

Chevron piped up again. "I'm more than willing to help where I can."

"We all are," Dryad added. "We can avoid washing out good soil with proper root systems from both myself and Manas."

Rhox gave a soft nod, lifting his head to the assembly. "I guess I just need to be more optimistic. Miranda and Chevron, could you set up a system to steadily weather away the flow?"

Both addressed nodded.

"And, Dryad—and Manas too, I guess—if you've got any plants that can survive without soil, root systems can always help break the rock apart."

The halfling and gnome gave their own nods.

"Now, Luna"—the elf lifted her head—"the last issue is the heat. Obviously," Rhox motioned to the swirling clouds surrounding the rotunda, "we've still got heat radiation from the cooling rock, but once that's finished we'll be left with black glass. In full sunlight, that will produce one hell of a thermal system. Do you think you could . . . I don't know, limit the sunlight?"

Luna gave a weak smile. "I could cut out sunlight to the region entirely, but that wouldn't be wise. Even discounting the proposed planting to the area," she motioned to Dryad and Manas, "sunlight is a necessary component of balance here. Too little and Chevron won't be able to work, too much and Miranda's will dry up before it has a chance to do anything. As with everything we do, we need balance."

Rhox nodded. "Do you think it would be a good idea to filter the light?"

Luna looked toward Miranda. "If you provide the clouds, I can filter the light much more effectively without forcing something horrendously unnatural."

Miranda gave her own nod. "We're going to be building storm systems over the area, I suspect for many years. We can work something out, I'm sure."

Dryad brought both hands to the edge of his armrests. "So we have a plan then?"

Rhox gave a wave. "It certainly sounds like it. Shall we adjourn?"

Chevron timidly raised his hand. "W-what of Salamandro?"

Dryad slumped back. "Right. Salamandro."

Manas raised his own hand. "So are we . . . ?" He brought it back down, folding both hands in his lap. Chevron shot him a glare. "There'd been talk of a tribunal? Why don't we bring him here to explain himself?"

Rhox bristled. "NOT now."

"Not now!" Manas raised his hands defensively. "But soon. We do need to learn as much as we can about what happened."

Rhox visibly relaxed, though he still spoke through strained teeth. "We do, I suppose." He shook himself down. "Why don't we give it some time? Discuss this at a later date?"

"I'm all for that if everyone else is." Manas peered around the semicircle.

Chevron shrugged. "I'd rather discuss it now but I understand, we're all still pretty hot about this."

"I'm up for whatever," motioned Dryad, "so long as we get some answers."

"It sounds like we might have a quorum. Luna? Miranda?"

Miranda gave her own shrug. "Sounds like the men have already decided."

"Well?" Rhox gestured in her direction. "I'm all ears."

"No, no, it's alright." Miranda gave a smirk. "I agree. I just thought it was a bit rude that we were left out."

"We weren't *trying* to—"

"Rhox, I'm messing with you," Miranda grinned. "You know I would've spoken up if I had anything to say."

"Luna? We don't want to leave you out either."

The elf gave her own little smirk. "Honestly, I'm good with whatever right now. I think a tribunal is a great idea." *It would be nice to get both sides of the story*, she thought to herself.

"Very well. Meeting adjourned until I feel like I can see that rat bastard without bashing his face in."

All assembled members stood, moving toward their respective chambers, except Dryad, who swiftly followed Luna. "Alright, what do you know?"

* * *

Justin collapsed at the foot of the carpeted stairs, eyes staring off at nothing in particular.

Angelo, carefully taking his weight off the handrail, took a seat next to him, bringing his knees up to his chest and wrapping his arms around them. "So."

"I don't know what to do. I was . . ." Justin shook his head slowly. "I don't know what I expected. I knew he wasn't going to help us."

"But he might have, right?" Angelo turned his head toward his companion. "I mean, Mickey said—"

"Mickey was just trying to be nice, I think." Justin closed his eyes. "So it's really all gone then."

Angelo lowered his gaze back to his knees. "Not like there was much for me to return to."

Justin sighed. "I'm sorry, Angelo. I'm not—I don't mean to detract from all that you've lost."

"No, you're fine. It's . . . It's devastating, isn't it? This feeling of loss." He lifted his head. "Kinda makes me want to try alcohol."

Justin cracked a slight smile in spite of himself. "Even if that were true, it's not like you could afford it."

"Why, is alcohol expensive?"

Justin gave a small chuckle. "It's more expensive than your standard juice, that's for sure."

Angelo lowered his head again, but this time, a glint caught his eye; he opened his eyes wider, spotting a small coin a few feet from the stairs. He pushed himself up onto still shaky legs, reaching down. "What if . . . What if I tried one of these machines? They're for gambling, right?"

Justin lay himself back, sprawling out on the stairs and staring at the raised popcorn ceiling. "Knock yourself out. Not like we could do much with that anyway."

Angelo looked at the coin in his hand—a ten-cent denomination token. He lifted his eyes to scan the large casino room; the sounds were near-deafening and the flashing lights were enough to dazzle anyone. Not knowing exactly what to do, the half-elf approached a nearby machine, a small slots box at the end of a long row. His eyes strained to make sense of the barrage of information it was trying to throw at him, looking for any sort of instructions. "I guess . . . Do I just . . . put the coin in here?" He slid the token into a coin slot near the top. "And then . . . I guess I pull this lever?"

Three large reels spun rapidly upon his release, so much so that he couldn't make out anything on any of them. One after another, the three reels came to a sudden stop: "Cherry, cherry . . . cherry?" He looked back toward the stairwell where Justin hadn't moved a muscle. "Justin? What does three cherries mean?"

The elf lazily waved his hand. "There should be a readout on the machine somewhere. Look at the tray underneath."

Angelo pushed himself off the fixed stool and dropped to his knees, watching as several coins spilled into that tray. "Eight, nine . . . Justin! I won a Moktle!"

"Congratulations." The elf lifted a hand into the air, pointing straight up and giving a sarcastic circle of mock celebration. One or two heads looked up from their respective games in the direction of the shout, unseen by the wizard. "Another two like that and you might be able to afford a shot."

Angelo gathered up the coins in the tray then righted himself, sitting back in the stool. It wasn't as though losing would affect him negatively, he reasoned, this was all gained capital. He slid another coin into the slot at the top then pulled the lever again more decisively. The lights and colors cycled as before, reels spinning, bells ringing: "Cherry . . ." He squinted. "Is that . . .bar? And . . . pineapple. Drat." But as he snapped his fingers, the machine lit up again in much the same way it had before. Three symbols lit up on the reels, one on each: All three the questionable "bar" symbol in a diagonal line down the display. "Wait, Justin," Angelo again shouted at his semi-comatose companion, "can you win with a diagonal?"

"Is it lighting up?"

"Yes."

"Then yeah."

The sudden sound of clattering coins overcame the din of the casino floor for the half-elf; he again looked below the shelf of the game and beheld a small avalanche of tokens pouring into that same tray. "Umm . . . Justin? I . . . uh . . . I think I broke it."

Several more heads lifted in the direction of the half-elf, and this time Justin's was among them. "What? What do you mean 'broke it'?"

"I-I don't know, it just—Oh man . . ."

Justin pushed himself off the floor, his existential crisis taking a backseat for the moment as he half jogged over to the half-elf. The moment he beheld what Angelo was talking about, he jumped back a good couple feet. "Angelo, what did you do?"

"I swear I didn't mean to! You don't think Mr. Kane will be mad, will he?"

"He will if you call him that. Look, we'll just explain what happened. We'll tell him that," Justin brought his eyes up to the game's display to get a sense of what Angelo might've done to damage this machine, "you won perfectly validly, and this money is rightfully yours! Angelo! Holy shit!"

"What? What did I do?"

Justin's mood flipped from dour to jovial. "Angelo, the only prize worth more than what you just won on that machine is the jackpot!"

"So . . . what, what did I do? What did I break?"

"You didn't break anything! Look, you see here, this line on the diagonal?" Justin shoved his hand forward over his companion, forgetting personal space in the moment. "See here on the end how it has this '3X' on it?"

Angelo gave a nod, eyes wide, genuinely curious.

"And over here, how this little paper shows the 'bar' symbol as the prize immediately above 'jackpot'?"

Angelo followed the elf's finger, again giving a terse nod.

"I mean, it's just a dime machine, but you might've just won," Justin paused, running the numbers in his head, "one hundred fifty Moktles!"

Angelo raised an eyebrow then ducked his head back under the machine. There was no way . . . He grabbed one of the coins. Sure enough, each of these tokens was worth one Moktle. "So . . . I can afford that drink now?"

"Damn, Angelo, you could afford my monthly rent with that payout!"

The half-elf gave a quick look around, scanning the area; a few patrons were beginning to approach the commotion, some curious, others interested in what they were sure they must have misheard. "Do you want to give it a try, Justin? I'm," he pointed toward a man in a waistcoat he figured must be an employee of the casino, "I'm gonna see what kind of beverages they have."

The wizard gave a shrug, still grinning from ear to ear. "I guess I'll give it a play or two. Are these—" He motioned to a small stack of tokens on the game's short shelf.

"Yeah, those are the 'dimes' I won the first time." Angelo was already limping backward toward the man he'd indicated before. Justin gave him a little wave of the back of his hand, and the swordsman nodded, turning back around and stepping as briskly as he comfortably could toward that gentleman. "Excuse me, sir?"

"What'll it be, kid?" The man smiled pleasantly at Angelo.

"So you do work here."

The man gave a curt nod. "I'm one of the attendants, sir." He motioned to a nametag that read "Chad." "So what'll it be?"

Angelo ducked his head, not wanting to offend this Chad. "Are . . . Do you serve drinks?"

Chad's grin widened slightly. "We certainly do, sir."

Angelo paused, lowering his head ever so slightly further. "Drink-drinks?"

Chad couldn't help but let out a chuckle. "Yes, sir. Soft drinks are a rarity here."

"What . . . um . . . I'm kind of . . . new to the area." Angelo cracked a smile, rubbing the back of his head. "What sort of . . . you know, drink-drinks do you offer?"

"We have just about anything you could think of. Go on, try me."

Angelo's cheeks flushed. "Well, you see . . . um . . . I'm . . . I'm kind of . . . new to . . . you know, drinking . . ."

Chad cocked an eyebrow, then gave another smile. "How about I surprise you? Maybe start you off easy?"

Angelo shrugged. "Could we . . . maybe . . . I'm kinda wanting something strong."

Chad raised his other eyebrow. "Well, if you're sure. Where are you gaming?"

Angelo gave a nervous chuckle but pointed back over his shoulder to where Justin was pulling the lever again.

"With that elf there? The small crowd?"

"Crowd?" Angelo turned his head to look and realized that indeed a small cluster of people had gathered around the machine. "Oh, uh, yeah, I guess." He turned back to the attendant. "So what, do I come find you or . . .?"

Chad gave a slight bow. "I'll bring the drink to you, sir. It's policy to distract our gamers as little as possible."

Angelo again provided an awkward chuckle, face still red. "O-Okay! That's fine! So I'll just . . ."

Chad smiled. "And I'll be by in a minute with your," he gave finger quotes, "drink-drink."

Angelo didn't bother responding to the minor dig, turning around and hobbling back toward where he'd been playing; Justin had whittled that stack down by just over a half.

"Dammit, Angelo, how did you win so much so quickly?" The elf only barely turned his head back to his returning companion. "I've not won a cent!"

"Don't worry about it. May I . . . Could I take the stool please?"

Justin's face seemed to snap back to reality. "Oh geez, Angelo, I'm sorry. With your win, I totally forgot about your leg." The mage turned away from the machine and hopped off the seat, quickly stepping out of the way.

Angelo sat back down, giving his bandaged limb a rub. "I know it'll get better but—"

"Well, don't touch it!" Justin moved to pull the half-elf's hand away from his own leg but stopped before getting there. If he wasn't careful, he might hurt the leg even more. "Just . . . Okay, so, what, we're waiting for your drink? You want to play some more? I, uh, I already put another coin in."

Angelo shrugged; he knew Justin was concerned about his leg. "Sure, I guess." He turned back to the slot machine and gave the lever a pull. The reels spun, and when all three stopped, the saddest little musical sting the half-elf had ever heard rang out. "I, uh. Guess I didn't win this one."

The small crowd gathered around seemed to confirm this, a chorus of disappointed groans rising from their collective bodies. One turned to head back where he'd been playing before.

"Well, you've still got a small stack of dimes there. If nothing else, you'll still walk away with the money in the tray." Justin propped an elbow on the side of the slot machine. "You might as well try those."

Angelo cocked an eyebrow. "I don't know if that's a terribly healthy way to look at it."

"Are you gonna try it again or not?"

The half-elf shrugged again, grabbing a coin off the stack. "I guess I might as well. But only because I'm waiting for a drink." He slid the coin into the slot, pulled the lever again and lined up three pineapples. A cheerful jingle, flashing lights, and a shower of coins below were accented by the small crowd cheering.

"That kind of luck, I can believe now that you survived." The voice cut through the crowd like a knife, sudden and unexpected. Angelo had only heard it once before, but Justin instinctively hunched his shoulders. Behind him, approaching from the bottom of those same stairs, was the very same Don Kane they'd met with mere moments ago.

"Don!" Justin quickly pivoted around to face the larger man. "I-I didn't expect you! I mean, I wasn't—I didn't think you came to the gaming floor! I didn't—"

"Stand down, Justin." Don Kane raised a closed-finger palm in front of him. "I don't normally. No reason to. But my boys, they were telling me about a commotion you two were creating. That the stranger was racking up an impressive streak on one of my machines, something not statistically possible." He gave a small bow. "I had to come see it for myself."

Justin tightened his back up against the side of the machine. "O-Oh, of course! Oh geez, this cuts into your profits, doesn't it? I—We didn't mean—"

"Angelo, was it? I have a proposition for you." Don Kane walked by the stuttering wizard, all but ignoring him. "I know you two are in dire straits. I said before that I couldn't help you, but let's say you were to offer me something in return?"

Angelo raised an eyebrow. "I'm listening."

"You've gathered quite a little crowd here in spite of such a short run." Kane motioned to the others clustered around the same machine. "Most folks would pay good money for someone who can do that."

"O-kay . . ."

"I can't give you much, but I could house the two of you in one of the hotel rooms upstairs." He pointed upwards. "I mean, I can't spare the big ones, but considering you don't really have anywhere to go . . ." He lifted his hands up, flat palms facing the ceiling, indicating a weighing of their options. "We've also got a world-class kitchen. I wouldn't mind comping a few meals a day."

Justin's jaw was practically on the floor. "You . . . Really? You'd do that for us?"

"On one condition: Angelo, how would you feel about gambling on a regular basis?"

Angelo shied to one side. "How regular?"

"Standard hours, nine to five, five days a week."

"To just . . ." Angelo looked down at himself. "To sit here pulling a lever?"

"So long as you keep up interest. And with that winning streak you just demonstrated, I don't think that will be a problem."

Angelo turned his head. "I mean, it's not like we have a choice."

"You *always* have a choice, Angelo. Just sometimes the right one is pretty obvious. So shall we prepare a room?"

Justin could've activated the tilt sensor on a pinball machine, he was nodding so hard at his companion. Angelo shrugged again. "Alright. I mean, we need a roof over our heads at least."

"Fantastic! Shake on it?" Don extended a hand, which Angelo took. "Very well! Let's see what we can do for these fine young men."

A familiar waistcoated man cut through the crowd behind the half-elf. "Sir? Sir, I have your drink."

Justin wrinkled his nose. "What the hell, I can smell it from here! What did you order?"

"I told him to surprise me." Angelo took the glass from the tray, giving it a quick swig. His eyes immediately widened and he pounded on his chest with his free hand. "STRONG. But . . . smooth?"

Chad nodded. "You asked for something strong. That's a Mekkit iced tea."

"A Mekkit . . . Angelo!" Justin pushed himself off the slot machine. "That's like six drinks!"

"Doesn't really taste like iced tea."

*   *   *

Justin let out a sigh as he slumped against the igneous embankment, sliding carefully down the obsidian face to sit and face the casino that had become his and Angelo's livelihood. His eyes scanned up the building, not really looking *at* it but more in its general direction. He knew they'd been lucky to still be alive but . . . now what?

Their options moving forward were limited, he knew. Stephen, his only hope for improving his own skills—and of course, Angelo's best friend—was dead, killed by his own brother at the behest of that immense dragon. The wizard shivered. Had he been John, would he have done the same? His knowledge of John's situation was limited: He knew the man had somehow been in contact with . . . What was his name? The half-orc had called him something like "Asmodeious." But even so, how long had this contact commenced? Did John truly have enough knowledge of the dragon to be that terrified of him?

Justin's gaze turned skyward. Asmodeious had certainly been terrifying in person. Such a large, powerful dragon. Had he any chance at all of surviving such an encounter again? Probably not, he realized; Asmodeious commanded magic to a level Justin couldn't even fathom. Hell, he *was* a magical creature.

But did Stephen truly have to die by his hand? Asmodeious had said it himself: He'd never told John to kill him. Were John not in the party, Stephen might have been able to escape the castle, much as he and Angelo had done. He might've had the chance to properly train him!

Justin shook his head, blinking the developing tears out of his eyes. None of this "what-if" mattered. Stephen was dead. His fate was sealed. He'd never become the master wizard his family desired him to be. And now, Angelo had truly lost everything. All because of a dragon and their ill-fated quest.

The mage opened his eyes in time to witness an elf push through the doors of the Road's End Casino. "Justin! There you are."

Justin climbed back to his feet. "May I help you?"

The new elf jogged over toward the wizard. "The family had heard you'd taken up residence here, but beyond that we didn't know where to look."

Justin raised an eyebrow. "The clan of Bailey?"

The stranger nodded. "The elders have been trying to catch up with you for some time, since about the eruption, I think." He handed the mage a folded piece of paper. "Consider this an official summons."

4

Dissociation

JUSTIN CAUTIOUSLY PUSHED the left double door open to the central chamber of the Bailey household. Hearing voices in the midst of what sounded like discussion, he quickly dipped to one side, standing hunched beside a gilded vase framing the path. He didn't want to interrupt.

A shorter, narrow man stood before the family elders, a man Justin easily recognized from the back as Todd McKearney. His distinctive sparse red curls swayed with every head bow he gave to the heads of the Bailey clan. Even as far back as he was, Justin could hear the desperation in his voice.

"Please, good sirs and madams! I do not ask for much. Our family is struggling to recover. Our homestead was in the path of totality!"

A platinum-blond cascade of hair wavered as one of the elders shook his head. "McKearney, you know we simply cannot. While our homestead survived the eruption, many of our family members spread throughout the city were hit every bit as hard as you were."

Todd wrung his cloth hat in his hands. "I do not mean to devalue your own losses, kind sir— err, gentlefolk." He motioned to the assembled audience, again bowing his head. "I simply ask to draw your attention to the suffering elsewhere. You know the unique position I'm in, the head of our clan." His grip returned to that strained hat. "I'm doing all I can to keep us afloat, but-but it's simply not enough! Already my kin are being driven from the city, destitute, starving!"

Another elf's hand raised. "McKearney, we apologize, but there is precious little we can do about that. And I loathe to say it—as I'm sure my colleagues would agree—but perhaps it's for the best that your family seek out livings in other cities where the eruption did not cause such devastation. I hear Topaz City looks lovely this time of year."

"Dammit, that's not the point!" Todd threw his hat to the ground behind him. "You have family all over the world but we've only ever held Monsoon City as our home. Our . . . 'assets' were centralized!"

The central figure took his turn to raise his hand. "Todd, if we cannot discuss this calmly, we have nothing to discuss."

The man shook his head, turning around to retrieve his hat before turning back to the elders, choking back tears. "It sounds like we didn't have anything to discuss anyway." He snapped back toward the doors Justin stood beside, speed-walking down the crimson carpet to their exit, barely tipping that hat to Justin in passing.

"Justin! Is that you?" A voice rang out from the end of the hall. Justin recoiled instinctively before holding up a hand in a nervous wave. "Come! Approach the assembly."

Justin quivered as he stepped up the same carpet Todd McKearney had just stomped through. "Uh, hello, elders! Yes, this is Justin! I'm-I'm responding to your summons."

"So we gathered."

Justin bowed his head instinctively. Or perhaps it was a reflexive wince; in the moment, he wasn't sure. "Right, of course, sirs. So. . . um . . ." He looked down at his feet. "Why exactly was I summoned? This is highly unorthodox."

"What was that?" One of the older elders put a hand to his ear. "Justin, approach! You know this room's acoustics only work to their full effect if you stand before us."

Yeah, so you can all sound like you're yelling at me without straining your collective voice. Justin unsuccessfully tried to hide a roll of his eyes and continued his walk, coming to another unsteady stop at the carpet medallion he knew his kin had meant. The structure of the room was designed for optimal acoustics in this location so one could speak in standard tone and have all the elders hear. "Is this better?"

"Much, young Justin. Thank you."

The elf bowed his head, deliberately this time. "So what is this about? Why was I summoned?"

"Justin," began a woman near one of the ends, "how've you been? We understand you've been under the care of sir Don Kane since the eruption."

Justin turned and bowed his torso in her direction. "Yes, ma'am. He's been quite generous, considering his own losses."

She waved a hand. "We've all lost a significant amount as a result of that incident, Justin."

You don't have to tell me again. I was just here, remember? "Of course, ma'am. I was merely praising the man, nothing more."

"And we've gathered that you've been living with a half-elf, nursing him back to health after a tragic incident with his leg." A different individual, a man now to his right, spoke up. "Don Kane even tells us you helped him through a bout of alcoholism."

"You seem awfully well informed as to how I've been." He turned to bow to this new voice. "Why, then, was I summoned?"

The elder in the central chair, Justin knew him as the patriarch of the family, leaned forward in his seat. "Justin, my boy, we've received some rather disturbing news. Some time ago. We hadn't pursued it until now because, frankly, we'd thought you were dead."

Justin scratched the back of his head, cracking a nervous grin. "As I'd told Don Kane, rumors of my death had been greatly exaggerated."

"Yes, as we see." The patriarch slumped in his chair, letting out a lengthy, breathy sigh. "Justin, we know."

Justin's expression became much more inquisitive. "Know what? What happened? What's going on?"

The patriarch gripped his armrests. "Justin, you can play dumb all you want but we have it from the horse's mouth."

Justin shrugged, shaking his head. "I genuinely don't know what you're talking about."

The patriarch practically leapt off his chair. "Dammit, boy, you know full well—" He stopped himself, lowering his head. "Justin, you and your friend, the one we hear is on the mend."

Justin had never seen the old man so riled up; it took him a moment to realize he was holding a flinched pose. *What did we do?*

The patriarch gave another sigh. "Justin, we know you participated in a direct assault against a member of the Revered."

"WHAT!?" It was the assembly's turn to flinch. "What are— That's simply not true!"

"Twist in the wind all you want," the patriarch declared, "we heard it directly from one of them. We know the eruption that caused such devastation to both Monsoon City and Flood City was a direct result of that attempt. You—Well, you and your friend, and we'd heard there'd been two others, the four of you took direct action against Them."

"Sir, I didn't! We didn't! And those two others, they died as a result!"

"Good riddance." The patriarch's ethereal eyebrows furrowed down at Justin. "But that very fact corroborates this claim, not that it needed it."

"No, you don't understand! There was a fire and—"

"Silence!" The patriarch slammed his fists against his armrests. "Justin, you've been nothing but trouble for this family! Your magic is atrocious, your skill is bad enough that our greatest tutors couldn't help you. You chose to live in a hovel outside Flood City to refine your skills—Oh, but wait, you've had a second home, rented from Don Kane here in Monsoon City this whole time!" The patriarch slumped back in his chair again. "You know he's sent his goons here to collect on *your* debts? YOUR mess. We've always been cleaning up *YOUR* messes. And now you go and pull something like this!?"

Justin's bottom lip was quivering; he had no idea Don Kane had done anything like that. No wonder his own family believed such a wretched lie. "I swear to you . . ."

The patriarch held up his hand. "Don't waste your breath, Justin. We're done with your lies. The elders have convened, and in light of these events, there was only one action we could take." He leaned forward, looking to each side before delivering his sentence. "Justin, you are no longer of the clan of Bailey. This council of elders finds you guilty of the crime of High Assault against the Revered, and for that, we excommunicate you."

* * *

Diablo took unsteady steps up the central hallway toward the Floating Edifice's main rotunda. It had been over a month since he first made this same walk; he dreaded this one far more. There hadn't been even an ounce of communication from the Revered since the eruption. True, he'd been trying to keep a low profile since then, but for a group that could instantly communicate with him telepathically—even just to chastise him—to not do so for so long, that fact made him especially wary.

As he emerged into the central chamber, his first instinct was to shy away. The other six members of the Revered were seated before him in much the same way as they were that first day.

"Salamandro." Manas motioned to the center of the semicircle. "Please step forward."

Diablo hung his head but did as he was told. He widened his stance subconsciously, preparing for a physical assault.

"Salamandro, it's clear you understand why we've called you here." Miranda spoke with an authoritarian air. "For the time being, you do not need to worry about physical harm."

"Speak for yourself." Rhox crossed his arms.

"Rhox, we agreed we'd conduct ourselves with maturity." Miranda looked toward her colleague. "May I continue?"

"Yes, ma'am."

"Salamandro, the fact is, none of us here knows entirely what happened that terrible day. We know the results, plain as day," she motioned out the open walls to where the obsidian flow was still visible from the elevated building, "but we only know pieces of what might have transpired to lead to it."

Diablo winced, looking out the open wall upon his—well, Asmodeious' handiwork. "So you want my version of those events?"

Miranda nodded. "This is an official Tribunal of the Revered. The way this works is we'll each give our own account, what we know and how we experienced the event in question. At the end, you may offer your own insight."

Diablo raised his head ever so slightly. "So . . . You didn't call me here to maim me?"

"Salamandro," Luna gave the smallest of smiles, "we're interested in justice. We don't like to pass judgment until we have every piece of information we possibly can."

Miranda nodded at the elf. "That's absolutely right. Now, who would like to go first? Rhox? I know you're just itching to say something."

The other half-orc in the room chuffed. "Luna called us all to the Edifice and there was an eruption taking place at Fire Mountain."

Miranda gave a rolling gesture with one of her hands. "Rhox, remember, we want everything. The stuff you knew leading up to that event is every bit as important."

"Look, what do you want me to say?" Rhox stood and walked to the center of the assembly, causing Diablo to shrink away. "None of us knew much of anything going into this. All we'd been given was that a group of four was supposedly on the warpath, and the next thing we know there's an eruption we have to divert!"

"Rhox, sit down!" Miranda pointed sternly at the empty granite throne. "We're trying to be professional here!"

"Oh what, your highness?" Rhox approached Miranda, arms spreading to either side of him. "If you didn't want me to speak my mind, you shouldn't have called on me! This whole Tribunal is fucking daffy, that's what I know!"

"Rhox!" Miranda stood herself, the noticeably shorter elf still managing to stare the half-orc down. "Seat!"

"As you wish, Eilafel."

The rotunda suddenly became deathly silent. The elf's shoulders shook with reticent rage. "When we are gathered here, Rhox, you address your fellows by their titles."

All eyes were on Rhox's massive frame as he took his seat once again. It was an uncomfortable minute before Dryad broke the silence. "Rhox, what the hell?"

"Dryad!" Miranda shot the halfling a look that could have stabbed him if he so much as moved. He put his hands in his lap. "Now. Rhox. Everything. Please."

The half-orc put his head in one hand. "That *was* everything. We were told this ragtag group was plotting to attack us. We called for an Inquisition—I don't even remember who it was who carried *that* out—and the very next day, Luna summoned us here to bear witness to that atrocity." He lazily waved his other hand in the direction of the visible flow.

"*Thank you*, Rhox." Miranda nodded toward him. "Would anyone else *like* to follow that?"

Luna timidly raised her hand. "Um, I can go, if that's okay."

Miranda sighed, visibly relaxing. "Very well, Luna."

The elf of light turned to Diablo. "I was one of two tasked with the Inquisition. The other was Dryad." She motioned to the still silent halfling now twiddling his thumbs.

Miranda forced a smile and nodded. "And what did that Inquisition find, Luna?"

Luna's gaze turned downward. "We . . . It was inconclusive."

"What do you mean 'inconclusive'?"

"We couldn't determine much of anything about the supposed plot. Certainly, none of the four made to attack us—err . . ." She paused. "Well, none of them seemed to be part of any sort of plot in any event. But of course, when one is asked directly about such things, it's not easy to trust such responses. So we . . . tracked them."

Miranda nodded again. "Tracked them how?"

Luna continued. "I placed a tracking spell on them so we could determine their intents from where they went. The four of them, all went straight for Feuerschloss, the home of Salamandro."

"So that sounds like it wasn't inconclusive."

Luna nodded. "It's certainly damning. But . . ." She paused again. "I don't know. All I know is two of the dots disappeared at Feuerschloss and the other two very shortly thereafter began fleeing the castle. That's when I realized the volcano was erupting."

"That's all?"

"Well . . ." Luna paused. "I did try to contact Salamandro at that time when I noticed the two fleeing the scene. Mostly I just wanted to make sure he was still alright. But . . . He seemed panicked. I suspected something must have gone terribly wrong. That's when I came up here to visually inspect Fire Mountain."

Miranda nodded once more, her face visibly relaxing. "Dryad, your take? You were the other on the Inquisition."

The halfling looked up at being called upon. He shifted his weight forward, moving to stand on his throne. "I really don't have anything to add to Luna's telling. If anything, she knew more than I did. I left her chambers long before the eruption occurred."

"You were one of the first ones here when Luna called, were you not?"

Dryad nodded. "I wasn't sure what to expect after the Inquisition, but whatever it was, it couldn't have been good. I'd kept myself at the ready from the moment I left. I . . . didn't sleep for almost forty-eight hours. It's a good thing, eh?"

Luna brought her hand to her mouth. "You hadn't slept!? You should have said something!"

"No, no, it was fine really!" Dryad grinned. "All I could do was run logistics on the evacuations anyway."

"Luna, while I share your concern—and, Dryad, you really could have said something—please do not interrupt." Miranda motioned back to Dryad. "You were saying?"

"Not really," he sat back down. "That was pretty much it."

Miranda gave another nod. "Very well. Manas? Chevron? Anything further?"

Manas shrugged. "Rhox . . . He didn't express it *quite* as I might have, but he covered all my bases. I knew literally nothing going into this."

"Same here," replied Chevron. "I mean, I guess I noticed the plume of ash before Luna summoned us, but I really didn't think anything of it at the time. Well," he rubbed the back of his head, "not until Rhox beat it into me really."

"Well!" Miranda clapped her hands. "This was far less formal than I'd hoped for, but I suppose we did get somewhere." She turned to Diablo. "Now. Salamandro. What we've said here essentially comprises our collective understanding of the events of the eruption. The fact of it is Rhox is not the only one who feels . . . that way, he's just more . . . vocal than anyone else about it."

Chevron shot Miranda a sideways glance.

"But what we do not know is your side of the story." She pointed toward the half-orc with her still clasped hands. "This Tribunal was called for that purpose. So go on."

Diablo swallowed the lump in his throat. These people . . . How many of them wanted to kill him where he stood? Or would they simply maim him well enough that Asmodeious gets suspicious and kills him himself? He brushed a bit of collecting sweat from his brow.

"Salamandro." Manas leaned forward. "Take as much time as you need. We want to know what happened—what *really* happened."

Diablo nodded to the gnome, giving himself a little shakedown. "Right. So as was described by Luna, those four individuals arrived at Feuerschloss much more rapidly than I was expecting. I'd been working on a trinket before they showed up, something to help me hone my magic—it's what I do in my spare time. Anyway, this trinket, it was a little bracelet elemental summoner. And so, when this group arrived, since I had this thing—"

"Wait, was that . . ." Rhox sat up. "Was that immense thing an elemental summon?"

"Yes! Well, it was at first a gigantic bird comprised of magma."

"The legendary Pyror . . ." Rhox fell backward into his chair. "*You* summoned the legendary Pyror?"

"Err . . ." *It wasn't really me . . .* "Y-Yes! But see, in the ensuing fracas the summoning bracelet was shot off my wrist—one of them had a crossbow—and fell into the lava. About then Luna contacted me and . . . well, you know the rest."

Rhox shot a glance at Manas; the gnome merely shrugged.

Diablo looked back and forth at the pair of them. "What . . . what did I say?"

Rhox waved his hand dismissively. "Don't worry about it. This sounds like the end of your side of the story. Shall we deliberate?"

Miranda looked to Diablo, who returned a single nod. "Very well! It certainly sounds to me like the whole incident was little more than an accident of power."

"You can say that again." Rhox rubbed his forehead in his fingers. "I've never . . ." He sat back up. "I'm still quite upset at the incredible damage this caused. Surely you knew summoning such a massive creature could go horrendously wrong."

It was Diablo's turn to shrug. "I really just wanted to end this threat."

Manas shook his head. "I suppose we don't know if the remaining two survived the incident?"

Diablo looked down at the floor, trying to recollect. "They jumped from the roof of the castle—it was a good fifty-foot drop. I do know they started running after that, but . . ." He looked up at Luna. "There's no way they could have outrun it, right? Certainly not as injured as they must have been."

Luna paused momentarily. "Well, maybe. My tracking spell wore off after a certain amount of time. I didn't see where they ended up." Her eyes darted over to Dryad for one fleeting moment. "Although you're right, it does seem unlikely."

"This is a great discussion and I'd be thrilled to have it in a moment," Miranda stood from her throne, "but can we deliver a verdict first? On the issue immediately at hand?"

Rhox nodded. "I think, given the accidental nature of the incident, we give him one more chance." He looked to Diablo. "I'm putting an awful lot of trust in you. Another fuck up like this . . ."

Diablo shook his head. "Of course! Never again! I doubt I even could!"

Manas was next to deliver a decision. "I'm on board with that. Besides, anyone who can summon . . . *that* really ought to be here, wouldn't you say?"

Dryad glanced at Luna. "I don't know. It was an *awful* lot of damage. Was it really justified to stop what amounts to two people?"

Luna sighed. "I agree with you, Dryad, but . . . I don't know."

"Look, what's to debate?" Manas stood on his chair. "We know that there was a plot to take us out. That requires *tons* of power to even *think* about it. I think it was only justified to throw his full power at them, it was self-defense!"

Luna looked at Diablo and at once he felt as though her gaze could pierce his very being. "Don't do it again. Do we have an agreement?"

"Yes, of course!" Diablo motioned to Rhox with his hands. "I just said—"

"I know what you said to him. I want you to swear."

Diablo swallowed. "Very well. I swear it."

Luna remained motionless for a few moments, staring daggers into the half-orc. "Very well."

"It sounds like we at least have a quorum, if not a consensus." Miranda looked to the only one who hadn't spoken. "Chevron?"

"Look, I don't know about anything like this. These people, they survived my blowing them out of the air, in a contraption *I invented.* I have to think he was at least somewhat justified."

"Fine, whatever." Dryad slumped in his seat. "I'll give you another chance. But *never* again."

Diablo turned to the halfling and gave an awkward bow, bending his rigid torso forward. "Of course!"

Miranda sighed. "Very well. At least for the time being, Salamandro, you are placed on conditional probation. From this moment forward, you *must* report to us on a regular basis so we may review your work and actions. We'll hold another council like this . . . let's say once a month?" Every head in the semicircle nodded. "Once a month. And the moment we discover you've taken such destructive means again there will be grave consequences."

* * *

Asmodeious paced the full length of his lowest laboratory, arms folded behind his hominid form's back. His pitch-black robes furled with each heel turn, a flourish that would look beautiful on most any form but his; a menacing scowl destroyed any such illusion.

"I can't believe it." He shook his head. "I still can't believe it!" He ran to one of his myriad shelves, swiping his arms across the one within reach and knocking various priceless artifacts to the warm stone floor. He turned back around and let out a roar that belied his true nature. "*HOW!?* HOW could he have *POSSIBLY* awakened his powers in that moment!? The moment when victory was all but certain!" He slammed his hands on the freshly empty surface, knocking a few more articles to the ground as a result. "His last ounce of strength. With his *dying breath*, he—" The transformed dragon grabbed a large glass vessel and threw it with his full strength, sending the thing flying clear across the room, where it shattered immediately upon contact.

The sound of breaking glass seemed to calm his rage at least a bit. "But he *did* die. There isn't a chance he can use that power again. And as for the rest of his entourage . . ." His gaze turned upward as he thought. "None of them could have done anything to me anyway, but even so, they're all dead anyway. No one could have outrun that lava flow. Plus, bonus! It did a lot of the work I'd meant to do with that tooth anyway!" His smile returned, more of a menacing grin than one of pure joy. "Yes, the destruction, the devastation. HA! Had *she* been alive to see it . . ." He brought his hands, clutched, to his chest. "'Oh, you want to bargain with your second-born as well? Oh please, madam, I can only take so many! Besides, you're *DEAD!*'" He threw his head back and let out a powerful laugh. "Your son is probably stronger than you ever were, woman! And it's all thanks to my tutelage!"

How many times had he had this same conversation with nobody in particular? He'd lost count. The last month had been spent stewing in his own strange sort of self-pity.

That last line though, his line of thought was brought back to the here and now, back to Feuerschloss. Back to Diablo.

"Where *is* that boy anyway?"

The dragon began the arduous climb back toward the main floor of the desolate castle; once he'd made it back to the grand foyer, a place with enough room to do so, he returned to his natural draconic form.

"Diablo thought he'd snuck out earlier. He should know better." Asmodeious peeked into his apprentice's much smaller laboratory. "Damn. Shouldn't have reverted. This freaking castle! It's like it was built for halflings!"

Even so, he was able to see what he sought quite readily: Diablo's still relatively new clairvoyance cauldron. He pressed his muzzle against the doorway. "Fire's Keep."

As before, the surface shimmered; he positioned his eye in the doorway again. "UGH, this is so frustrating!"

Even so, he was able to make out the controls. Unbeknownst to Diablo, he'd even taken the liberty of mapping his apprentice's genetic signature to the cauldron for this exact sort of thing. "Find Diablo."

The surface of the material shimmered again, and within moments a clear image of the half-orc was visible. "Wait, where the hell . . . ? Cauldron, zoom out."

The image shrank and more of the surrounding environs were visible. Asmodeious squinted; from this angle he couldn't quite make it out, but it seemed like an opulent sort of palace or temple. Ornately adorned stone floor, immense marble columns supporting, he couldn't see it but he had to assume there was a roof of some kind. It almost looked Grecian, but he knew no such structure existed in the mountains. And it would have had to be in the mountains if those were indeed clouds he was seeing outside.

But upon zooming out, another, more immediate, question entered his mind: "Who are those other people he's with? Sound on!"

"Very well. At least for the time being, Salamandro, you are placed on conditional probation."

"Who the hell is Salamandro? Is that what they're calling Diablo?"

"From this moment forward, you *must* report to us on a regular basis so we may review your work and actions. We'll hold another council like this . . . let's say once a month?"

"Report to them? You report to *ME!*" Asmodeious pulled his head out of the narrow walkway and let out an angry roar that shook the very foundation. "You are *MY* apprentice! Who are these people who presume to take you away!?"

The dragon again placed his eye to that doorframe, trying to catch the end of the conversation. Looking at the scene again, however, he realized something.

"These people . . . They're all *incredibly* powerful." He pulled back again, mulling this over. "Not quite as powerful as me but . . ." He pondered. "Almost like . . ." He shook his head. There was no way! But then he cocked an eyebrow. "They *did* find Diablo . . ."

He put his eye back to the door. "One, two . . . six. Six others. Is this . . . What had they been called, the Revered? Something like that?" He studied each as closely as he could, being sure to save their "signatures" to the cauldron.

"Six. Six total. Together they might pose quite a threat." He again pulled back into the main foyer. "But separately they're easy pickings. I'll show them. And I'll show *him* for thinking he could possibly get out from under my wing!" Asmodeious returned to his hominid form to begin descending the grand stairs to his labs.

"I can't do this while he's here. He can't know that I'm attacking his newfound 'friends.' I don't want to test his allegiance. He's been a good apprentice, and I'd hate to have to kill him."

5

Outset

JUSTIN ROLLED ONTO his side on the mattress, bringing his knees up to his chest, causing the crisp white casino sheets to bunch up underneath him. He could practically feel the bags under his eyes as their center of gravity shifted, sagging toward the side of his face. The light coming through the window behind him lit the room well enough that he could see Angelo's bed was empty. It was morning, late enough that his companion was already at the casino floor.

He closed his eyes for the umpteenth time since crawling under the covers last night, clenching them tightly, feeling the hint of tears roll down his nose and temple. He'd not gotten an ounce of sleep. He pulled the sheets up over his head, bending his chin down toward his chest.

They were his family. They had been his family, his very own flesh and blood. And in the moment he needed them most, at a time when he was most vulnerable, they'd tossed him out on the street. And for what? Because someone had told them he'd attacked the Revered?

Who'd told them that anyway? Who *would* have told them such a bold-faced lie? And why? It had to be someone with some clout, someone the council would believe. He shook his head. It just had to be someone they would believe over him. That wasn't exactly difficult, apparently.

He thought back to the Inquisition. It was clear the group was concerned about their trek to Feuerschloss, but had Dryad and Luna truly believed they intended to attack them? If so, why had they been dropped off practically at the castle's gates?

Whatever had happened at Feuerschloss, it definitely had to do with the Revered. The new panel on the altar, the new symbol on his map. What did it mean? And what did it have to do with their quest? Why would someone either believe they intended to do harm to the Revered or else benefit from that lie? What was going on that they weren't seeing?

Justin pushed the sheets back off his face, in one motion rolling back onto his back, kicking his legs back down, and straightening his arms along his sides. Did any of that matter? Was it important in the moment? The fact was the Bailey clan had excommunicated him. He no longer had a family. The closest thing at this point would probably be Angelo. Or Don Kane perhaps.

What was he to do? Stephen was dead. His family wanted nothing more to do with him. He stared at the eggshell popcorn ceiling above him, shadows of the morning light casting the subtle points of the texture as massive peaks by their shadows. What was there *to* do?

His gaze fell back in the direction of Angelo's empty bed. His friend had no idea of his current predicament. He'd not said anything, preferring to keep it to himself until he could come up with some sort of answer.

His mind came back to that altar. His old "domicile" outside Flood City. Did it remain? The underground portion had been sturdily built; it's possible it survived the eruption, if nothing else. He at least had *things* there. Perhaps.

He sat up in the bed, looking out the window at that black expanse. People *had* crossed it already, they needed to. There was plenty of trade between the two cities to warrant such treacherous trekking. Could he? Could he bring himself to do so?

His eyes focused on the horizon, where he could just make out the barest outline of Flood City. It was something. It may not have been the best thing, but it was a thing to do. He nodded to no one in particular.

He'd brave the barren obsidian wasteland. He'd try to make the journey to his old home to piece together his own belongings. He could decide a direction from there. For now, this was enough. This was a plan.

His eyes closed again and the elf fell backward onto his pillow. In seconds, he was out.

*　*　*

Dryad lay back in his throne, staring at a coat of arms that hung on the opposite wall; the banner shield was decorated with a series of symbols relevant to his clan, the primary field dominated by a sprawling verdant tree with multiple trunks contained beneath a black isosceles triangle, the upper point of which was garnished with a spire. His brow furrowed, the fuzzy caterpillars that were his eyebrows inching closer as he contemplated the series of events that had recently been instigated. The big picture, or what he could make out of it at least, reminded him heavily of the story of his people, that shield's primary tale. It was something he'd never really understood; indeed, many points of the story seemed impossible or at least illogical. Nevertheless, he recognized the symbolism contained within, and it was in that symbolism he now sought to discover some sort of hidden meaning behind this recent chain of seemingly unrelated happenstances.

Feuerschloss, he knew, was the building on the triangle, the shape itself representing Fire Mountain. "Teinemeall" they called it in the old tongue, a peak that contained at its core what they called a ley-line culmination of magical energies of the flame. His people were its progenitors, taking the rock from the very slopes of the mountain itself, carving it a radiantly black facade. They resided within its massive halls, protected from the heat of the fire by the building. A formerly migratory people, the halflings of this clan came across this land far before anyone else had even pondered approaching the mountains; the power they felt radiating from it, it is said, was more than enough to convince them to settle.

The ancients had built this magnificent place, large enough to contain everything they would ever conceive of requiring for sustenance. Water was not bountiful, so it had to be carried in from nearby rivers and streams, stored in massive holding tanks below the keep; the lower the tank, the warmer the water, each level being used for its own purposes. Whether bathing or taking care of the more exotic flora they had brought from near the ocean, warm water was a precious commodity they did not take for granted.

With the focus of fire energy surrounding the castle, the forefathers knew a balance had to be maintained; the people who were gifted with the ability to use magic concentrated their efforts on that of plants, maintaining a regular food supply for the halfling clan while simultaneously somehow utilizing the fire magics toward another, very different, purpose, diverting the excess by reshaping it. This is one aspect of the story that Dryad could never wrap his head around—certainly a balance needed to be kept, but what was this magical energy they were diverting? There were no such things as ley lines he knew; why did this one feature so prominently in the tale?

These people continued their lives quite happily for many years until one fateful day. The magical energy they had been using became tainted somehow. The fire raged, intent on consuming instead of radiating. The volcano erupted, claiming many lives; the castle was built for sturdiness and protection, but it was as if the fire sought to inflict damage. Indeed, the very earth rumbled beneath the foundation, and there was little anyone could do but run, hoping to save themselves. There was no time to make sure loved ones could escape; a few later found each other, but ultimately the clan had become decimated by the events. They knew they could no longer return safely.

The survivors remained together for companionship and safety, but they were no longer fit to be nomads as their ancestors had been. Having come to rely on a steady supply of readily available food, they were incapable of hunting. Being so heavily reliant on the confluence of ley lines for magic, many of their wizards could no longer conjure even a simple sprout from what few seeds they could scavenge. To make matters worse, the expanse of plains they now fled across was rapidly drying out as if the very water was fleeing the land. Those streams they had grown to trust had now become parched paths of dirt winding through the dying foliage. They provided something of a trail for the fleeing clansmen at least, but the fluvial nature of the former rivers was disorienting and quite grueling to navigate. It was as though the entire world had suddenly, inexplicably turned on them.

Just as the few remaining survivors were about to give up hope, it is said a miracle was granted to the clan. The morning sun greeted the exhausted halflings with less intensity than it had left them the evening before. As they awoke, the clan was startled to discover a tree had grown in the very spot they chose to rest, easily twenty feet tall and with giant flat leaves that caught and deflected the sun's harsh rays. They recognized the species to be a kind of banyan fig, a sacred tree even at the time for its ability to shelter; however, none before or since had ever displayed the same intense rate of growth this specimen exhibited. Deciding to take this boon as a blessing, the people went out into the surrounding plains on their own, and each brought back some form of meager food; when they returned to prepare their daily meals, the tree had already spread its branches over a thirty-foot radius, several aerial roots trailing down for eventual support.

They were not the only beings to recognize this miraculous event; indeed, a family of sparrows was discovered nesting among its branches that evening, and the morning saw much more in the way of fauna congregating at the tree, seeking food and shelter. The second day brought with it the first blossoms, and plenty of insects got to work immediately, pollinating as they sought their own sustenance. The early blooms were producing figs by the end of the second day, the tree's impressive girth providing more than enough room for all creatures who desired its shelter to rest beneath its boughs. The clan chose that second night to make this their new home, naming the tree Gealbhanmeall as a tribute to both their first sighted companions and the mountain keep they had left behind.

Dryad himself was born beneath this very tree he knew. He could remember running through the support trunks in childhood games, the other youngsters shouting, "Bring us back the biscuits, Galan!" He'd climb the tree to eat figs when he was playing hooky with his studies. He'd always had an innate knack for the sort of magic the former wizards of the clan had left behind, and from a young age had earned the name Sprouttalker for his ability to start plants from seed. He knew he owed his current life to the tree; had it not sheltered him when he was infantile, fed him when he was hungry, or intrigued him when he was growing, he could never have taken the post of Dryad.

That fact, however, had little to do with why he was reviewing the tale over and over in his mind. The eruption, the desolation, and the sudden miracle—except for the last part, it all seemed quite familiar to what was going on now, though perhaps not to scale. What happened back then to cause the eruption? Perhaps a better question, he reasoned, might be why they thought it wouldn't erupt in the first place. Did the desert truly form as they fled their former home? What had caused such an immense catastrophe, and what was at the heart of this one? He knew he needed more information. Perhaps Rhox, much more familiar with the nature of the Earth, might have some clues, the diminutive halfling determined. Sitting up in his throne, he made a mental note to discuss certain events with the other member of the Revered.

*   *   *

Asmodeious knelt in the middle of the stone floor. This chamber had started out as one of his many laboratories, but it had become something of a meditation room for the dragon. It was a place where he could mentally prepare himself for a particular challenge.

And boy, was this a challenge. He'd decided, in Diablo's absence, to go after the member of the Revered who appeared to show the most skill. After one or two periods of observation, this appeared to be the one designated as Rhox. Moments before, Asmodeious had determined this particular half-orc was at a location in the desert on the other side of the mountains, something that made him a relatively easy target. Everything was just perfect.

Opening his eyes, Asmodeious rose to his feet, his robes flowing back down over his ankles. He stretched his neck, shaking out his arms, before ascending the stairs to the rooftop. He gazed out in the direction he'd seen Rhox's particular "palace" to be. He couldn't see it over the mountains but he knew it to be there.

The creature returned to his natural form, giving his wings a stretch before leaping from the castle; using the thermals from the magma body below, he quickly rose into the air, a perilous shadow blighting a cerulean sky. Rising well above the cloud line, he folded his wings behind himself, entering into a dive straight at that point he'd seen in the cauldron.

Asmodeious recognized the half-orc seconds before arriving at his destination; this sandstone structure, while ornately carved, lacked a roof of any kind, making such sight much easier. He had plenty of time to adjust his trajectory.

Rhox heard it, a soft whistling in the air. His brown-green ears swiveled, the half-orc turning his head this way and that, trying to see what it was he was hearing. In a moment, an incredible force slammed him into the floor, claws piercing flesh, ribs cracking under the immense weight of the dragon.

The half-orc came to remarkably quickly; his head slowly rolled back and forth, the weakest of utterances coming from his mouth before the great beast reared up off him onto his hind legs. A swipe of a forelimb and the half-orc's body rolled along the abrasive sandstone floor, only coming to a stop as his back slammed into a massive column.

Asmodeious grinned, shifting himself to his hominid form; he knew Rhox was more durable than this, that he would not only survive but try to fight back, and did not want to betray his own identity to this being. As Rhox's eyes began to open again, the dragon brought both hands to one side of his body, readying a fireball.

The half-orc shook his head. *What just happened?* He lifted himself on a shaky arm, pushing himself back upright, and scanned the area; his eyes fell on this intruder and he immediately realized he was preparing another attack. Pushing himself onto one foot and one knee, he swiftly brought his arms up to cover his face. "Stone Shield!"

No sooner had he sputtered the spell than Asmodeious hurled the fireball straight at him with such force and speed he could hear the very air crackle around it. The sphere struck his arms, knocking the half-orc off his feet and onto his back.

"Ahh!" Rhox rubbed one of his forearms with the opposite hand, the skin on both singed bad enough to be first-degree burns. For a fireball to have the kind of heat that it could do this through his Stone Shield . . . *Who is this?*

He rolled over to the side opposite that sandstone pillar, narrowly dodging another fireball and inadvertently jamming his arms into his damaged chest. "Ah, *FUCK!*" He coughed up a splatter of blood as he pulled his arms out from under himself, pushing himself to his hands and knees. He looked behind himself, seeing through defocused eyes that the robed figure held the same pose.

Rhox wasn't Chevron but he'd picked up enough wind magic from his peer to use the spell he spoke next: "Towering Leap!" He shoved himself off the ground with weakened limbs, flying into the air just as another blast of heat nearly seared his front.

He winced as he tucked his arms back under his chest in the air, twirling to retain control over his trajectory. That, unfortunately, made little difference: Asmodeious was already preparing yet another fireball. He flung this one into the air, striking Rhox's legs as he fell.

The bones splintered, the fire burning down to his very muscle. Rhox let out a shriek of pain; he landed on his back, rolling haphazardly along the ground.

Surely he's not dead yet, Asmodeious pondered. *We've only just begun!* He stepped toward the limp being, preparing another spell just in case.

Rhox groaned weakly before vomiting onto the floor beside his head, blood and bile swirling in the chunky mess he could barely see. His first thought was on how cold this floor was; his next was the realization that he could no longer feel his legs.

Asmodeious placed a foot on the weakened half-orc's arm. "I thought you'd've had more fight in you." He put his weight on that leg and Rhox whimpered a breathy cry.

"Rhox? You here?" A diminutive halfling wandered out of an alcove.

Asmodeious cursed under his breath. He recognized the voice, and in a moment he was able to confirm: this was the one they called Dryad.

"Hello? Hey, wh—" Dryad stared at the scene before him. "What are you doing!? Who are you!?"

Asmodeious didn't want to fight a battle on two fronts. Sure, Rhox was mostly incapacitated, but he was still more than capable of hurling spells if he wanted to. Their combined power, he wasn't sure how well he'd fare. The dragon leapt from the side of the palace, immediately running out into the sand of the expansive desert.

"Rhox!" Dryad ran to his colleague, dropping to his knees beside the massive limp body. "Rhox, buddy! You okay? Speak to me!"

The half-orc's eyes barely opened. "D-Dryad? Is that you?"

"Yes! Come on, stay with me, big guy . . ." Dryad looked out over the side that strange figure had jumped from; he was nowhere to be found. "Damn! Oh geez, what do I do?" He looked over Rhox's form. He recognized that his friend was gravely injured, but beyond that . . . His specialty was plants, not animals.

"Alright, big guy, let's . . . Let's get you to the Edifice . . ." He looked behind himself to where the teleportation pad was located. A good fifty feet. He cursed to himself. "D-don't worry, I've got you. Your pal Galan has you. We just . . ." He grabbed Rhox's arms and immediately recoiled from the scorched flesh. "Oh, man. Okay. It's okay." He stood back up, shaking out his arms. "It's all gonna be okay. Just gotta get him there."

He reached back down and grabbed those arms again, shuddering at the crispness of the half-orc's skin under his fingers. He gave Rhox's body a tug, barely moving him an inch. "Fuck."

Half an hour later, Rhox's breathing had grown laborious, but Dryad had managed to get him to the teleportation pad. In a moment they were back on the Edifice. "Hello? Anyone out there!? I need some help!"

The door to Rhox's meditation chamber flew open. "Dryad! I thought that was you." Diablo stepped forward, followed shortly by Manas. "What's all the—HOLY—"

Manas' jaw dropped. "Is that . . . Rhox?"

"*Please* help me get him to the rotunda."

Diablo ran in, grabbing one of the other half-orc's arms and wrapping it around his shoulders. "What the hell happened to him?"

"I-I don't really know! He was—There was this other guy and—"

"Wait, other guy?" Manas ran around behind Rhox and hefted his legs. "Are—Are you saying he was attacked?"

"I think so? I didn't really see it very clearly. By the time I got to Rhox's side, he was gone."

"But it was just one guy? Just one person did this to him?"

Dryad shrugged. "I can't imagine it myself, but . . . that's what it looked like."

6

Regrets

LAUGHTER ECHOED ACROSS the front of the short row of houses, a young half-elf chasing after a colorful ball his father had thrown across the yard. Hands outstretched, running stiff kneed behind the bouncing toy, the boy stumbled, quickly falling to his side. Carlos rose with a start but relaxed when he heard the boy's giggle rise from his collapsed form. "Angelo, where's the ball?"

The half-elf rolled over onto his back. "I can see it, Daddy!"

His father placed his hand on his own waist in mock exasperation. "Well? Are you going to throw it back to me?" He took a lumbering step toward his supine son. "Or is the dad monster gonna have to get it?"

"Oh no!" giggled the child. "Not dad monster!"

"Uh-oh . . ." Carlos growled. "I think maybe the dad monster's gonna have to come over . . ." He trudged across the grass. "He might even be . . . a tickle monster!"

"Nooo!" Angelo rolled back and forth, giggling before his father had even gotten to his knees. "Daddy, wait, don't tickle me!"

"Well, okay, if you insist!" Carlos flopped in the grass beside his son. "Do you not wanna play ball anymore?"

Angelo grinned. "I just thought this felt nice!"

"You're not wrong."

The half-elf giggled again, laying his head back down, staring up. "Dad, why is the sky blue?"

Carlos folded his arms behind his head, looking up at more or less the same patch of sky as his son. "Well how do you know it's blue? Someone else might see it as purple or green."

Angelo laughed. "Green? Daddy, that's just silly!"

"Hey now, maybe I see the sky as green!"

"Do you?"

"No, but maybe I did! You don't know that!"

Angelo smiled and lay his head back down. A moment of happy silence passed between the two. "Dad, why did you name me Angelo?"

Carlos' expression changed rather quickly. "Why do you ask?"

"I'm just curious."

Carlos sighed. He stared up into the sky, not sure if he was searching for the words there or just stalling for time. "I . . . I wanted to be able to protect you even when I cannot. And I thought that maybe if you were named after the angels they might help look after you as one of their own."

"Does that work?"

Carlos stared into the sky, watching the clouds float by for a moment. "I sure hope so."

Angelo just smiled. "But, Daddy, you'll always be able to protect me!"

Carlos winced. "I wasn't able to protect your brother."

"Brother?" Angelo rolled over onto his elbows. "I have a brother?"

The man shook his head, putting a smile on. "Never mind that, let's find that ball."

* * *

"Angelo. Angelo, come on."

"Hmm, what?" The half-elf shook his head.

"It's your bet." The dealer motioned toward a pair of cards in front of the gambler.

"Uh, is—is it open?"

The dealer nodded. "It's your call, sir."

"Err, where are we?"

"It just opened, we're at lowest bid."

"Err, alright, sure, whatever." Angelo tossed a chip toward the center of the table, lifting his drink to his lips with his other hand.

"Sir, are you sure? You've not even looked at your hand."

"It's fine, just go."

Angelo reached forward and pulled those two cards toward himself, lifting the corner and giving them a cursory look, promptly forgetting what the cards were. A blink, and suddenly three cards were on the table, his eyes having difficulty focusing on them. He shook his head again, reaching over to grab another chip off his stack; a moment later, he opened his eyes again, vision obscured by shaded green felt. Was he upside down? Where was he?

"Angelo! Come on, boy, wake up!" It took him a moment to realize someone had grabbed him by his shoulders, shaking him side to side.

The half-elf, barely conscious enough to not realize the dealer was the one holding onto him, slammed his fist on the table, using the sudden movement as propulsion to throw his head and torso back up. The sudden action nearly knocked the dealer to the ground and threatened to teeter Angelo backward off his stool. Light infiltrated his eyes, the scene revealing itself before him once again, and he vaguely remembered where he was.

Monsoon City. Road's End. Justin.

Where's Justin?

Angelo's head snapped back up in momentary sobriety. Justin. Where was he?

Right. He'd said he was going to brave the obsidian flow to survey the damage at his old place. The half-elf shook his head. He doubted much remained of any structure above ground; the thing was falling apart as it was. He'd been amazed the slightest breeze hadn't knocked it down years ago. But underground?

That bunker maybe. Justin had clearly designed the thing to withstand some serious damage. He'd wanted anything within to survive . . . something. Maybe a magical blast? He shook his head again. Knowing Justin, he wanted to save that space from himself. Angelo knew the wizard would never admit it, but it had to be true.

"Angelo?" The dealer snapped his fingers before the gambler's eyes, his other hand remaining on his shoulder. "We alright?"

Shit. "Shit. Uh, yeah. Sorry." He scanned the table again, eyes struggling to focus on any one thing. "Um . . . Where are we now?"

The dealer sighed, lifting the hand on Angelo's shoulder to give a nonverbal halt to a man bringing yet another full glass to the table, a glass he had to hold somewhat away from himself to keep from fainting. "Angelo, I need you to focus on the table or I'm going to have to ask you to leave. We can't have this large a distraction at the tables."

The half-elf nodded, giving his cheek a light smack, trying to bring himself back to the present, to the table. "Right, right, of course." He squinted, again scanning the felt. "So . . . Where are we?"

The dealer stood, giving a light shrug to the rest of the table. "The flop's on the table. It's your bet."

Angelo nodded. Of course Justin was away, how else would he get away with drinking this heavily? "Right, so . . ." He peeked at his cards again, retaining the information a bit better. "Alright, I'll call."

His brother. The Revered. Angelo found his mind wandering once more. Was that other man, that half-orc, was he really his half-brother? And what did he have to do with the Revered? With the fire? He shook his head swiftly and took another swig.

The altar. Justin had predicted—well, "predicted"—the ending of their journey using that altar and a related map. His brother was at that end. As was that . . . monster.

The giant black dragon. "Asmodeious" his brother had called it. Powerful enough to corrupt the hearts of men, or so it seemed. He shuddered, taking another gulp.

But the Revered seemed to be involved as well. In addition to the map, there was the Inquisition. That strange halfling. Justin knew exactly who he was.

"I'll raise." A voice from across the table snapped Angelo back to reality; he groaned softly, gripping the side of his head. Who turned up the lights? Where was his next drink?

"Fine, whatever." The half-elf tossed a small handful of chips toward the pot, a number that seemed to approximate whatever the other individual had dropped. The dealer tossed a chip back at him to even it out.

Why had the Revered, whoever they were, been interested in their quest? Did *they* have something to do with Springsboro? Or was it just his brother? Or the thing living with him?

"Alright, showdown, folks. Let's see 'em." Angelo hazily flipped his cards; in moments, a small stack of chips was pushed in his direction.

Something wasn't adding up. But maybe Justin had a lead.
I hope he's doing alright.

*   *   *

"Shit!" Justin stumbled to his knees and the distinct sound of ripping fabric let him know his robes had finally given up holding together against the razor-sharp volcanic glass. He'd had the foresight to wrap his hands and knees in a tear-resistant fabric tape, but there was precious little he could do about his clothing.

I could've tried to enchant it against tears as well. Hush, you. Justin shook his head, shakily pushing himself back to his feet. He would have been every bit as likely to disintegrate his clothing as enchant it properly.

He looked down at himself, arms out to either side, trying to keep steady on the slick glass surface. *I mean, if this keeps up, the result will be the same.* His robes weren't in *bad* shape, all things considered; a couple deep gouges but still holding together somehow. But he'd not made it terribly far either; he carefully peered over his shoulder, still quite able to see Monsoon City.

You're used to not seeing the city until you're right on top of it, he reminded himself. With the jungle gone, the scenery was . . . different. It was one thing to survey it while standing at the edge, it was quite another thing entirely to be navigating this flow. No readily available fruit, no shade-providing trees.

No spiders, he shrugged.

He pulled his robe out away from his neck, letting the fabric drape away from his chest for a moment; a wave of heat poured from beneath, the stink of his own sweat assaulting his nostrils. He silently gave thanks for thinking to bring water with him.

His eyes scanned the sky as he took another unsteady step forward. *What happened to the rain?* Wasn't Miranda trying to weather this thing down? That seemed to be the reason for the otherwise regular storm systems in almost exclusively that region. Sure, Monsoon City had earned its name, as had Flood City, but the rains seemed to be far more focused on the slab rather than either location at either side. He'd read Miranda's original treatise on the storm systems of the region; this had clearly been magical intervention. Had something happened? Did the Revered decide it wasn't worth the effort?

I mean, people are *finding their way across.* Nobody else *today* it seemed, but he'd seen the caravans. And now here he was, making the same trek. Shakily, in fits and starts, but making it nonetheless.

He scanned the distant horizon, recognizing some faint landmarks through the thermal haze rising off the obsidian. *Will I be able to bring the altar back with me?* That'd been the original impetus, but it was a massive chunk of stone; it'd been a haul to bring it there from the ruins of River City, and then he didn't have to worry about walking on shattered glass. He'd had shade, places to stop and rest. He could slide it along on mud.

Another step and his foot slid out from under him again.

"SHIT!"

Back on his hands and knees. *Well, perhaps this slick surface lacks traction enough that it'll be similar.* He shook his head again, a bead of sweat dripping off his nose and evaporating near instantly on the black glass below. This was hell to get across *by himself*, much less with a gigantic monolith in tow. In shove? However he might think to move it.

The map at least. It wasn't quite as impressive but it was far more mobile, and it *did* have some information on it.

He noted a slick wetness under his hand; bringing it up for inspection, it drooled red. "Son of a . . ." *Do I drink it? Conserve water, conserve iron?* Another head shake. Bandages. He looked back down to his robes. Bandages. He hurriedly reached down, grabbing two corners of fabric on either side of a tear and yanking them apart, widening the rip but providing a ready strip of material. He began wrapping it around his wounded hand but stopped after two turns.

How am I gonna tie this off?

He squeezed the partially wrapped hand, blood immediately drenching the fabric. *Shit. Wait!* He wrapped the material a few more times until he was near the end; he then took one free end in his mouth, using his free hand to awkwardly form a knot around the taut length. *It's not perfect but it'll work. Just gotta be careful with it.*

He looked at his other hand, not gouged but certainly roughed up. *Gotta be careful in general. Would this be easier on hands and knees?*

He took another look behind him. It'd be humiliating, but if he can make it, what did that matter? Using his non-bandaged hand, he reached into his robes, pulling out a canteen, uncapping it and bringing it to his mouth. *Gotta replenish what I lost at least.*

*   *   *

"Sure seem to be calling plenty of these 'emergency meetings' lately." Chevron forced a smirk.

"Well that tends to happen when *someone actively attacks one of our own*." Dryad leaned toward the dwarf, brows furrowed in a dire expression, motioning with one arm toward the bed in the center of the chamber. "Right after," he whipped his head around to glare daggers at Diablo, "a major catastrophe caused by *another of our own!*" The half-orc shrank in his chair, a makeshift wooden construction someone had pulled out of a closet somewhere. Chevron pulled back, staring down the halfling.

"Fucking damn, I was just trying to break the ice!"

"With what, a joke?" Dryad leapt up, standing on his tree-branch armrest. "A joke about a dear friend and colleague who, might I remind you, is *two goddamn steps from being in a body bag!?*"

It was Chevron's turn to stand. "God DAMN, man! I was just saying! Calm the fuck down!"

"Saying what? That this is *such* an inconvenience for you? That you'd rather be whittling away a fucking useless hunk of glass, not thinking about the fact that it could be you next, lying like a goddamn lump in the middle of our assembly hall or *worse!?*"

"Dryad, Chevron!" Miranda sprang from her throne, putting herself between the two. Behind Dryad, Luna had also jumped from her seat, putting her hands on the halfling's shoulders. "That's enough! Both of you, sit!"

Dryad shook free of Luna's hands, putting up his own hand palm back toward her. "Sorry . . . Sorry. I'm just, this has me all kinds of keyed up, okay?"

Miranda looked down at her smaller colleague. "We all are. I certainly haven't been able to think of anything else."

Dryad looked back to the center of the chamber, to the narrow bed with a white sheet draped over the still unconscious Rhox. His eyes began to wet. "If I'd've been there just a bit sooner . . ."

Chevron inadvertently muscled through Miranda, putting a hand on Dryad's shoulder. "We're lucky you got there when you did, before any more damage could be done. I—I'm sorry, too. I wasn't trying to make light of this."

Dryad reached up and squeezed that hand. "I know. You have the habit of trying to break tension with comedy. In some cases it works, but right now . . ."

"I know. I'm sorry."

Miranda rapidly shook her head, grabbing her forehead. "So can we talk about this now?"

"Holy shit!" Chevron turned back toward the elf. "I'm so sorry! Are you okay?"

"Yeah, just good to know I would've been absolutely no roadblock if you wanted to go after someone."

Chevron cracked a smile. "Look at you, breaking tension with comedy. Seems I'm rubbing off on you."

"Don't you dare."

Diablo's cheeks flushed.

"Look, this is cute and all," Manas broke his own silence from the end of the semicircle, "but is there any chance we can get to the meat of the problem? Dryad may have been a touch emotional but he was still *right*. We've got one of our own completely disabled. Likely scarred for life. And Chevron's right too: we got lucky. Dryad happened to be in the right place at the right time this time. Emphasis on *this* time."

"What, you think this could be a serial offender?" Miranda looked inquisitively at the gnome.

"Well, let's look at the facts. A short while ago a group of folks assembled to attack the Revered and succeeded in attacking Salamandro, right?"

Diablo hadn't caught the cue, instead looking over at Miranda. "Diablo?"

The half-orc started. "Huh? What's that, Manas?"

"You were attacked by a group of folks, right? That's what caused the aforementioned 'catastrophe,' was it not?"

"Oh! Y-Yeah. I . . . um . . . Two of them were dispatched, and the other two, I can't imagine they survived . . . you know, *that*."

"But what if they did? You didn't confirm their deaths, did you?"

"How could I have?" Diablo shrugged his shoulders. "If they perished, what's left of their charred bones is buried under about twenty feet of obsidian."

"Dryad, Luna, you two performed the Inquisition, right?" Manas gestured at the pair.

"Err, yeah." Dryad rubbed at a temple. "They weren't . . . They were surprisingly tight-lipped about their intentions. Only one of them seemed to know who we were though."

"So, what if—and I'm just spitballing here—what if the pair managed to escape and attacked Rhox as something of a continuation of their quest?"

Dryad contemplated. "I mean, I guess it's *possible* . . ."

Luna reached over and squeezed at Dryad's hand.

"Did you get a good look at his assailant?" Manas extended a hand as though offering Dryad an opportunity to expound.

The halfling looked toward the white-linened lump in the middle of the room. "I really didn't. He—They, this person, was wearing dark robes but otherwise . . . They . . . looked white?"

"Not even a guess as to their race?"

"I mean, whoever it was did a lot of damage, mostly fire. I assume it was magic. So if I *had* to guess, they might've been an elf?"

"And you're *sure* it was just the one?"

Dryad threw his hands up. "Hell, I don't know! I only saw one figure. There might've been others present and I just didn't see them?"

"So it *could* have been the two attackers who *might* have escaped from Salamandro."

"I mean, I guess . . ."

"Hey now, come on, Manas." Miranda spoke up from the middle of the semicircle. "We don't know anything about who might've done this. We can't act on wild speculation!"

"But we can't just sit here and do nothing!" Manas jumped from his sod, walking toward Rhox's prone form. "We came dangerously close to losing someone this time. We can't just do nothing!"

"Yes, we can!" Miranda rubbed a temple. "Look, this is a problem, and it's obviously a serious one, but we can't just start attacking random folks on speculation!"

"It's not random folks! We know who it might be!"

"If they're even still alive, which they may not be, what proof do we have that they did this? None! This is *speculation!*"

"Very well, what do you suggest? We sit here and wait for another of us to be attacked?"

"Of course not! But after we wiped out half of Monsoon and Flood cities, we can't just take preemptive action like that again!" Miranda sat back down in her chair, not realizing she'd pulled so far forward. "We need to observe. Talk to our contacts, see if anyone knows about any leads. Anyone who wants any of us, particularly Rhox, dead. Hell, they might've just been after him for all we know. See? We know next to nothing about this!"

Manas sat back in his own seat, propping his chin up with a hand supported by his armrest. "So just observe, huh?"

"Observe, inquire. Learn more than we presently know!"

"Alright." The gnome shrugged. "Where do we begin?"

7

Counter

THE MORNING SUNLIGHT filtered through the open hatch in the ceiling, orange glow dancing through particulates directly into Justin's closed eyes. He stirred, moving to yawn and immediately hacking himself awake.

Everything above ground had been thoroughly decimated by fire as Justin had expected; still smoldering rectangles of broken black charcoal remaining the sole testament to any structure having been there previously—though if he was being fair, Justin knew the structure they implicated belied the old shack. A thin layer of black dust coated the brown earth, itself belying the true extent of the obsidian flow from a distance. Little was as it seemed.

The same could be said for the little bunker upon which floor Justin now found himself wheezing. He'd expected the destruction up top, sure; he hadn't expected quite the damage underground that he came back to. He'd left the hatch open out of necessity—when he'd opened it the night before, a thick cloud of soot poured from the sealed entrance.

All his papers, years of research, and in that moment the most important thing to him, his cot, had all combusted from the sheer heat of the lava flow immediately outside the chamber. Indeed, had the chamber itself not been made of stone, it might've caught just as readily. Hell, Justin was amazed it hadn't simply melted, upon seeing the destruction within.

Precious little had survived. The altar was still intact, itself having been made of stone and what Justin could only assume was magic; further, to his own surprise, the map had survived as well, minor singeing to the edges but otherwise still plenty usable. He'd misremembered—the map was made of a parchment, not paper. That simple fact had apparently allowed it to survive.

Justin, still choking on aerosolized coal, struggled up the ladder, poking his head out the hatch and taking a deep breath through his mouth, his nose having been plugged with blackened snot throughout his slumber. He'd thought about sleeping above ground, but as cold as the nights were getting and as much rain as *should* have been falling on the area, he'd felt it better to brave the soot than the elements. Besides, that way he might have a chance of being alerted if anyone tried to secret away his belongings, what few were left.

The elf looked back down into the hole at the top of the altar. There was simply no *way* he was getting that all the way to Monsoon City, frictionless or not. His bloodied shins bore witness to just how difficult it had been to get here, sore and bandaged hands adding their own proof; he'd be lucky if he could make it back in one piece by himself.

This left the question of the map. Would it survive such a trip? He had to assume the worst, that no matter how hard he tried, the map would regularly wind up in a position where the obsidian might cut it. Would it? If it did, would it be noticeable? Would the map still hold up? Would whatever magic that allowed the map to function retain itself over such damage?

He climbed back down the ladder into the still sooty room. Surely the magic wouldn't be damaged by something as banal as obsidian, right? But then, would it survive his attempts to repair it? He pulled the parchment out and unrolled it on top of the altar. *Maybe?*

The question then became what value would the map serve at this point? It had been little more than a glorified trinket when he'd found it and brought it here; truly its first bout of true worth had come when Stephen *et alii* arrived in Flood City. Would it be useful in the future?

And as if to answer, Justin's vision suddenly went black.

"Oh damn it."

*   *   *

Luna paced inside her chamber. The events of the emergency meeting still troubled her. Manas was correct, at least somewhat—Stephen, Angelo, John, and Justin had made their approach on Feuerschloss, and at least according to Salamandro, they'd attempted to attack him. He was able to confirm both Stephen and John had died; while he did not specify anyone by name—why would he have?—he'd nailed the exact number of the party who'd died, and they had certainly died inside the castle well before the lava flow began. There was no reason to suspect him of lying at that point, he'd simply let himself get carried away.

Except the Inquisition still gnawed at her. It had been the reason she'd saved Justin and Angelo; she wasn't sure, but it didn't seem like the party was particularly vested in the Revered's destruction. Justin had even *praised* them. The other three . . . It was like they'd only just heard of the Revered. They didn't know what was going on. Surely someone intent on destroying the Revered would *know* about them, at least enough to recognize an Inquisition.

Justin had. He knew. But then again he seemed the most innocent of the four. When she saved him and Angelo, he was the one who told Angelo to sheathe his blade; he had been the one to show deference. He knew, but he knew better.

Angelo, on the other hand, had been hot-headed in both their encounters; she'd seen his sword twice now. The half-elf had been the most combative in his responses and seemed to have the most hate in his eyes. Even so, he didn't seem to be angry specifically at the Revered save that she and Dryad had pulled them from their quest; no, he seemed angry at the situation, at something external. He was still young for a half-elf. Had something happened to him?

And again, when Justin told him to put away his weapon, he did so. That would not be the act of someone who genuinely wanted a member of the Revered dead for the fact of being a member of the Revered, *especially* considering how hot-headed he'd been.

Luna thought back to the incident that seemed to spark this conflict: Salamandro had told Chevron of a plot to destroy them, and as a result Chevron literally blew a plane out of the air. When confronted later, Salamandro and Miranda had both corroborated three conspirators on the plane, with a fourth having joined them in Flood City.

Which one was that?

Given John, Angelo, and Stephen's near total ignorance, Justin seemed the most likely, but then he was a wizard. He *must* have known about them regardless. Maybe he'd kept the others ignorant?

Stephen and John seemed unlikely; the two were clearly brothers. While it was possible they might've met up with either at the much larger city—Topaz was barely a blip on the map—families tend to stick together. Humans in particular were deeply invested in family; sure, elves had their own massive clans to whom they might be loyal, such as her own rae'Arkeneamitore, but humans didn't live anywhere near that long and still held on to the concept of family as important, perhaps even more so.

That left Angelo and Justin, the two who survived. Even then, Justin seemed the more likely. Angelo, being a half-breed, would be far less likely to have come from such an urban area; generally, interbreeding is heavily frowned upon in elven clans, and those who wish to do so tend to elope. A city might seem like the best place to hide, but quite the contrary, eyes are everywhere.

This left her with the same burning question: if Justin had joined the party *after* the plane crash, *how would the other three have been involved in a plot against the Revered?* They barely knew the Revered existed; what little knowledge they had *must* have been given to them by Justin.

Things didn't add up. She didn't have the whole story and she knew it.

Did they? Justin and Angelo, were *they* aware of what was happening? If Manas was right in his accusations, they must, but she still had doubts.

She stood from her throne. She knew what she had to do.

"Oh damn it." A flash of light and Justin was before her. Another flash and a familiar half-elf collapsed to the floor on his left. "Shit! Angelo!"

"Um . . . Is he gonna be okay?" Luna sheepishly pointed at Angelo's crumpled form. "Pretty sure that wasn't me."

"No, it wasn't—" Justin immediately straightened his posture, facing the luminous elf. "My apologies! Luna, what—Why have you summoned us?"

Angelo gave a half groan from the ground.

"Could you . . . check on him please?"

Justin's eyes fell to his companion a moment before he dropped to his knees. "Angelo, come on, buddy." He gave the half-elf a light slap on the cheek. "Wake up, come o—OH!" The elf winced and immediately pulled back.

"What is it? Is he alright?"

"He's alright, he's just . . ." Justin shook his head. "*Unbelievably* drunk. He fell off the wagon again. DAMMIT, Angelo! I was only gone a day!"

Luna peered at Angelo from the side of her face. "Look, I need both of you present, so . . ." She raised her hand in the air, then rapidly slashed it down and to the side.

Angelo immediately gasped, eyes going wide. He coughed, curling into a ball on the floor. "*HOLY*—What did you do!?"

"I banished the alcohol from your body." Luna paused. "Well, *technically*, I banished ethanol from the realm of this palace, which should've been sufficient to sober you up, but—"

"Why!? I was perfectly fine!"

Luna flinched but rapidly regained her composure. "Setting aside your apparent alcoholism . . . I need you. You and Justin. I needed you both here, and by that I mean I needed you both *here*, not floating through the stratosphere on drunken euphoria."

"She thought she'd hurt you." Justin smacked the back of the half-elf's head. "*I* thought you were hurt!"

"Ack! Fuckin' . . ." Angelo picked himself up off the ground. "I get it, I'm sorry!" He turned to look at the woman who'd brought them here and his pained expression sank. "Oh damn it."

Luna furrowed her brow. "I *brought* you here," turning to Justin in an attempt to include both of them, "because I need your help. There's no easy way to do this, so I'll just muscle through. Do you two know of any . . . recent attacks on the Revered?"

Justin looked down at his feet. "I mean, I know of what happened with *us*, at Feuerschloss . . . But that wasn't an attack! I swear!"

Luna put up a hand. "I don't mean that, you aren't on trial. Not this time." She looked off to the side. "I mean like, in the last few days. Do you two . . . know anything?"

Angelo began to approach. "Now listen here, I already don't appreciate being suddenly sober—"

"Angelo!" Justin ran over to put himself between his companion and Luna. "No, ma'am. We've not heard anything. Has something happened?"

Luna hesitated. "Look, what I'm about to tell you is *not* to leave this room, understand?"

Justin and Angelo both nodded.

"The other day, there was an attack. Rhox was . . ." She paused again. "Incapacitated. It appears to have been by strong magic, though the assailant might have dealt more direct physical damage as well."

"Rhox? Holy crap, is he okay?" Justin turned back toward the other elf.

"He . . . survived. He should pull through." Luna shook her head. "But I wanted to ask you two . . . Listen, if you know of *anything* that might've caused this . . ."

It was Justin's turn to shake his head again. "I can't imagine anything that might've damaged Rhox."

Angelo's gaze turned distant, unfocused. "What about . . ." The half-elf shuddered.

Justin turned back around. "What do you—" Seeing his companion's sudden change of emotion, he stopped. "No . . . No, it *couldn't* be . . ."

"What is it? Do you know something?"

Justin turned back to face Luna. "I suppose it *is* possible . . . Listen, there might be something, but . . ."

"Could you help me stop it?"

Justin immediately stopped his train of thought. "Wait, what?"

"Whatever it was, I cannot stop it myself. And if you two know what it is . . ." Luna paused again. If they know what it might be, they might still be implicated. She thought quickly. "Okay, look. I'm going to let you two go with the knowledge I've given you, again with the understanding that none of it is to leave this room. What you do outside is entirely up to you. But if you know how to help, I—" She paused. "We, the Revered, would greatly appreciate the . . . assist."

Angelo snapped back to reality. "W-wait, help? Oh-oh no, I-I can't, I can't, not again." He began shaking his head slowly, backing away from Justin and the woman. "I can't. I'm not. I'm not doing—NO!"

"Angelo!" Justin grabbed the half-elf by his shoulders. "It won't be—Look, I can go to River City like we'd planned before! I might find something!"

Angelo's gaze remained defocused. "I can't. I'm not gonna do it." He screwed his eyes shut. "I'm not gonna do it!"

Luna slumped. "Is this why he was drunk?"

"It's a significant—Yes," Justin responded over his shoulder. "Look, can we go back now? I'll handle him."

"Oh, uh, sure. Do you want to return to where you were or . . ."

Justin turned back to Luna, keeping one hand on Angelo's shoulder. "Can we both go back to where he was? I think I might need to reprimand a bartender or three."

Luna cracked an awkward smile. "Sure . . ." A snap of her fingers and the pair was gone.

They might know of something that could have done that much damage to Rhox. Luna clutched her hands together. *Have I made the right choice?*

But she knew too. If they might be involved, another of her comrades could fall, but she'd know.

She'd know.

8

Confidence

THE SUN'S EARLY morning light filtered through the trees of the Emerald Forest, the dust of the road catching and dispersing the rays. The still wet grass splashed dew against Angelo's feet and ankles, the young half-elf running around his front yard with energy and exuberance. Swinging a stick "sword" around his head and in front of him, he was "vanquishing" an invisible threat that morning when a small family walked by the fence.

Four humans, like his father, seeming to just be enjoying the morning experience; two older, a man and a woman, held hands as two younger, both boys, ran ahead and yelled various exclamations at each other, shattering the silence otherwise punctuated only by birdsong. The two seemed to be having fun together, a fact that intrigued the young Angelo.

"Hey!" he shouted, stumbling up to his side of the weathered picket fence. "Hello!"

The two other boys stopped their raucous exchange, the older boy grinning and nudging the younger toward the fence. "Go on, he's calling for you. You're about his age anyway."

The younger boy blushed softly, rubbing the back of his head. "H-Hello! Sorry about all the noise . . ."

"No, it's fine! You—" Angelo paused, looking down at his feet. "You looked like you were having fun."

The two elders, clearly the boys' parents, had since caught up and were now stopped in front of the house. "Hey, it's Angelo, isn't it?" the man inquired.

Angelo nodded, puffing out his chest. "Angelo Villalobos!"

The man chuckled. "Steve, do you want to invite him along on our morning walk? We know his parents. I'm sure it would be okay with them."

The young boy's eyes lit up. "Can he come along?"

The man just held his grin. "Only if he wants to. Go on, ask."

The boy turned back to the stranger on the other side of the fence. "Do—Do you want to come along with us? It'll be fun!"

Angelo's smile spread from ear to ear. "Yes!" He jumped in excitement before bolting for the front gate. "I'm Angelo!"

The other boy extended his hand. "I'm Stephen, but you can call me Steve. Steve Doe."

*   *   *

"Come on, Angelo," Justin nudged his companion, "we have to discuss what we're going to do about this."

The half-elf collapsed on the casino room's bed, bringing his knees to his chest. "No, we don't. We don't have to discuss anything because we don't have to do anything. Even what's-her-name—"

"Luna."

"Luna, whatever. Even she's not sure what we should do, much less what we even can do."

Justin kicked the bed. "Dammit, Angelo, don't you understand what's going on!? The Revered believe we're trying to attack them—someone *is* attacking them. Put two and two together!" He turned around and slammed his fists against the top of the dresser. "They think we're doing it. They're accusing us of doing this again! We know we're innocent but they don't. If they continue to suspect us, the next time one of them is attacked, they might decide to take more direct action." The mage took a deep breath, walking back over to the side of the bed. "Angelo, they'll kill us if we don't prove our innocence."

It was Angelo's turn to yell, leaping off the bed at Justin. "Oh what, and that . . . that THING, facing that would be better!?" He stabbed his fingers into the elf's chest, punctuating his words. "It. Killed. Stephen!" He shoved Justin back, turning and walking briskly over to the window overlooking what remained of Monsoon City. "I'd rather take my chances doing nothing."

Justin approached the half-elf with the same sense of urgency. "And let the Revered believe we're actively attacking them!?"

Angelo swung back around to face his roommate. "I don't care! I don't care what they think! I just don't want to—"

His screaming was interrupted by a sharp pounding from one of the walls of the room, accompanied by a muffled, "Shut the hell up!"

Justin sighed, gripping Angelo by his shoulders. "Look, I'll—I can go investigate the ruins at River City for any sort of clues."

Angelo sniffled, eyes locked on the floor. "What good will that do?"

"It's a start, okay? And you don't have to do anything at all, just stay here and keep playing for the casino. I'll do all the work. River City was obviously an important location for the Revered before it was destroyed. The altar's presence says that much. There might be something there that might shed some light on why anyone would even *want* to attack them."

Angelo's eyes lifted tentatively, barely meeting Justin's. "I don't have to do anything at all related to this? I can stay here?"

Justin patted the half-elf's shoulders. "I knew you'd like to hear that. Don't you worry, I'm sure I'll find something."

*　　*　　*

Light. The light was the first thing he could see, piercing through the shadows, melting away the darkness. The half-orc's eyelids fluttered; he could hear a muffled sound, at once distant and right at his side. The light split by further shadow, shapes seeming to have difficulty forming on his retina.

"Rhox? Rhox!"

The figure on the bed squinted, bringing that shadow into focus, revealing a face he knew: Dryad. Dryad was here.

Where was here? What had happened? His eyebrows furrowed, rattled brain trying simultaneously to remember and reveal. Light. Ample light. White light.

He'd been at his palace when . . .

Rhox bolted upright. "Dryad! Where . . . Where!?" Still half blind, he reached over and grabbed where he assumed the halfling's shoulders should be.

Dryad struggled with the sudden weight having fallen on his head, fighting to keep his companion on the bed. "Where what? Calm down! You're in the Edifice."

"The Edifice?" Rhox, completely unaware of how close he'd been to landing on his face, growled. "Did he follow you!? Are you hurt? What did he do!?"

"Calm down! You're safe. He ran when I showed up." Dryad laboriously hefted his friend's center of mass back over the mattress. "What all do you remember?"

Rhox paused at the question, and in that pause suddenly realized the extreme amount of pain his body was in. "HOLY—Son of a—" He began panting. "What—*OW!* What happened? I remember—"

Dryad pulled a sprig of something from beneath his robes and immediately began tying it around the gaping wound on Rhox's arm; the pain quickly lessened there, but only just bearable. "Be careful, okay? You've sustained a lot of damage."

Rhox's eyes screwed shut. "No shit." His breathing grew less and less shallow as Dryad continued applying his herbs. In a minute or so, the half-orc was present enough to properly respond. "I was—I remember I was attacked. It was . . ." He squinted again, trying to remember the details. "It was a surprise ambush. I don't . . ."

Dryad placed a hand on the half-orc's forehead. "You don't have to strain yourself trying to remember. You need rest. It's good to see you awake, but you need to rest. Your body needs to heal."

Rhox nodded. "How . . . how long was I out?"

"A few hours."

"Shit." Rhox's eyes screwed shut again. "That's *really* bad for you."

"You needed the rest, trust me." Dryad rested his hand on Rhox's. "Besides, it can't be any worse than what you've gone through."

Rhox winced. "Did you get a good look at him?"

Dryad shook his head. "Unfortunately no; he'd started running across the desert before I could get close enough." He paused. "Are . . . Do you know if it was . . . one guy?"

"How do you mean?" Rhox's vision was growing hazy again; he lay his head back on the provided pillow. "I hate to admit it but . . . yeah, it was just the one."

Light again. Sheer bright white light. He was still in the Edifice, wasn't he? In an instant, a familiar shadow came back into his vision. "Dryad, is that you?"

"Yeah, I'm here, big guy." The halfling gripped his compatriot's hand in both of his own. "Still here."

"Where's here?"

"You're still in the Edifice, remember? You took a beating."

"SHIT, was I unconscious again?"

Dryad nodded. "I told you, you need rest."

"For how long?" He tightened his face, trying to wake himself up further.

"Maybe . . ." Dryad looked off to one side for a moment, toward the sun. "Probably four hours or so?"

"Dammit." Rhox tensed his arms, trying to push himself upright.

Dryad immediately put his hands up, trying to encourage the half-orc to remain reclined. "Whoa, whoa! You're gonna hurt yourself!"

"I *need* to get up, okay?" Rhox shook his head and things got foggy again. "Augh, I can't—I *swear* I've got a concussion. I can't—I can't keep falling asleep."

Dryad nodded, reaching down below the surface of the bed to pull a knob; suddenly, the entire mattress contorted, angling Rhox's torso up and elevating his legs. "That better?"

"Much, thank you." Rhox took a moment to breathe, careful not to close his eyes this time.

Dryad remained seated on a stool beside the bed, a mildly comical sight given his diminutive stature. He didn't want to interrupt the half-orc's train of thought, whatever it might be.

"Dryad?"

The halfling snapped back, not realizing he'd let his own mind wander a bit. "Yes?"

"Why were you there?"

Dryad paused. "What do you mean?"

"I mean, why were you at my palace? If it weren't for you, I might be dead." He winced again. "So why were you there?"

Dryad had almost entirely forgotten in the sudden emergency. "Oh! I just . . . I had a question, is all."

"What was it?"

The halfling hesitated. "I don't know if you're in the best condition . . ."

"What was it?" Rhox repeated himself, looking at Dryad this time.

"Well . . ." Dryad thought. "So I was thinking to myself about this old story I'd been told and . . . I mean, it's not important but . . . You know the desert you live in?"

Rhox nodded.

"Do you . . . Do you happen to know its age?"

"Its . . . age?" Rhox lifted an eyebrow.

"Yes. I just . . ." Dryad looked down. "This story, it was the story of my people, and it involved the desert. It's a stupid question, I know, but—"

"Hardly!" Rhox cracked a grin in spite of his pain. "If anything, it's such a good question. I've never had cause to ask it. I honestly don't know."

"Oh . . ." Dryad's expression continued to fall.

"Hey, listen." Rhox put a finger under the halfling's chin, easily lifting it back up. "I promise, once I can I'll look into it, okay? If it's that important to you."

Dryad nodded, cracking a slight smile. "Thank you. It's just . . . It might answer some questions. It might even be related to . . ." He gestured down Rhox's body. "All of this."

Rhox chuckled, a sound Dryad never expected to hear. "I can't imagine how the age of a geological formation might be related to my being soundly beaten to within an inch of my life, but if you think so, then there must be a connection somewhere! Maybe when I'm more sapient you'll have to tell me what it is."

Dryad chuckled a little himself. "Perhaps, my friend. Perhaps."

*   *   *

"Welcome to the Castle of Eternal Spring!"

Diablo scanned the immense grand chamber, slack-jawed. "Manas, it's . . . It's gorgeous!"

The gnome cracked a grin. "Were you expecting maybe worse?"

"Oh, uh, no, of course not!" Diablo frantically shook his head. "It's just, I've never seen anything so beautiful! Except maybe the Edifice."

Manas smirked, extending a hand out to the room. "The finest in gnome architecture."

Giant stone columns stretching toward the sky supported an open pergola-style "roof," intricate carvings all over their surfaces almost entirely obscured by long, trailing vines. Leaves and flowers the likes of which the half-orc couldn't begin to identify filtered the sun like stained glass, rainbows of color falling upon all manner of grains and grass covering the floor. Between fields of amber and green, paths covered in hardy, soft succulents snaked across and around the open-air chamber.

"It must be hell on anyone with hay fever."

The gnome laughed. "Thankfully, I don't get too many visitors."

Diablo looked out to his left, through the "wall" to the spanning field outside. "Yeah, I've been meaning to ask about that. You guys are called 'the Revered.' Do you, like, hold audiences or anything like that?"

"Rarely, and never at our palaces." Manas stepped toward Diablo, the gnome's head barely cresting above the half-orc's waist. "We have special places in most major population centers."

Diablo cocked an eyebrow. "But, I mean, isn't this place kind of . . . obvious? I'd imagine a lot of folks might just show up."

"Oh no, Luna's got some sort of cloaking thing around it. Sure, we're plonked square in the middle of the flattest contour on the planet outside of the ocean, but nobody can see this place. Well, outside the Revered of course."

"Luna can do that?"

It was Manas' turn to cock an eyebrow. "I thought we went over that. She's done the same to the Edifice."

Diablo nodded. "Right, right. I guess I'm still new to this whole thing."

"Well, that's part of the reason I asked you here today. I didn't think anyone's really given you the 'grand tour,' as it were, especially not in the fallout of your little . . . 'accident.'"

Diablo's eyes dropped to his feet.

"Which is the *other* reason I wanted to talk."

"Wait, what?" The half-orc's eyes came back up.

Manas nodded. "You did that to fend off an attack, right? From those four, what were their names? Justin, Angelo . . ."

"Err, right. Two of them died."

"Yeah, yeah. So do you think the two remaining ones really attacked Rhox?"

Diablo stuttered. "W-why do you ask?"

Manas shrugged. "Well, they attacked you, right? And I mean, you leveled half the countryside fighting them off. You think they're capable of doing that much damage to him?"

The half-orc paused, cheeks reddening.

"Diablo, you're a terrible liar."

"Wh-what?"

"Did they even actually attack you?"

Diablo's face began to darken. "Wh—of course they did!"

"But . . . ?"

The half-orc sighed. "They . . . had their reasons. It's . . . unlikely they're the ones who attacked Rhox. Even if they had, I doubt they could've done what was done to him."

"*There* it is." Manas nodded. "I knew something was screwy with that whole thing."

"You . . . You did?"

"Oh yeah." Manas shrugged. "It seemed weird that four—well, two now—random jagoffs would try to pick a fight with the Revered and actually win."

"I mean, they *are* skilled."

"Well sure! Hell, you wouldn't have rewritten the entire face of the world if they were pushovers."

Sure, I wouldn't have. "R-Right."

"So is that why you're so interested in finding the real attackers?"

Diablo's eyes looked off to one side, where he could see a plume of smoke rising off the mountains. *I'm worried because Asmodeious might find out if they ever show up, and then, regardless of who it is, he'll kill me.* "Look, whoever it was, they did a number on Rhox, right? And it must've happened in seconds or I'm sure he would've retaliated accordingly. Hell, if it weren't for Dryad, they easily would have killed him!"

Manas nodded, rubbing his chin. "It's certainly a predicament." He reached out and took Diablo's hand. "Well, look, you obviously have your reasons for opposing those two. I won't pry any deeper. But we have the same goal regarding the real attacker. Let's work together to find them, yes?"

Diablo looked down at his contemporary. "Y-Yeah. Thank you."

"Don't mention it." Manas stepped forward on the path, indicating to the half-orc to follow him. "Now, on to business, hm? Let's walk and talk. I need to tend to my gardens."

Diablo rushed up to Manas. "R-Right! I was wondering about that too. Do you water them yourself?"

"Rarely." Manas inspected a nearby ear of corn. "No, I rely on the rains, Miranda's domain, to do most of that." He motioned to the rest of the chamber. "The winds of Chevron to bring said rain and fresh air, the potent light of the sun and moon, Luna's bailiwick. The powerful stone pillars and wooden beams, Rhox and Dryad, to support everything." He winked at Diablo. "I even rely on fire."

"Wh—Fire? Why?"

Manas smirked. "Without the cleansing of fire, plains can be choked out by encroaching forest. The heat activates some embryos; the flames scarify certain seeds. Even the ashes that remain help fertilize new growth. You may think of fire as largely destructive, but it has a heavily creative element to it as well. Everything is like that. It might destroy, but think of what might grow in that place now that it's clear."

Diablo nodded, considering. "I suppose you're right. I . . . I never thought about it like that."

Manas smiled at the half-orc. "There's a reason we wanted you in the Revered. Sure, a few were concerned with controlling fire's destructive nature, but some of us recognized its incredible restorative nature as well."

"So . . ." Diablo thought about how to pose his question as the two continued to walk. "I mean, what exactly is it that the Revered do? I don't know that I ever got an explanation."

Manas stretched his hand out across the chamber again. "We are the force that harnesses the elements for the good of all beings." He cracked a smile. "Well, that's the explanation I was given, anyway. I mostly just research my plants. But of course, all of that goes into producing better quality food for millions, improving strains to increase yields, that sort of thing. Not to mention the quality-of-life improvement that comes with observing incredible beauty."

Diablo nodded. "I guess kind of like with the . . ." He cleared his throat. "Incident. When everyone was working together to reduce casualties."

"Right, exactly!" Manas grinned. "I mean that was a catastrophic event, those tend to be pretty rare. And I don't know that any have been *caused* by the Revered before."

Diablo's eyes fell again. "So what should I be doing?"

Manas patted the half-orc's forearm. "Hey, big guy, we chose you *because* of what you do. You specialize in fire. You may be a good all-around mage, but you *know* fire. Keep learning. Keep improving your craft. You might've had a bit of a rocky start, but we still expect great things from you."

The half-orc's eyes grew misty. "Th-Thank you, Manas."

"Hey, don't mention it. And if you want to know anything else, don't be afraid to ask, okay? We're colleagues now. We help each other."

Diablo nodded. "Of course."

9

Decisions

ASMODEIOUS PACED THE grand chamber, steps thundering throughout the castle, a scowl apparent even on his draconic features.

"I should have killed him." The great dragon let out a growl, turning into a roar as he slammed both forelimbs against the front door. "I should have killed him!"

He returned to pacing the length of the room. "I should've checked. If I'd've checked, I could have avoided this. I could've avoided . . . *RAAAGH!*" With a swipe, the dragon flung a table clear across the room, the wooden furniture shattering in a shower of splinters against the stone wall.

"Well, they're definitely keyed up now. They've all but vacated their various homes, off at . . . whatever place it is they meet. That great palace? The cauldron can't trace them anymore." He peered up at the door to Diablo's chambers. "Even *he's* been absent since."

He furrowed his brow. "Does he know it was me? If he did, would he say anything? To me or *them?*" He shook his head. "No, if he said anything to them, they would've broken down the door by now. He probably doesn't know."

Asmodeious paused, taking a deep breath and slowly exhaling. "Rhox won't be an easy target anymore. They've whisked him off to . . . wherever it is, probably to heal. I won't be able to take advantage of his weakened state."

The dragon gripped the railing on the upper balcony, pushing off the ground with his hind legs as he shifted into his humanoid form, landing both feet on that balcony. He strode down to Diablo's room, making a beeline for the cauldron.

"Let's see . . . Dryad hasn't returned either. Ahh, but what's this?" He centered the view on another target. "Of course, they're still trying to weather down the obsidian flow."

He turned away from the cauldron with a flourish. "I need some time, but I think we can do this! Once they let their guard down in the slightest . . . Thank you ever so much, my apprentice, for leaving your tools unattended!"

*   *   *

Justin hefted the bundle onto his back. It wasn't much—the blankets off his bed and a small wad of notes he'd managed to scrape together from various pockets of various robes he'd managed to save—but its size made it awkward. He'd felt bad sneaking some food from the buffet to pack as well, but he knew it could be some time that he'd be sequestered in the ruins of River City.

The straps on the "backpack" he'd fashioned from the robe that had otherwise shredded while trying to traverse the obsidian flow seemed to hold up. He'd figured they would—the problem was size, not weight—but it was still relieving to see they'd work. He turned away from the window, opened the door to the room, and after peering both ways to make sure nobody who might care would see him essentially stealing casino property, hurriedly ran to the stairs.

Angelo wasn't difficult to find this time—the half-elf had taken a seat at what Justin had dubbed his favorite slot machine, the one that had started their tenure there. Again checking against potentially angry employees, Justin rushed over to his companion.

"Angelo? You doing alright?"

The half-elf barely acknowledged the wizard, pulling the lever of the machine almost mechanically. "Yep."

Justin rubbed his eyebrows with his fingers and thumb. "Angelo . . . Look, I don't know what I'll find, okay? I might not find anything."

"Right." Angelo inserted another token.

"So . . ." Justin made a rolling motion with that same hand. "Look, I don't like asking this of you, but I need you to practice."

Angelo pulled the lever.

"Your . . . swordsmanship."

The half-elf looked up from the game for the first time since Justin had approached, a light show encouraging his gaze to remain. "My swordsmanship?"

Justin nodded as tokens poured into the shelf below the wheels. "You know my magic isn't reliable. While I'll make every effort I can to fight alongside you, there's every chance you'll essentially be fighting alone."

"Fighting . . ." Angelo's eyes defocused. "Alone?"

"Angelo, we've gone over this." Justin put a hand on the half-elf's shoulder, who responded by screaming.

* * *

The sound of shattering glass. Angelo ducked instinctively behind a hedge. Looking back up, he recognized the house whose window he'd just broken with a well-placed but poorly chosen rock.

Stephen.

"Why must you throw rocks at my window? You knew this was bound to happen. I tell you every time not to do it again, but you never heed my warning. And now, of all things, the window *does* break!"

The half-elf peeks sheepishly around the hedge. "I'm so sorry, Steve. I figure that you're a heavy sleeper so you wouldn't hear me hit the door. So I hit the window instead."

He knew where he was. He recognized this scene, this dreadful scene. The half-elf began to sweat.

"Now, what do you want to do so badly that you had to wake me up by breaking my window?"

He could run. He could turn around and run, and sure, Stephen would think less of him for a moment but maybe . . . maybe things would turn out different. He could leave town, go get his mother and father and just leave.

But what about Steve? Here he was, blissfully ignorant of their future. Cross about a broken window, taking for granted that there'd be a home for him to return to. Could he come too?

Angelo shook his head. He knew this was only a memory, a shadow of the past in his own head.

"I wanted to go hunting in the woods around the town. I just got a new longsword and wanted to try it out. You always bring good luck to my hunting ventures, so I was wondering if you wanted to come along."

Stephen had brought good luck on their hunting ventures in the past. Was what happened that day good luck? They *did* survive after all. But . . .

He shook his head again briskly. It wasn't too late, was it? He could flee, right?

But he knew. He couldn't change his past any more than he could change the path on which he'd been placed. He and Stephen had to go out hunting because that's what happened. He and Justin had to seek out that dragon because that was the only way to continue living.

You have no choice.

Angelo screamed and blacked out.

* * *

"Angelo! Angelo!" Justin violently shook the screaming half-elf. When he didn't respond, he slapped him in the face. Angelo snapped back to reality, eyes moistening.

"Wh—OW!"

"Angelo!"

"What!?"

"You scared the piss out of me!" The elf sighed. "Are you going to be alright? I know this is asking a lot."

Angelo shook his head briskly, then nodded. "Yeah, I-I think so. I'm not—Sorry, I just—Bad memories."

"Angelo." Justin put his hands on his compatriot's shoulders. "I'm serious. Are you going to be okay? I won't be here, possibly for some time. I want you to get help if you need it."

Angelo crossed his arms and pushed Justin's hands off him. "I'll be fine. I was fine when you went to get your stuff, right?"

I'm not so sure about that. "This is different, you know that." He lowered his head, sighing again, before raising it back. "Practice. Okay? I cannot do this by myself."

Angelo nodded again. "Okay. You don't have to worry about me."

"Promise?"

"Yeah."

Justin repositioned the heap on his back. "I'll try to get back as quickly as possible."

10

Haunt

SUNLIGHT FILTERED THROUGH the trees as Justin broke through the overgrown underbrush, stumbling forward at the sudden lack of resistance. He lifted his eyes to take in the familiar sight before him.

An immense gorge dug into the very rock spread out easily over a mile before him, the other side rising up a sheer cliff, the edge of the continent. Below, a vast river delta split and meandered across the fertile, verdant soil of the floodplain. Dotting this picturesque vision, small charred skeletons of buildings spiked out of the ground like hundreds of miniature black karst peaks. Scaling the cliff face beneath him, the former city rose almost to meet him, dwellings and structures hugging the very rock, etched into every crevice anyone could find.

The ruins of the delta settlement known as River City.

Justin stepped cautiously to the cliff face, taking off his parcel and tossing it down to the next level some twenty-odd feet below; it bounced, rolling right to the lip, then slid down another drop.

"Shit."

The elf turned around and dropped to his hands and knees, carefully backing off the edge, lowering his feet down to find purchase on the rough rock face. Sure he'd found good footing, he hefted the rest of his body back, white-knuckle gripping the rock as his center of balance shifted. It was only a twenty or so odd feet drop but that still wasn't a drop he wanted to make alone like this. Angelo likely wouldn't send a search party.

A few shaky minutes later, Justin jumped off the rock face, falling flat-footed the remaining few feet to that next ledge. The whole city was laid out like this. To maximize use of the fertile delta land, they'd built the bulk of the city into the otherwise unusable rock faces to either side. In some places, such as this ledge, they'd clearly cut into the rock itself to produce a good-sized shelf, a place to put roads, perhaps buildings, if there was enough room.

He hurried to that next edge, peering over to spot his makeshift bag resting inside the remains of a structure. A house of some kind most likely, furnishings upturned, scorched, ruined by centuries of exposure to the elements. Justin had pondered in the past whether the years of exposure or similar years of regular usage would have destroyed such materials faster; it was a surreal thought, the idea that such things might've been left behind in such a rush by the entire city to flee.

The disaster that had struck here must have been massive in scale and incredibly sudden. Justin had investigated everything he could to find the answer to what exactly had happened, but records of that event simply didn't exist. He reasoned it must have had something to do with an immense fire, but then, wouldn't someone somewhere have documented that? If it had been a devastating raid by the nearby Assimmian culture, wouldn't *they* have documented that? Rather, it was as though the city had disappeared overnight. One day, all mention of River City simply ceased. He'd spent years sifting through the remains upon finding them, looking for any clues, but that puzzle piece seemed to have been lost with the city.

The elf sighed as he bent over to pick up his dropped cargo, hefting it over one shoulder and strolling out what must've been the front door of this abode all those years ago. The city itself was surreal in its own right; even had it been the bustling center of population it once was, descending into the delta canyon below would always seem magical, Justin imagined.

After what must have been over an hour of wandering judging from the position of the sun and his past experiences with the place, Justin finally came to a familiar structure, one of the only such places that still had a roof above, at least in most places. He almost always came to this place once he'd found it, a safe spot to set up camp for however long he'd be staying at a given time. It seemed like sheer luck that this place was down the street from the city's old library, the place Justin most often frequented while here; though most of its ancient inventory had been either burned or looted, what remained was an intriguing look into the distant time of the city.

The elf pondered as he unrolled his—err, the casino's—bedsheets on the floor. Should he try the library first? It seemed like a good location, but he'd picked it mostly clean by now; while he'd left what he found—Justin felt it wrong to loot such an immense store of ancient knowledge and history—he couldn't remember any mention of anything that might help their present situation.

What would *help our present situation?* Justin paused, looking down at the bedroll. He had to admit to himself he wasn't sure. What would help their fight against a massive dragon bent on their destruction? What would assist their case with the Revered that they weren't guilty of these charges?

The elf hung his head. This was going to be a greater task than he'd thought.

*　　*　　*

Everything was pain.

Angelo tried opening his eyes, lids immediately slamming back down. His eyes hurt.

He tried lifting his head, reaching up under his pillow and pulling the padded headrest around his pointed ears. His ears hurt.

He tried rolling over onto his side, facing away from the window, to kick his feet off the side of the bed in a feeble, half-hearted attempt to get out of bed. His very muscles ached.

A groan escaped his lips and regret filled him. Even his lungs burned. He felt like he'd ingested literal fire.

The half-elf carefully, oh so carefully, pulled the veil of his eyelids back once more, squinting through half-focused pupils at the nightstand. He said a silent prayer of thanks—he'd had enough presence of mind the night before to leave a decanter in arm's reach.

His eyes darted behind those lids, calculating his next move carefully. As quickly as he could, he lunged forward, hand grasping that glass container. He sat up, wincing, and brought the neck to his lips, pouring the clear brown fluid straight down his throat. The swallows were involuntary and largely unnecessary; his head was slammed back, little if any of the stuff pooling in his mouth. He hardly tasted it.

He wasn't sure how much of the stuff had been in the bottle, but it was long gone by the time he finally stopped nursing. The ache was still there, still pulsing through his body, but it had been muted to a dull roar, a subtle reminder of what might happen again should he let it. Angelo looked over, surprised to see he'd managed to put the empty vessel back on the nightstand in such a way it wasn't going to fall even.

That's much better. He shook his head, wincing again at the slight pain just behind his eyes, and tried standing up. A hand shot out and instantly his entire weight was on that nightstand, pushing the small wooden furniture to the wall and threatening to topple the bottle he'd been so proud of placing mere moments before. His chest heaved. He closed his eyes slowly, then reopened them, looking at his hand, looking at the edge of the veneered wood. His mouth hung open, and he took another swallow of air.

Slowly, painfully slowly, agonizingly slowly, Angelo brought one foot closer to the nightstand under his weight. He pushed down, pushing himself back up, back upright. He brought that hand to his face; he hadn't felt the furniture leave its touch, yet there it was, back to full ambulation. He could feel his cheeks pulling taut, feel the air on his teeth as he smiled. He was upright! He was standing!

The half-elf sighed. *Hard part's over.* Raising both arms to each side, he carefully lifted a foot and lunged forward, landing on that same foot nary a foot ahead. A single pleased chuckle rose from his throat. The next step was about as fast but more sure, more stable. Then another and another.

He paused, facing the door. He balled his fists, taking shallow, sharp breaths through his teeth. *One, two, and* . . . He grabbed the handle and yanked the door open, eyes slamming shut in anticipation, lids immediately casting their red-orange glow on his retinas.

He waited a second before letting his eyelids slowly, cautiously open once more. Certainly, the light in the hallway was considerably more than the room had been, but that "shot" of Dutch courage had done its job.

Arms still elevated, the half-elf made his way down the flamboyant red carpet to the wide mouth of the stairwell; his knuckles death-grip white, he held the railing and side-stepped one stair at a time down, down toward the main floor, down toward a responsibility.

A familiar, if disheveled, head of brown-blond hair stumbled its way from the stairwell, sitting in the first chair it could find. A small commotion rose at a bar nearby and a red-vested gentleman walk-ran in its general direction. Angelo looked up and the young man drew back.

"A-Angelo! It really is you! Where've you been?"

The half-elf grunted his reply, a noncommittal guttural sound.

"You—" The man brushed his own hair back. "Nobody's seen you in almost a week. Are you alright?"

Angelo shook all over, turning back to face whatever he'd sat down at. The others at the roulette table stared at the threadbare half-elf who'd taken a seat with them, one or two wrinkling their noses. "'Ave a whiskey."

The vested man cocked an eyebrow. "I'm sorry?"

"I'll have a whiskey," he enunciated. His right hand lifted to the side of the table, fingers and thumb grasping at a glass that wasn't there.

"O-Oh." The man hesitated but bowed. "Right away, sir."

He hurried back to the bar, eyes never leaving the bartender. "He . . . uh . . . He wants a whiskey."

"Well, how is he?"

The waitman paused. "He . . ." His eyes fell before returning to the bartender's inquisitive gaze. "We need to send housekeeping up immediately."

Angelo slowly woke over the next hour at the roulette table; most other patrons gave him a wide berth. His usual luck was still with him—he managed to win a fair sum—as was an old-fashioned glass. He stood, eyes more open, and turned around deliberately, bracing himself on the table with his non-glassed hand; careful not to stumble on the stool, he stepped away, eyes defocused, not paying attention to where he was going next.

Another table, craps. He sat, another vested individual rushing in to refill that glass in his current state of mild stability. The games were something, a mild distraction, a means of doing something else, something that wasn't . . . He took another deep swig. His eyes fell on a pair of red, translucent dice pushed underneath him by a narrow rattan hook. The last caster had rolled snake eyes it would seem.

He stared at the cubes, and they stared back, unblinking. In an instant, those eyes were familiar and he reached out, jaw quivering, reached out to grab him, to bring him—

He snatched the dice up, shook them in his hand, and haphazardly tossed them back onto the table, making the dealer step back. The larger gentleman sighed. "Seven out."

* * *

Luna gripped her orc compatriot's hand tighter. "We'll do it, okay? We'll find them. I swear it."

Rhox brought his other hand up, running his fingers through the elf's hair. "I appreciate it, but I hope you'll afford me an opportunity to get a hit or two in myself." He cracked a smile, a sight that made the elf smile in turn.

"If you insist. But get well." She snuck a quick glance at Dryad. "We need you, but more importantly, we all want to see you get better."

Rhox nodded, laying his head back on the bed. "Yeah, I know. I appreciate the visits. I hate that I can't help you guys out."

"Don't worry about that." Luna smiled, holding the larger man's hand in hers. "Just worry about healing." She looked back up at Dryad again, the corners of her lips dropping. "Are you *sure* you're okay?"

The halfling nodded. "I'll be fine. Thank you for the food."

"If you ever need it, you know I'd be more than happy—"

Dryad shook his head. "There's no need. Trust me, I'm good."

The elf stood, golden robes cascading down her frame as she stepped around the bed, eyes never leaving the defiant hobbit. "You're not understanding me. You need sleep. You need to get up, to get out, to take your head out of this. Let me take your place."

Dryad closed his eyes, sighing. "I knew what you meant, and my answer is still no." He looked her in the eyes. "I'm. Fine."

Luna's typically calm facade cracked for an instant. "I'm not worried about *you*, I'm—" She paused, taking a deep breath. "Fine. If you insist, I won't press."

Dryad's eyes widened just a touch. "Luna." He reached out, taking her hand. "I'm fine, okay? Thank you for your concern, I truly mean that. But this is something I want to do."

She gripped his hand tightly. "Okay. Just . . ." She looked back at Rhox. "Take care of yourself, okay?"

Dryad nodded. "Of course I will." He put his other hand on top of hers. "If I need relief, you'll be the first to know."

The elf smiled. "Thank you."

Dryad released her hand, and she turned toward the other side of the rotunda, toward the hallway that housed her room, toward where, unbeknownst to her, two other individuals patiently waited their turn.

Manas cracked a melancholy smile toward the elf; Diablo—no, in this space he was Salamandro—rubbed at the back of his arm. Luna's cheeks flushed for just the slightest fraction of a moment before she closed her eyes, straightened her posture, and strolled straight past the two without as much as a second look.

Salamandro followed her out with his gaze. "Is she . . . Is she mad at us?"

Manas shrugged, shaking his head. "She's not mad at us." He looked up toward Dryad, the slightest smirk crossing his lips. "She just gets that way sometimes."

"If you say so . . ."

The two approached the bed in the center of the dial, the half-orc keeping a little more distance than his gnome friend. Rhox tilted his head in their direction, forcing a grimaced smile. "Manas, Salamandro! Where've you been?"

Manas, short enough that he was having difficulty seeing over the bedframe, placed his hand where he hoped Rhox's might be; after a few fumbled grasps, the prone half-orc rolled his eyes and grabbed the gnome's hand, ending this little play. "Err, thank you. We—we'd come to visit you before but you were always . . ."

Salamandro nodded, smiling. "It's good to see you awake."

Rhox chuckled. "What, you thought a little magic could keep this ox down?" He flexed his other arm. "I'm still in my pri—" His word was interrupted by a cough, then another, another, the bedridden man hacking. Dryad jumped off his stool, only for Rhox to yank that same arm up and away from him. "I'm—I'm FINE."

Salamandro recoiled slightly; the red liquid now occupying his bedsheets might have suggested otherwise. Manas let go of Rhox's hand, stepping around the bed to Dryad's side. "Has Miranda seen him yet?"

Dryad nodded solemnly. "She . . . Her specialty is water, so she could only do so much. Besides, she has to attend to . . ." His eyes briefly broke in Salamandro's direction. "Other things." He sighed. "This wouldn't be such an issue if she was still—"

"But she's not, is she?" Manas interjected, grabbing Dryad's chin and looking straight into his eyes. "We just have to do what we can, alright? He's . . ." He let go, looking back up at the large mass on the bed. "He's gonna pull through, I'm sure."

Dryad sighed again. "At least he's aware, he does seem to be improving."

"That's the spirit." Manas returned his attention to the bed. "Listen, big guy, you're gonna pull through this, alright?"

Rhox turned to his other side, looking down at Manas again. "You're damn right I am."

Salamandro took that now vacant hand on his side of the bed, squeezing it. "Listen, I don't—" He paused, taking a deep breath and closing his eyes. "We're going to find whoever did this to you, okay?"

Rhox, starting to grow weary of all this division of his attention, remained looking in Dryad and Manas' direction. "Salamandro, I—" He sighed. "Look, you're new, and I know you feel bad about what happened with that lava flow, but you don't—"

Manas quickly jumped up, grabbing the side of the bed and pulling up enough to look his colleague in the eye. "Rhox, he speaks for both of us here. While I'm sure . . ." He grunted, dropping back to the floor. "While I'm sure some of his motives might lie in his own past actions, I do believe he means well and wants to act in all our best interests. That includes finding whoever attacked you."

Rhox smiled. "Well, thank you. Thank you both. Just coming to check up on me means a lot, honest. And when I'm feeling better, I'll join you in finding them. That's a promise."

"Salamandro? Surely you're not here by yourself."

The half-orc's face immediately grew a deep red, his head dropping below his shoulders. He took a quick, shallow breath, straightening up and swiftly turning around to face that familiar voice. "Miranda! How—How unexpected!"

"Unexpected? Salamandro, one of our own is laid out. Of course I'm going to check in on him."

"Miranda!" Dryad and Manas appeared around the head of the bed, the halfling smiling wide. "Yes, I'm still here, and Manas is with us too."

"I see that now." The elf sighed. "Is he still . . . ?"

Rhox grunted as he rolled himself back over to that side. "Hello! I understand you've been quite the help."

Miranda ran forward, pushing Salamandro out of the way. "Rhox! You're awake!"

Rhox managed a taut smile. "Starting to get tired of hearing that."

The elf lifted her half-orc compatriot's hand to her face, her throat gently quaking. "I didn't—After doing what I could, you were still unconscious. I wasn't sure if you would—"

"Again, seems to be a common sentiment. But I'm fine, really. Thank you for your help. Sorry I distracted you from your post."

Miranda closed her eyes and grit her teeth. "It was nothing, really."

Manas cocked an eyebrow at Salamandro, who hadn't taken his eyes off Miranda this whole time. "Listen, Miranda, Salamandro and I are going to see if we can find any more leads about who attacked him. Don't worry about it."

Salamandro straightened his back, his cheeks flushing again. "Uh, y-yeah! I'm sure we'll find something."

Miranda sniffed softly, then carefully putting Rhox's hand back on the bed, turned to face the two. "Thank you both for doing this. I know you—Manas, you in particular, but it seemed you were gung-ho about it too, Salamandro—are ready to go toe-to-toe with the two individuals who *might* have survived their earlier bout, so please take care to examine all the evidence. After all, we honestly don't have a good description yet."

Salamandro averted his gaze. "Err, yeah, you're right. It could be literally anyone . . ."

"Exactly. We don't want to go chasing someone—someone who might already be dead, mind you—and wind up losing more of our ranks in the process."

"You can count on us!" Manas brought up his arm in a flex across his front.

"I sure hope so." She turned back to Rhox. "Listen, don't push yourself, okay? Relax, let yourself heal. I'll be back to replenish your fluids if need be. Dryad," she looked up at the halfling who'd returned to his stool, "don't hesitate to call me for anything. I'm never too busy for this."

Dryad smiled back. "Of course. Thank you again for stopping by."

Miranda nodded to him, then to Rhox, before turning back around. "I've got other matters to attend to, gentlemen. Besides, I think Chevron wanted to come by too. I don't want to have neither of us working on this."

She strode out of the chamber, almost floating across the floor, Salamandro following her out with his eyes. Once she was out of view, Manas jabbed him in the shin with his elbow. "Ow! What?"

"Oh, nothing."

"Salamandro? You came to visit Rhox and Dryad on your own?"

The gathered ensemble turned the other direction to see Chevron emerge from the other side of the Edifice. Dryad smirked. "Right on schedule."

"What's that?"

"Oh, nothing. We were just talking about you."

"What, you and Salamandro? What did you have to talk about?"

"I'm here too!" Manas ran and jumped up at the side of the bed. "I can't help being so short!"

"Ah, okay, that makes a little more sense. But why were you talking about me?"

Dryad chuckled softly. "Oh, it was nothing really. Miranda was literally just here and had mentioned you might want to stop by, is all."

"Oh! Well, I'm glad it must've seemed like we coordinated then! I assure you this was a complete accident."

"You know how Miranda is. She's got a sixth sense about these things sometimes."

"Heh, you're not wrong." Chevron turned his gaze to Rhox. "How're you holding up, big guy?"

"Not quite strong enough to pummel you yet but give it time." Rhox winked, then quickly covered his mouth, starting to cough again.

"Well, he's well enough to joke around at least." The dwarf cracked a smile. "I was worried I'd have to help you breathe, your chest was so screwed up."

"Oh yeah? You gonna hook one of your bellows up to my throat?"

"The thought had crossed my mind!" Chevron gave the half-orc a playful punch in the arm and Rhox immediately winced and recoiled. "Oh shit! S-Sorry! I forgot your arms—"

"You're fine, you're fine!" Rhox managed to squeeze out through his teeth. "I'd forgotten myself actually. Everything's kind of a dull roar right now. Can hardly tell where it's coming from most of the time."

"Oh geez, I'm so sorry. I mean, you certainly looked like hell when Dryad brought you in. I guess I shouldn't be surprised."

"So I'd surmised. Apparently everyone had visited while I was out. Sorry to make you all worry."

Chevron shook his head. "No, don't worry about it! Trust me, we're just all glad you're okay. No matter how many beatings you've given me this month."

Rhox grinned again. "There'll be more where those came from if you shirk your erosion duties you know."

"Aw, c'mon! This gives me the only excuse I have!" Chevron chuckled, and Rhox had to hold back a chuckle of his own.

"Okay, but consider this a warning!"

11

Foray

THE DEEP-BLACK CLOUDS settled over the blacker stone of the keep in the distance. The black dragon's lips pulled back into a tooth-filled grin. For him, there was no such thing as revenge for the sake of deterrent. Deterrents don't work.

Death tends to be a good means of stopping further transgressions.

Asmodeious strode up the side of the volcano, proudly stomping as he did so, making sure the very rock beneath him announced his presence. He wanted them to know. He wanted them to come out swinging. It was always more fun when they put up a fight.

Indeed, with the keep in view, he could make out the front door opening and a pair of humanoid figures emerging—guards, he presumed. One hurried back inside and the other stood waiting for the dragon to get close enough to shout: "What business have you here, dragon?"

Asmodeious smirked. "Don't act so innocent. Don't think I haven't noticed. The stink of elf infiltrated my territory. I've tracked it to this location."

"We're careful to note any bestial territory and avoid it if need be. If we've trespassed, it would have been a one-time thing."

"Oh, you've got that right." Asmodeious continued striding confidently forward, puffing an ember from his mouth.

"Dragon! We have no quarrel with you! We will leave your territory be."

"Yes, you will." He continued up the slope.

The guard—Asmodeious could see now that he was an elf just as he'd thought—drew his sword. "This is your last warning, dragon! More of our number are preparing inside. You will not win a fight so easily!"

"Doesn't matter." Asmodeious stopped less than a hundred feet between himself and the castle; he widened his stance, threw back his head, spread his wings, and bellowed out a roar that shook the very foundation of the building. In an instant, that door flew open and out streamed a battalion of similar elves, all decked out in armor and wielding a number of different bladed weapons—several kinds of swords and numerous polearms. Above, along the parapets, a row of archers rose, interspersed with the occasional mage. Every weapon available was pointed at Asmodeious. "Oh good. I was worried you were going to make this *too* easy."

"Last chance, lizard! Turn around and walk away!"

"Do you honestly believe all your blustering will change anything? Every last one of you has chosen death." He lowered his head and charged straight at the fortress.

Several elves in his direct path managed to dive out of the way, but as he removed his head from the shattered rock wall, the bloody mess he left behind included more than one body. Swiftly, he swept his neck to the left, exhaling a burst of fire hot enough to scorch the very earth, and a chorus of wails rose into the blotted sky.

Above, as the archers recovered from the sudden shock to their foundation, several began to fire down at the black-scaled beast, watching in horror as every last arrow bounced right off his hide. Even those more adventurous, taking aim at his wings, watched slack-jawed as with one impressive beat he merely knocked them out of the air.

Turning now to face the remaining army trying to pin him against the walls of the keep, he swiftly swung his tail. The cracked wall crumbled, opening the inner chamber to the elements in one swift motion. Screams and cries echoed out the new portal and Asmodeious smiled—in their attempts to pin him, they'd ensured their kind no escape. They'd made his job that much easier.

Once more he belched a fireball at the assembled army. At the very least, it seemed the elves had had enough foresight to enchant their armor against the flame, but that did precious little to save exposed flesh, those closest to him witnessing their very bone through the new scalds. Many found their limbs no longer responsive, hanging limply from blackened joints.

Those in the rear charged forth and Asmodeious paused in his onslaught, allowing them—this was hardly sporting otherwise. Swords raised, spears thrust, and all bounced harmlessly off his scales. "You're going to have to do better than that."

On the roof of the keep, archers fell back as the mages took over their front. Several, misguided, hurled their own fireballs at him, all of which fizzled against his scales. "Ha! You think to use my own weapon against me?" As he turned to taunt them, one took particular aim and Asmodeious winced, the flame shot straight at his eye. "Oh-ho, you're too clever."

He spread his wings and leapt upward, the gust of wind from the downbeat of his wings knocking all on the ground onto their backs. He landed on the roof behind the wall of assailants, alighting as lightly as a feather, then drove a clawed forelimb down into the set stone. With a rumble, the floor before him split from the rest of the structure, crumbling and bringing the full backup battalion down with it, howling in despair before being suddenly silenced against the very rock upon which they once stood.

Asmodeious once more leapt to the ground, claws digging divots into the igneous earth as he charged the remaining soldiers, head down and horns bared. Feeling the slightest hint of resistance, he stopped and threw his head back, shaking several bodies free and bellowing his triumph. He looked back and surveyed the land. Bodies littered the ground and fallen face of the castle, one or two still managing to limp, hobble, and crawl but the vast majority lifeless.

He turned back and began approaching the keep once more, being sure to crush those still moving figures underfoot as he strode. Coming to the gaping hole he'd created in the front of the structure, he smiled a wicked smile. It had been a good fight, one he'd have to remember. And with little effort he'd made the rest of his work that much easier:

The dragon took a deep breath, letting it roil deep in his lungs and throat. Putting his face inside the crumbled keep, he pursed his lips and exhaled.

The flames were instantaneous and omnipresent around his head in the otherwise enclosed space. In an instant, they drove through the keep, wooden structures disintegrating and the bodies of those still trapped within charring beyond any scope of recognition.

He had taken out the hornet's nest and utterly decimated its population. As the flame and smoke cleared around him, Asmodeious took note of what remained. "I can see why you leeches took residence here. Aside from my destruction, it's a nice place. Surprisingly cool given its proximity to the magma. Well-built, fortified. Yes, yes. It would make a fine cave for a dragon such as myself."

He pulled his head free and turned his back to the keep once more, spreading his wings and throwing back his head in a glorious roar. In that moment, unseen, one surviving mage raised his hand and threw a final spell.

"What was that?" Asmodeious turned back to see the would-be assailant. "Did you honestly believe that would hurt me?"

"It . . . wasn't meant to . . ." He pointed at the sky, where the formerly gathered clouds had begun to grow dark.

"What do you mean? Inform me of your grand plot before I snuff your life."

"Curse . . ." The mage hacked into his hand, a chunk of something the size of a kiwi fruit slapping wetly into his palm. "Warn . . . Warn others. A storm shall . . . storm shall be your . . . harbinger."

The dragon smirked as a bolt of lightning shot across the sky, illuminating and outlining his already imposing figure. "How truly convenient. Maybe with this folks who have no business with me will leave my territory be. Indeed I must thank you properly!"

He lifted his forelimb and slammed it down against the rapidly fading wizard.

"And I can think of no more fitting reward than a swift death."

* * *

"Diablo! Where are you when I need you?"

Asmodeious shouted from the grand staircase of the keep up to his apprentice's chamber. He didn't truly need the half-orc for anything in that moment; rather, he was testing the waters, determining if indeed the coast was as clear as it seemed to be. Diablo knew better than to keep his master waiting, no matter the reason.

The cry would determine if he was in. His lack of response indicated he was not.

Asmodeious grinned. Diablo had been staying out for longer and longer periods of time now that that other half-orc—what had his name been? Rhox?—was laid up. He hadn't finished the job, but these regular absences were cause for celebration. He may not have killed his target but he'd done enough damage that the rest were up in arms.

This was indeed good news. Rhox had been the physically strongest of the ensemble he'd noted, even beating Diablo in that regard. That he was able to do that much damage to him that quickly meant the remainder wouldn't be difficult. He almost felt disappointed—the challenge, the thrill of the fight wouldn't be there at this rate.

But by the same merit, this revelation had a drawback. Diablo's regular and continued leaves meant they were keyed up. He'd alerted them. They'd be on the defensive now. The element of surprise was a difficult one to recover.

This of course meant that same challenge he'd hoped for might be present after all.

He paced the great hall in humanoid form, arms folded behind his back as he pondered what little he knew of his adversaries in this moment. There were two locations of theirs that he'd had difficulty seeing with the cauldron—a place that seemed associated with the one called Luna and a more . . . centralized location. He presumed the place he'd seen before that was no longer visible. He'd had to assume Rhox had been taken there to recover; it made the most sense. Luna was no doctor. None of them were individually. Dryad might've been the closest in their ranks, and indeed he'd been noticeably absent from his usual haunts as well. Every time Diablo left, Asmodeious had checked in where he could and Dryad was the only one he hadn't seen once since his attack.

He rubbed his chin. That had been the biggest problem with his failure, Dryad's sudden presence. What had he been doing there? He needed that information to avoid such a scenario from unfolding in the future, and it seemed doubtful Diablo would divulge anything about his new clique.

He needed the element of surprise again. That was the biggest guarantee of success.

There was the one known as Chevron. He and Diablo seemed about equally matched in physical strength. Of course, the biggest concern he'd had was magical strength, in which case it seemed either Luna or Miranda would take the cake. In that regard, Chevron was something of a wild card. His magical strength was unknown. All he'd been doing since Asmodeious had been checking in on them was using his prowess over the wind to weather the obsidian slab he'd created. That might have been the extent of his strength, but it seemed highly unlikely. With Dryad and Luna effectively unknown in location and the gnome Manas palling around with Diablo, that really narrowed his choices down to two.

He looked up at Diablo's lab. A plan was hatched, and once more a wicked grin spread over his face. This would work, absolutely.

*　*　*

Stephen pushed the double doors open on the one off-color building on the street—the one structure that didn't match the color scheme for which the town had gotten its name—a small bell on a spring announcing their presence. Inside, behind a counter, his back to the door as he stocked shelves on the back wall, was what might as well have been a clone of Stephen. Even when he turned to face his new "customers" Angelo had difficulty noting any immediate differences. "Hello, welcome to John's Shoppe. How may I help you?"

John Doe. Stephen's brother. He turned to face them with a huge false smile the likes of which only a merchant could master. Angelo hung back in the doorframe.

"Steve?"

"Yes, John, it's me!"

"Steve! How've you been? Long time no see!"

Angelo resented that smile. That joy. The seemingly innocent ignorance. They'd assumed in that moment that he'd had no idea what had just transpired a day's journey from his new home.

He must have known something. How long had he been plotting with the enemy?

"John, there's nothing left of Springsboro. It was burned to the ground."

"Burned to the ground? What do you mean?"

Don't you lie to us, you sorry son of a bitch.

"John, it's gone. Springsboro . . . It's gone. Something came, and when we got back . . ." Stephen's chin vibrated as he fought back the tears Angelo was letting fall freely. The half-elf watched the stranger's face, a surprising mix of emotions passing over his facade. He must've been a remarkable actor. Why else would he have . . .

"I'll give you all the supplies you need for free under one condition: I come on the journey."

You slimy, slippery fucker.

"You? Why? Don't you need to keep an eye on things here?"

"Oh, come on, Steve! I grew up there and now it's destroyed! I have to do something even if it turns out to be fruitless!"

You knew. You totally knew.

"I need this quest and you need supplies. It's a win-win situation. I can help."

Angelo crossed his arms and strode confidently toward the stranger with a familiar face. "Really? What skills can you offer to aid our cause?"

"I can offer you—"

"No. I don't like you."

"Angelo!" Stephen rushed between his friend and his brother. "We need his supplies, and he has every right to—"

"No, he doesn't, Stephen. He knows what happened. He's been communicating with the enemy this whole time."

"Wh-what do you mean?"

"Our enemy is . . ." Angelo paused. He shook his head.

That's not what happened. That's what I wanted to happen. I wanted to call him out from the outset but I deferred to Stephen's judgment. And now . . .

Angelo curled his arms up over his face as he lay on his side on the bed, his pillow already wet as he began sobbing.

I couldn't stop him. I couldn't stop it.

And now you're gone.

I couldn't stop it.

* * *

Diablo once more found himself admiring the innate beauty of the Castle of Eternal Spring. Eyes gazing over the abundance of life, given aid and range to thrive by his new compatriot; the sight made him more than a little jealous.

"Why?"

"Hmm?" Diablo looked down at Manas, the significantly smaller gnome still managing to keep up beside him.

"Why do you feel jealousy gazing upon my work?"

"Oh geez, did I say that out loud?" Diablo's face gained a decidedly ruddy hue.

Manas smirked and shook his head. "It was painted all over your face. You didn't need to say it."

Diablo hung his head. "I just . . . You've created so much, made such a wonderful palace, and contributed so much to the world it looks like. It's enough to make anyone jealous."

"So again I ask why?"

"What?" Diablo looked back down at the gnome. "I don't understand what you're asking."

"Salamandro, sit down. Your strides are wearing me out anyway."

The half-orc took a seat on the manicured grass path, crossing his legs. Manas walked around to his front to look him in the eye.

"Salamandro, I've seen what you're capable of. We all have. There's a reason we invited you to join our ranks!"

Diablo looked to the side, finding himself appreciating the particularly feathery seeds of a nearby plains grass. "I guess, but . . . there's a big difference between potential and achievement."

"Sal—Do you mind if I call you Diablo? It's much shorter."

Diablo shook his head. "Not at all. I'm still not quite used to the title anyway."

"Diablo. Your achievements are already impressive. I have affinity toward stem plants and grasses in particular. That just happens to be my bailiwick. Dryad's is the more woody trees. He understands their growth far, far more than I ever could. Our specialties are so similar and yet he could never hope to do what I do. Nor I, him."

Diablo nodded, gaze still distant.

"Rhox's specialty is stone and earth. While soil conservation relies on plant life, that's only one aspect of his whole sphere. And even then, while he might recognize the best type of plant life to protect a given land, he still defers to our—that is, mine and Dryad's—expertise on that matter. We can work together to save a particularly diverse wetland, but no one of us could do it by ourselves."

Once more Diablo nodded, having brought his eyes back to Manas. "I suppose, but what does that have to do with me? Or my jealousy with your obvious accomplishments?"

Manas smiled. "There's an old saying: 'If you judge a fish by its ability to climb a tree, it will spend its whole life believing itself to be worthless.' Your achievements are quite different from mine, but to you they're mundane. You do them all the time, you think nothing of them."

Diablo nodded once again.

"You're like a fish swimming in the ocean. Except you might more accurately be described as a shark. You're streamlined, specialized, perfect for what you do. To you it's just swimming, eating, and sleeping. But to others you're a powerful creature to be admired, respected. Revered." He winked. "So you can't climb a tree like Dryad or increase food yields like myself. That doesn't make your accomplishments any less! Besides, you summoned *Pyror*. Do you have *any* idea how jealous that made Rhox?"

"Wait, what? Rhox was . . . jealous of me?"

"Diablo. The level of magical skill and discipline needed to even summon that creature, much less control it as long as you did, is almost unheard of. It requires a prowess that, frankly, our ranks has been lacking."

But that wasn't . . . "Manas, what about Miranda?"

The gnome cocked an eyebrow. "What do you mean?"

"Well, you described yourself, Dryad, and Rhox. But what about her?"

Manas smirked. "How about I fill you in on everyone? After all, they all know you're Diablo Villalobos. It's only fair you understand their various contributions, names, et cetera. Hell, having your unique view on their lives might lend us some assistance in finding our mystery assailants."

Diablo's cheeks flushed again but he nodded. "S-Sure. I guess I *have* been curious."

Manas nodded. "Well, since you asked about her first, let me tell you about Miranda. She's obviously an elf, and you might've caught her first name during our little Tribunal after that . . . incident. Eilafel, clan Ousseaear. Oh, elves have family units called clans. Don't know how familiar—"

"I'm not but I guessed."

"Right. Her mastery is obviously water. And I don't just mean plain old pure water. She could tell you the exact salinity of the Sapphire Ocean for just about any location. She understands the weather patterns of the known world better than anyone else, a collaboration between herself and Chevron. She might've been the earliest of the present Revered to join our ranks, I'm not sure. But she earned the title Miranda for mapping out in exquisite detail the weather patterns that coordinated the twinned water efforts of Monsoon City and Flood City. She discovered that the air broke near perfectly against the Cliffs of Chevron, causing a sudden pressure differential that lowered its saturation abilities, causing immense rainstorms that subsequently ran through the jungle to provide for Flood City's fertile fields."

Diablo's eyes had grown wide and not quite focused on the gnome anymore.

"And that's too much detail, isn't it?"

Diablo slowly nodded.

"Okay. So she's good with water and knows just about everything there is to know about water. How's that?"

"I mean that's certainly better."

"Being one of the earlier members, I don't know much more about her. I wasn't involved in her selection. But there are certain things you learn. It's hard to miss the crowning achievement that ultimately decided their current position. Take Chevron, for example. He's a dwarf named Lantham Brander. Originally from a small smithing family in Topaz City, he gained fame by inventing the airplane."

"Wait, Chevron *invented* the airplane?"

"Oh yeah." Manas closed his eyes and nodded. "You want to talk about an overall improvement to quality of life. Trips that used to take several days through some of the most unforgiving terrain on the planet now take little more than a few hours. Plus, it's an immense boon for dealing with . . . well, the giant obsidian flow. Planes can't carry a whole lot of cargo and they're an immense initial investment, which is why a lot of merchants would rather try to send a caravan even now. But Chevron's improving on the design all the time. I can't imagine where we'll be in a few decades because of him."

"Yeah, no kidding." Diablo shook his head. "Geez, now I'm jealous of him."

"Diablo."

"Yeah, yeah, I know. But I can't help it! You've all done so much."

"And you'll have your chance."

"Well, what about . . . Luna?"

"What about her?"

"I jus—"

"Right, right. Man, Luna's got a name. Oh, what was it . . ." Manas closed his eyes and lay his head back. "Rua . . . Rualibrar? Elves have such weird names."

"Rualibrar? Sure, it's odd, but that's not—"

"Yeah, but her clan name. Eilafel was of the clan Ousseaear, but Luna was . . ." Manas screwed his eyes shut and rubbed at his temples. "I'm gonna be super impressed if I can remember it correctly. She's from clan . . . rae'Ark . . ."

"You mean rae'Arkeneamitore?"

Manas looked up at Diablo, slack-jawed. "HOW did you know that?"

Diablo shrugged. "I recently . . . had a run-in with a half-elf. And he said something to me, which made me curious about elves and their clans. So I did a bit of research."

"Oh yeah? Speaking of, what kind of orc name is 'Villalobos'?"

Diablo hung his head. "It was my dad's name. He was human."

"Ah, I was gonna say." Manas folded his arms behind his head. "That's right, you half-orcs tend to be born outside tribal structure. Even Rhox was born in a human city, Monsoon City I think. But he retained a strong orc name, Ougigoth Greymatter. I guess his dad was an orc. Or maybe both his parents were half-orcs? I don't know."

"What, we're just moving on then?"

"What—Oh yeah, Luna. I don't know, she was the one who joined immediately before me. She works miracles with light. Literally. I'm pretty sure she's cloaking the Edifice. She tried to explain it to me one time . . . Something about a whole lot of infinitesimal tubes through which light travels, so light itself still moves in a straight line but that line is curved by the tubes? Except it's all over the surface in all directions. The mathematics involved is more than enough to make my head spin. She and Rhox have that in common, both attended institutions of higher education and have just unbelievable prowess with things like math and physics."

Diablo nodded. "I guess you'd have to have that sort of background for light."

"Now Dryad, I was involved with his selection. Galan, Sprouttalker of Gealbhanmeall. His was remarkable. Gealbhanmeall is a singular giant, sprawling tree deep in the Forest of the Unknown. He once told me it was a special kind of fig tree, something about growing roots off its own branches and extending them to the ground to keep its spreading canopy supported. Like, you know the four principal trees, right?"

"Err . . ." Diablo rubbed his chin. "I guess you mean the four really big trees."

"Yeah, yeah. We call them the principal trees. Dryad and Chevron actually live in them, one in each. Chevron calls his the Tree of Wind, on top of the Cliffs of Chevron. Dryad calls his the Tree of Life. Gealbhanmeall isn't anywhere near as tall as any of them, and in fact if you look over the Forest of the Unknown—I guess you can see it pretty well from Feuerschloss—it's the big sprawling forest past the desert to the east of the mountains."

"Oh, sure. I always wondered what was that way."

"You and about the rest of the world. The forest is dangerous. Only the halflings of Gealbhanmeall have been known to live there, and then entirely because of the protection of that one tree. And you'll never be able to pick it out from the rest of the forest, but I've heard it easily spreads half the distance from Dryad's Tree of Life to the other tree in the south."

"Oh geez, that's . . ." Diablo looked up, pondering what he could remember of that view. "That's huge!"

"Yep. And the other thing is apparently none of the halflings there know the tree is protecting them."

"Wait, what? What do you mean?"

"Dryad told me one time. He'd earned the name Sprouttalker for the same reason he became Revered: he's able to use his magical influence to reach into seeds, determining if they're viable, and even able to coax them into germinating. The way I describe it, it sounds easy, but that's an unbelievable amount of magical energy required to do that, and extreme discipline. I don't even know how he managed to do it, and I have an extremely similar bailiwick. But he's told me it's something like having a conversation with the plant itself. And he's said he'd had conversations with Gealbhanmeall too. That's how he learned that the tree is protecting his people."

Diablo looked out over the various fields in the castle. "Man, if you can do all this and not know how he does that . . ."

"It's *really* impressive. Frankly, Dryad might be the strongest out of all of us. Just he uses that strength in a different way."

Diablo nodded. "So what about you?"

"Hmm?"

"You've told me everyone else's name. What's yours?"

Manas nodded. "Ah yes, of course. My name's Boddyo Plainsmyth. And you see my accomplishment before you."

"Right, right." Diablo put his head in his hands. "I guess now I'm just wondering . . . why me?"

"Diablo, sometimes an individual is selected for their pure, raw potential. Especially if they've shown affinity for a particular aspect of the world, even more so if that aspect hasn't been covered by one of us yet. You fit every one of those boxes. We expect great things from you."

Diablo thought about Asmodeious. "Right. I'll do my best."

"That's all we can ask."

*   *   *

Chevron squeezed Rhox's hand. "I'd heard Manas and Salamandro are looking into who might've attacked you."

Rhox nodded. "Yeah, I'm honestly a little surprised. The two of them seemed so ready to take on a potential bogeyman, but they seem to be taking this search seriously. And I'm kind of impressed by Salamandro." He looked down at himself, at the sheets covering his damaged body. "I honestly didn't expect much out of him, especially after he . . . well, you know."

Chevron chuckled. "We told you, he's a good fit. I hope Manas is taking the time to show him the ropes though." The dwarf looked out over the side of the Edifice toward the volcano. "With everything that's happened, I don't know that we've had much of a chance."

"That's true. Manas seems to have taken him under his wing." Rhox looked to Dryad, then back up to Chevron. "He's responsible. I'm sure they're working these things out."

"Right, right."

They paused.

"Well look, I've got to—"

"Get back, yes. Can't leave Miranda on her own for too long. Thanks for stopping by."

The dwarf nodded, then turned to Dryad. "Are you sure you don't need anything? I can—"

The halfling put his hand up in front of him. "I'm good really. I've been fed and whatnot by Luna. She's been keeping pretty close tabs on me. But if I need anything, I'll let you know."

"Alright, alright. Just gotta check, you know?"

"Believe me, I get it." Dryad smiled. "Thank you for asking. And for checking up on us of course."

Chevron nodded, turning toward the hallway back to his chamber. "Okay, well, I'll see you guys later. Keep resting."

"Not like I have much choice."

The dwarf smirked as he left the room, strolled down the hall, and entered his meditation chamber. He put forth a hand, palm forward, fingers together and pointing up; he closed his eyes, concentrating, then brought his hand down in a swift motion. The wind that had been whipping out the door settled, providing him a walkway on thin air to the pad in the center of the space.

He stepped on the pad and closed his eyes as a circle appeared on the floor, beginning to glow. He felt the air on his skin change and opened his eyes to the familiar scene inside his own temple at the top of the Tree of Wind.

And suddenly something of immense weight pounced on him from behind.

Chevron didn't have enough time to react, his body thrown across the central hall, slamming violently against the opposite wall. He fell backward, chunks of the stone he'd just collided with falling to the ground with him. Eyes bleary, he rolled onto his stomach, trying to get back up, only to be suddenly pinned to the marble floor. The weight on his back shifted and he shrieked as he felt several ribs shatter.

The dwarf shuddered; he'd never been aware of just how cold this floor was. He tried to open his eyes to look to his side to perhaps catch a glimpse of his assailant, but all he could see was shadow.

And then suddenly, in an instant, that shadow was replaced by the most brilliantly blinding light and the cold of the floor was replaced by the most intense, painful sensation he'd ever felt. He blacked out in less than a second, more than enough time for his flesh to be blackened and cracked by Asmodeious' flame.

The dragon kept his fire breath on the dwarf for as long as he could exhale, plenty long enough to have killed his mark; he didn't want to take his chances this time. Rhox had gotten away from him. This ambush, on the other hand, had gone perfectly, exactly according to plan. He put a little more weight on the body to be absolutely certain, feeling the spine separate in several places beneath his foot and the stone beneath cracking under the pressure.

"Good. One more threat down." As much as he wanted to savor the kill, he didn't want to risk another incident like last time. Asmodeious leapt off the charred heap and galloped down the hall, throwing himself out the same window he'd opened to gain entry, spreading his wings against the familiar pelt of rain.

It had been a clean kill. Quick, efficient. The dragon smiled to himself as he soared east, back toward Feuerschloss.

In the hall, Chevron weakly coughed up blood.

*   *   *

Miranda sighed, resting a hand on the railing in front of her. She'd been holding this same pose, standing with both hands outstretched and gently guiding the storms across the obsidian flow, for hours now and her muscles ached. Shaking her head, letting her black wavy hair flutter around her shoulders, she pulled the other hand to her back and stretched. She looked up at the Tree of Wind's canopy. "I swear, Chevron. I want a break from this just as much as you do, but the difference is I know better."

Typically she could feel his influence in her storms. While his position was one of direct wind erosion against the surface of the flow, she'd still had to compensate for it in her own efforts. But for the last three hours there'd been . . . nothing. Simply nothing to account for.

"Dammit, you'd better not be fucking around with Rhox and Dryad . . ."

She turned from the southern balcony of her palace, striding briskly toward the magical pad at the very center of the Lake on the Pillar. In a flash, she was surrounded by familiar waterfalls and the swirling pool of her meditation chamber.

She practically threw the door off its hinges, stomping her way down the hall to the central dais. Seeing Rhox's bed, she quickened her pace. "Chevron, I swear on the elements if you're in here—"

Both Dryad and Rhox turned their heads at the surprising, loud vocalizations. The halfing hopped off his stool and ran around the bed to meet the elf. "Miranda! Geez, you look like hell."

"Dryad, if you're covering for him so he can get out—"

"Covering for who?"

"Chevron! I know he's here!"

Rhox laboriously rolled over onto his other side to see the commotion. "Miranda, what are you talking about?"

Miranda gave a quick sweep of the room with her eyes, then hung her head. "Then did he just leave?"

"Miranda." Dryad, having reached the elf, grabbed her wrists and looked up at her. "What. Are you. Talking. About?"

She looked down at the halfling with a sigh. *"Chevron."*

"What do you mean Chevron? What about him?"

She looked up at Rhox. "Is he seriously not here?"

"Miranda, Chevron hasn't been here for several hours. He stopped in to check up on us, see if we needed anything. It was a quick visit, like ten minutes. He knows better than to leave you—you'll pardon the expression—high and dry like that." Dryad took a step back. "Why? Did something happen?"

Miranda's eyes hadn't left Rhox's supine form. The color drained from her face. "He went back to his palace?"

"Yes, yes, I swear it!"

The elf briskly shook her head and began striding across the dais. "Miranda, what's going on? What's happened?"

She didn't break her eyes' fix on the opposite hall. "I pray nothing . . ."

*   *   *

The first thing she noted as she emerged in the familiar teleportation chamber was the smell. Altogether unpleasant, like someone had burned a pork roast and then tried to piss the fire out. Wrinkling her nose, she opened her eyes and spotted a massive furrow in the wall opposite the portal. And just beneath this . . .

She bolted forward, collapsing on her knees and trying to jam her fingers in under the blackened lump on the floor, recoiling at the still wet yet somehow crisp feeling she encountered there. The realization hit her a moment later—it was cold. Tears began welling up in the corners of her eyes.

She stood back up, bringing a hand to her mouth. "What—What do I do?" Her mind raced. "Chevron!" She shouted into the otherwise empty hall. "Lantham, please . . . Please answer me. Please tell me this isn't . . ."

The faintest groan echoed off the marble floor.

"Lantham!" She dropped to her knees again, hands scrambling over the barely formed mass. "Where . . . ?" She crawled a few feet, changing her position before searching over the body again. "Where are . . ." She gasped, then held her hands where she thought she'd felt . . .

She felt it again. The slightest of breezes. The faintest of breaths.

"Lantham! You're . . ." Those tears streamed down her cheeks. She looked over his form, then glanced over her shoulder. She wasn't going to be able to . . .

"Salamandro!" She called into the void. "Salamandro, can you hear me?"

Several agonizing seconds later—what might as well have been an eternity for the elf—she heard a response. "Miranda? Is that you?"

"Salamandro!" Her words caught in her throat and she wept. "Salamandro, it's . . ."

"Miranda? Everything okay?"

"It's Chevron!"

"This . . . doesn't sound like Chevron . . ."

"No, I mean—" She cursed under her breath, her face turning red. "I need your help! It's Chevron, he—Please come to Chevron's Palace right now!"

A few more seconds passed in silence. "Manas says—So the meditation chamber? Which? Right next to—okay! I'll be right there!"

Miranda slumped forward onto the charred pile. Her tears flowed freely. "D-Don't worry, Lantham. We're gonna—You're gonna be fine, just hold on a little longer . . ."

Several minutes passed, the only sound that of her gentle weeping before it was interrupted again. "Miranda?"

She hurriedly lifted her head and looked around. "Salamandro?"

"Miranda, how—This room has no floor! How am I supposed to—"

"Just walk forward! You'll be fine! Just please, hurry!"

A second later, she heard the familiar sound of the transportation spell. "Oh man, what died in here?"

"Salamandro!"

The half-orc's eyes fell on the scene just outside the door, the elf clinging to what he'd initially thought might've been a pile of burned leaves. "Holy—" He ran forward, dropping to his knees beside her. "Is this—What's—"

"This is—I'm pretty sure this is Chevron. I need your help getting him to the Edifice."

Diablo looked at the mass in front of them. "Miranda, I don't know how to tell you this but—"

"He's alive! He's breathing!"

"What? How!?"

"I don't know, but—" She stood up. "Salamandro, every second counts! We need to get him—"

"Right, right." Diablo winced as he wriggled his fingers in under the body, trying to find purchase. "He's cold but I can feel his breathing. You're right. I can't believe it, but you're right. He's alive."

12

Languish

THE SOUND OF the door of Chevron's meditation chamber being blown clean off its hinges was plenty sufficient to get Dryad off his stool. "What the SHIT—"

"Dryad!" Miranda burst through the doorway, racing down the hallway. "Dryad! Dryad, we need a bed!"

"Miranda, what—" The halfling met her at the entrance to the central chamber. "Bed? What's going on? You left with that look on your face—"

"There's no time! We need a bed now!"

Rhox stirred, having dropped into sleep since she left. "What's going on?"

Dryad tried to catch Miranda's hand but the elf broke away from him, eyes flitting around the room, mind racing. "What do I do, what do I do!? Dryad, where did we get this bed?"

The halfling looked up at her, bewildered. "What—We got it out of the back. Remember, we'd had that thought about maybe setting up stuff so we could retreat here—"

Before he could finish his thought, the elf was gone. He scratched his head, then heard another sound behind him, a deep grunt of effort. He turned back around and his jaw dropped.

Salamandro looked up at the now familiar room from the hall through one squinted eye, teeth bared, stance wide, a strange black shape draped over his shoulders. "Wh-where'd Miranda go?"

Dryad just stared. He'd never seen Salamandro put forth this much physical effort before.

"D-Dryad. Miranda?"

"O-oh! Uhh . . ." The halfling pointed back behind himself at the opposite hall, eyes never leaving the half-orc. "What . . . Uhh, what's that you've got there?"

Salamandro paused, bracing himself on his shoulder against a pillar. He took several labored breaths, his own eyes never leaving that hallway. "Chevron."

"Wait, what?" Dryad cocked his head. "What about him?"

The half-orc closed his eyes, chest still heaving. "He's . . . a lot *heavier* than I'd expected."

"What d'you . . ." Dryad looked at the black mass on Salamandro's back. "Wait . . . Wait, no . . ."

The half-orc nodded, his eyes snapping back open the moment he heard the familiar racing footsteps coming back.

"Salamandro, bring him here!" He saw Miranda return with a bed similar to the one Rhox was on.

Dryad continued examining the unrecognizable lump as the half-orc grunted, pushing himself up off the pillar. He took a labored step forward, then another.

Rhox's eyes focused on the strange sight. "Salamandro, Miranda, what's going on?"

Dryad shook his head. "No . . . No, it *can't* be . . ."

Salamandro plodded past the occupied bed, not responding to either of his colleagues. As soon as he was lined up, Miranda ran up behind him and grabbed what she could only hope were Chevron's shoulders. "Okay, on three?"

The half-orc nodded.

"One . . . two . . ." Miranda braced herself. "Three!"

The two of them moved in tandem, Salamandro tilting toward the bed as Miranda guided the shape down onto it. As soon as the weight was off his back, the half-orc collapsed to the floor. Miranda lifted the two extensions that had to be Chevron's legs up onto the bed.

"No . . . holy *shit* . . ." Dryad ran forward, up to the side of the newly occupied bed. He certainly couldn't recognize it but laid out like this he could now tell this was a person. Salamandro had just carried a full-grown adult body through the bulk of the Edifice.

And the context clues were all there. Dryad brought a hand to his mouth, shaking his head.

"Salamandro, Miranda, will somebody please tell me what's going on?" Rhox rolled over onto his other side, eyes falling first on Dryad then on the lump on the bed, watching Miranda rush around it as she tried to straighten it out.

Salamandro grunted from the floor, having dropped to a prone position. "Sorry I didn't respond earlier, Rhox. I honestly wasn't sure if I would've made it the whole distance if I'd've stopped to say anything." He took a deep breath. "*That* is Chevron."

"Wait . . ." Rhox squinted. "Wait, what? I don't understand."

Dryad bolted out of the room. "I'll be right back!"

"It's Chevron." Miranda closed her eyes, tears squeezing past her eyelids as she readied a simple spell. "He must've been attacked, same as you."

Rhox's eyes slowly grew wide. "Holy *shit.*" His nostrils flared and he recoiled on the bed. "Augh, holy SHIT! What the fuck!? Was he—Was he burned alive!?"

Miranda nodded as Salamandro once more responded from the floor. "Yeah. Frankly, I'm amazed he's still alive. As much damage as was done and as long as he'd lain there like that, he shouldn't be."

"Salamandro, I understand you've done a lot, but could I get your assistance here? I'm not nearly as familiar with fire-inflicted wounds as I expect you are." Miranda moved her hands over the charred body, small gentle jets of water pouring off her palms and fingers over his cracked flesh.

The half-orc on the floor groaned but got his hands underneath him, rolling himself onto his back. He closed his eyes, took a sharp breath, then heaved his torso forward, sitting up. With more vocal protests, he managed to get a foot under him, pushing himself up off the ground. "I—Sorry, I've never tried to carry someone before."

"I understand but please . . ."

Salamandro looked over the body on the bed. "To be honest, I don't think I've ever seen damage this extensive. Err—" He stopped himself. *It probably would be untoward to mention the bodies I'd found in the back rooms of Feuerschloss.* "Yeah. I mean, washing the burn is a typical first-aid treatment, so you're good so far. The water isn't too cold, is it?"

"It's my body temperature."

"Is that close to his? I don't know the intricate physiological differences between elves and dwarves."

"I . . . think so? Yeah, probably."

"Okay, that should be fine. We just don't want it too cold. That can actually do more damage. And of course, we don't want it too hot either. Oh shit!"

"What, what is it?" Miranda stopped her cleaning.

"Oh, no need to stop. Just . . ." The elf resumed. "I just realized. We need to make sure he's getting enough oxygen. It's likely the fire consumed the air around him, which almost certainly suffocated him."

"Wh—How do we do that?"

Salamandro shook his head. "I'm not sure, honestly. The person to ask would be . . ." He waved a hand at the body on the bed.

"Right."

"Guys, here!" Dryad reemerged from the hallway, running as fast as his legs would carry him. In his hand, waving it around over his head, was a large tightly coiled vine, and in his other hand appeared to be several thick green dagger-like leaves.

Salamandro cocked an eyebrow. "Bandage, I guess? He'll need it, sure."

The halfling paused, putting the hand with the vine on his knee. He held up the other hand. "Aloe. I remember hearing one time—"

"It's good for burns, yeah." Salamandro looked at the spears, then back at Chevron's body. "I sure hope you've got more where that came from."

"Yeah, yeah! I've got 'em growing like bromeliads on my tree." He looked up and saw the half-orc's inquisitive glare. "What?"

"I thought you were the Revered of trees and whatnot."

"It looks nice! Plus, I mean, I'm good with all kinds of plants."

"Right, whatever. Just . . . here." Salamandro held out his hand. Dryad furrowed his brows but handed the aloe spears over. The half-orc set the bulk of them down on the bed, taking one and squeezing at its tip, producing a dollop of clear goop from the cut end. He snatched this up with a finger, rubbed it between his hands, then began massaging it into the parts of Chevron's skin Miranda had cleaned.

The mass moaned, causing Dryad to jump back and even Rhox to wince. "Holy shit, he *is* alive."

Neither Miranda nor Salamandro responded, both working feverishly to treat their fallen comrade. Salamandro tossed the first leaf over his shoulder, grabbing a second and smearing its contents on his hands once more. As soon as Miranda moved on to a new spot, he swooped in to treat the affected area. Every once in a while he'd dip his head down near the recognizable head of the body, ear hovering over Chevron's mouth, simply making sure he was still breathing before continuing.

After what must have been an hour of cleaning and treating, both stepped back and cleared the bed of their hands. "Okay, Dryad, he's ready to be bandaged."

The halfling nodded and moved in, starting at the dwarf's feet, beginning to wrap the vine he'd brought around the body to attempt to protect his dermis as it tried to heal. Being careful not to disturb too much, Salamandro lifted both legs so Dryad could get the vines in underneath him as well. The moment they got to his pelvis, the groan they'd heard before repeated, significantly louder.

"Hold on, Salamandro. Something's . . ."

The half-orc gently bent his own legs, lowering himself slowly, then lifted back up again at the same rate; the louder sound of protest repeated again. "Shit. He might've broken something."

"But it couldn't have been his legs—he didn't make a sound while we were working on those."

"No, I think . . ." Salamandro reached up underneath Chevron's lifted back. The moment his fingers contacted the flesh there, the dwarf began to writhe. "Shit."

"What did you do!?" Dryad grabbed one of Chevron's arms as Miranda ran forth and grabbed the other.

"I just barely touched his back. I think he broke something in his spine."

"Oh, fuck me."

Miranda looked down at what must have been Chevron's face. "I mean, judging by the damage to his surroundings, he probably hit the wall pretty hard . . . Not to mention the damage to the floor beneath him when you picked him up, Salamandro."

The half-orc nodded. "Yeah, that was my thought too."

"Wait, damage?" Dryad let go as Chevron's movements settled. "His palace is like pure marble! What do you mean 'damage'?"

Miranda's eyes began welling up again. "The wall right outside his teleportation room had a huge divot, like he'd been thrown into it. And the floor . . ."

"I don't know what to make of the floor damage we saw," Salamandro contributed, shaking his head.

Dryad took a step back, running his fingers over his head. "Wha . . . How . . ."

Rhox closed his eyes. "No, I believe it."

Salamandro and Miranda looked over at him, both nodding solemnly. "There's just no other explanation for what we saw. And now this . . . He's probably got other broken bones too." The half-orc put a hand on Chevron's front, causing him to squirm again. "Yeah, that's at least one broken rib."

"What the fuck!? Don't hurt him more!"

"If I don't do this, we run a major risk of doing more actual damage." Salamandro shook his head. "He must've been thrown across the room with enough force to smash that wall. Frankly, I'm amazed this is all he broke."

Dryad swallowed, taking a step back toward the bed. "Well, what do we do now? We can't bandage him up like this."

"I don't know. I've never treated anyone else for burns like these."

"*Else?*" Miranda tilted her head at the half-orc's strange verbiage.

Salamandro froze. His eyes darted for a moment. "W-well, sure. I mean, I work with fire all the time."

"Right." Miranda closed her eyes. "Sorry, I'm just—" Her words caught in her throat and she collapsed to Chevron's side.

Dryad leapt to her side. "Miranda! Are you . . ." He paused, then stepped back, hearing her gentle sobs.

"I just . . . I could've checked on him earlier." Her back shook as she inhaled sharply. "I thought he was slacking. I should've known something was wrong . . ."

"Miranda, he's alive." Dryad put a hand on her back.

"I know." She sniffed. "I know, and I'm so glad for that. But . . ."

"Miranda." Salamandro stepped around the bed. "I don't know that you could've done anything about this. If you'd've checked on him before you did, he would still be in this state. And if you were present when he was attacked . . ."

"You might have been right there beside him," Dryad continued the thought. "Hell, we might not have found either of you for days. You might both have died."

Salamandro nodded. "All we can do in this moment is be grateful he's alive. There's no sense pondering what-ifs and maybes."

Miranda paused for a moment, then nodded. "You're right." She stood back up, legs shaking a little with the effort. "You're right. He's alive." She looked over the half-dressed body on the bed. "Maybe . . ."

She reached over and grabbed the white sheet at Chevron's feet, pulling it over him, tucking it at his shoulders. "Maybe we just leave him like this for now?"

Dryad and Salamandro both nodded in agreement. "Dryad, you're going to be here anyway, right? You can—"

The halfling put up a hand. "We need to have a meeting."

Miranda nodded in agreement. "We have a lot to talk about."

*   *   *

Justin squinted his eyes against the morning mist, diffusing the light of the rising sun into a faint, omnipresent glow. He glanced down, moving a foot forward onto a nearby rock in front of him. The rock gave under his weight, shifting as the mud beneath squished up around it. Filthy water burbled up from the ground, covering his foot. "Ah, dammit."

He looked back up, eyes meeting the small outcropping of overrun grasses and scrub trees that signified, he hoped, a proper island. A piece of dry land in this quagmire. He closed his eyes, taking a deep breath. "Three, two . . ."

He lunged forward, pushing off the rock with enough force for it to sink deeper, absorbing the grand bulk of the energy he'd intended to use to move forward. The elf collapsed face-first in a rivulet through the muck.

"FUCK."

He got his hands underneath him and pushed, removing himself from the ground with a wet squelch. On hands and knees—hardly any reason to try keeping himself clean and dry at this point—he crawled forward the few remaining feet to that outcrop. Indeed, as he'd hoped, fingers digging into tufts of grass for purchase found dust beneath. This piece of land was dry.

He clambered up onto the "shore," flopping down onto his back and sighing. He'd made it across, but his desire to do so with minimal mess had not come to pass. He looked down at himself, at the brown mud now caked to the front of his robes. He let his head fall back against the ground, closing his eyes in mild frustration. He then opened them again and looked to his right.

Every once in a while, the mist would clear just enough and he could see it, a massive wall, a formation that hadn't been there the last time he'd tried to traverse this landscape—the obsidian flow. Much as it had cut through Monsoon City and Flood City, it had bisected the sprawling delta as well, forming a wall as tall as the cliffs surrounding the region, having begun to cool by the time it reached the area.

He cursed under his breath. He'd thought about using the wall to simply climb across the delta to his destination but decided the sharp glass-like rock wouldn't be good for such. This was an inconvenience; that would have done serious damage.

"But at least I would've been dry," he explained to the empty mist.

He rolled over onto his side, pushing himself back up off the ground again, and surveyed his surroundings. The fog made this difficult; it had been particularly thick this morning, but he'd noted it every day since his arrival. The region had been humid before but the presence of the obsidian flow seemed to trap the moisture in the valley, allowing it to condense as soon as the sun's rays began warming it. Or at least that was his best guess. He'd only seen it this thick once or twice before. It's what made the most sense.

He knew the layout of the delta better than most anyone else, but with the air this heavy with water, he was having difficulty figuring out where he was going. The flow didn't help in that regard either. The river still flowed, and instead of simply moving straight to the ocean, now it had to cut across itself. A small lake had formed at the base of the wall, and the rest of the delta had entirely shifted as a result. Formerly obvious rectangular fields had been completely overrun, and areas where weeds had taken over were now submerged.

He shook his head. That wasn't the only part he was having difficulty figuring out where he was going. Several days in the delta had yielded nothing useful yet. He didn't even know where to begin. He'd been half-assedly looking through the buildings on the approaching cliff face, trying to put off this exact trip. He didn't want to venture into the delta proper with all this fog, but as the days passed it became more and more obvious he wouldn't have much of a choice.

A crow cawed from a nearby tree, startling him out of his reverie. "Fucking . . ."

He strode across the tiny island to the other side, peering out through the mist. He couldn't see much but he could make out the faintest outline of a decaying shack. He tried to think. Did it look familiar? He shook his head and squinted, but no further detail made itself known to him.

"Dammit . . ."

That was another problem the obsidian flow presented—having cut through the delta, it had flowed over a good chunk of the former city, parts he'd gotten to know quite well. While there hadn't been much there—being the bottom of the delta, it was the richest farmland and so there weren't many buildings—there was still history. There was still the possibility of some clue.

He put his hand to his forehead and closed his eyes, feeling the cool fog condense on his skin.

The only reason he was here looking for clues was the provenance of River City's destruction. It had fallen to an immense fire, a "clue" he'd thought, given the way Springsboro was lost. Similar circumstances: two centers of civilization, both torched seemingly overnight, with no survivors.

Except for Stephen and Angelo of course. They'd somehow managed to beat the odds.

He opened his eyes again and peered in the direction of that structure he'd seen before. The mist separated just enough to reveal its blackened surface, charred beyond original recognition.

Was it one of the buildings in which he'd found bodies? Some of them he'd found huddled together as if they knew what was coming, but most had been caught oblivious. Plentiful bodies lying in bed, toasted in their sleep. Others, they'd just started their day, walking out the front door to begin the day's business, or strolling down the street on their way to various places of commerce. Rain washed away most cinders but blackened bones remained, a macabre reminder of the horror that transpired here.

He shook his head. It wasn't a building he recognized.

"Well that just means it might have something, right?" he inquired of the crow that had been watching him this whole time. The bird cocked its head, then took off from the branch.

"What I wouldn't give to be able to do that," he muttered to himself as he stepped down from the dry land mass, back into the waterlogged mire.

* * *

Thrones pulled into a tight circle around the now two beds in the center of the primary dais, the five still fit Revered gazed over their comrades. The once white sheet that had covered Chevron's body had stained red along his torso, less so at his legs. Rhox, still awake, reclined on his bed, eyes closed but listening intently.

Luna broke the silence. "And we're *sure* his assailant was the same?"

Manas shrugged. "I can't imagine who else it would've been."

Dryad nodded at the gnome. "I hate to agree, but the burns Rhox sustained on his forearms are remarkably similar to . . ." He motioned at Chevron with a lazy hand. "All that."

Luna sighed. "I mean, it's obvious someone attacked him, and it would make the most sense that it was the same person or people who'd attacked Rhox—"

"Person." Rhox lifted his head, straining against the bed.

"Rhox, be careful!" Dryad leapt off his chair and put his hands on the half-orc's torso.

"Rhox, I appreciate your input as much as anyone here," Luna began, "and I have no reason to doubt what you say, except that you and Dryad were the only two so far who've seen the assailants . . . I just . . . I have a hard time believing any one person..."

"Listen, I don't know—" Rhox pushed up against Dryad, easily lifting the halfling in spite of his injuries. "I'd be right there agreeing with you if I hadn't seen it myself!"

"Okay, alright! I'm sorry." Luna bit her lip. "Just . . . don't hurt yourself please."

The half-orc settled back down. "I'm sorry too. I can't believe it myself."

Manas leapt from his sod throne and peeked under Chevron's sheet. He immediately jumped back, dry-heaving as black flakes settled through the air to the floor.

"Manas! What the fuck!?"

"S-Sorry . . . h'OHman . . ." The gnome turned and braced himself on his throne, taking several deep breaths, eyes screwed shut. "I . . . I didn't believe . . ."

"You can *see* his head!" Dryad sighed, rubbing his temples.

Manas took a few more breaths before sitting back down. "So we're all in agreement that *has* to be magic-induced damage, right?"

"Manas!"

"I'm just trying to get the story straight!" The gnome stood on his chair. "We need to know what we're up against here! We need to know everything we possibly can!"

Salamandro, having remained silent, hunched over, lifted his head. "Yes, Manas. It . . . It almost certainly had to be magic damage."

Miranda nodded in agreement. "Even though Chevron's palace is made of stone, I'd expect to have seen other signs of fire, at all. That fact alone means an accidental fire of that size is almost impossible." Her eyes flitted to the sheet-covered body on the bed, then quickly darted away. "It . . . It had to be instantaneous."

Manas nodded. "I mean, this still doesn't rule out . . ."

Luna's eyebrow twitched. "Are you suggesting . . ."

Rhox looked back at the two. "What? What do you mean?"

"Sorry, Rhox, I forgot you weren't privy to that conversation." Manas slumped back down. "We'd postulated before . . . Well, you know the Salamandro incident with the obsidian?"

"I was hit pretty hard but not *that* hard."

"Right. Well, he said he'd done it to stop an attack on his person. By a group of four. The four we'd had an Inquisition about prior to the event."

The half-orc nodded. "Right . . ."

Manas continued. "Two of the four are confirmed dead. We know for a fact they're dead, confirmed by both Salamandro and Luna."

Rhox nodded again. "And the other two?"

Dryad shook his head. "I still can't imagine anyone *surviving* that . . ."

"Wait, surviving the eruption?"

Manas nodded. "It's just a thought but—"

"That's ludicrous!" Rhox tried sitting up again, immediately wincing and settling back down. "I couldn't stand the heat, and I was a fair distance in front of it. And if it weren't for Luna's magic, there's no way I could've kept ahead of it as well as I did even while we were actively cooling it! Nobody could've outrun that flow!"

Manas gripped his hands together, fingers intertwining, pointer fingers sticking up. "Right, right." He began moving those pointers to one side, then the other. "BUT *if* they did . . ."

Rhox grunted and nestled into his bedding. "Luna, was one of their number a wizard?"

The elf lowered her gaze. "One of them, yes. And he *is* one of the two unaccounted for."

Miranda leapt from her seat. "But that's not proof!" She turned to Manas. "We have absolutely no evidence they survived! And even if by some unknown miracle they did, how, HOW can we know that they perpetrated these acts!?"

Manas put his hands up in front of himself. "Whoa, whoa! I'm just speculating!"

"You said it yourself, Manas. We need to know everything we possibly can." She turned around, rubbing her forehead with a fist. "And we can't do that if we . . . follow some random thread that by all logic already presented *makes no earthly sense!*"

The gnome shrugged. "Then what do you suggest? That we wait for the next of us to be attacked?"

"Of course not!"

Manas jumped back to his feet again. "Then what!? We have to investigate *something*. We can't just sit here waiting for death!"

Miranda put a hand out to her side, palm down, fingers tight together and straight out to the side. The room immediately became silent. She waited a few seconds, letting the silence linger before she spoke.

"I will not allow another of our number to fall like this. But I will not allow our Revered council to stoop so low as to waste time on a wild-goose chase." She sighed, looking back at the two beds in the center of the room. "These were deliberate attacks, coordinated even. I would not deny that they were likely perpetrated by the same . . ." She paused again. "Person. And I do believe that you and Salamandro should continue your discussions and searches for any lead."

Manas felt the tension he didn't realize had built leave his body as he sat back down. "I'm sorry, Miranda. Speculation is helpful in an investigation like this, but you're right. It seems unlikely we need to worry about those two."

The elf looked around the room at those gathered. "We have five remaining among us. At this point . . ." She swept between the individuals, aware and not. "I'm sorry, Rhox, but I assume you'll agree with me that you're in no shape to hold your own in a fight like this."

Rhox closed his eyes but nodded. "You're not wrong."

Miranda continued. "So truly that leaves us with five. Manas and Salamandro, you've been working together and I expect you to continue—do *not* leave each other's presence."

It was Salamandro's turn to stand. "Now wait just a minute—"

"No, *you* wait." Miranda pointed at the half-orc, who promptly sat back down. "We don't know what we're up against but we know they're dangerous, dangerous enough to take out a single one of us probably before he even knew what happened."

Salamandro looked at Chevron's body. "And I'm sure the only reason he wasn't killed is because the assailant thought he had been."

"Exactly. At this point, we can only assume whoever this is wants any and/or all of us dead. And we're far stronger in numbers. So. You and Manas. Together."

Salamandro closed his eyes. *Asmodeious isn't gonna like this . . .* "Okay. You're right. It's the only way to ensure our safety." *And the best way to ensure Asmodeious never learns of this group.*

"Thank you. And, Luna," she turned to the other elf, "I presume it won't be too much to ask to have you stay here with Dryad?"

Luna paused. "No, of course not, but . . . What about you?"

Miranda rubbed her eyebrows. "I'll be fine."

"Miranda." Luna stood and grabbed her companion's wrists. "You just gave an impassioned speech about strength in numbers."

"Look, I have to keep working on eroding this obsidian!" She threw her wrists down, breaking out of Luna's grip. "With Chevron . . . incapacitated, I'll be the only one doing it. It's something I *must* do."

Luna looked at Chevron's sheet-covered form, nodding. "Okay. But only if I come down to check on you every once in a while."

Miranda took a shaky, shallow breath. "Sure. That's fine."

"Let's say once an hour?"

Miranda nodded. "S-Sure. Dryad, is that fine with you?"

The halfling waved his hands in front of him. "You two, you decide what you're going to do. Whatever is fine with me."

"Okay. Luna will check in on me once an hour then."

Luna nodded. "It's not much but it's something."

Miranda looked around the room. "Are we all in agreement then?"

Everyone nodded.

"Okay then. Meeting adjourned, I guess."

Miranda was the first to leave; this whole ordeal had been completely exhausting, and while she knew she needed to work on eroding the obsidian flow, she needed sleep first. Manas and Salamandro nodded and took their exit next, each peering at Chevron's form in reminder of their duty. This left Luna and Dryad to watch over Rhox and Chevron as they healed.

Once Dryad heard the door to Manas' meditation chamber close, he waited a few seconds to be absolutely certain everyone else had left. "Okay, Luna, what aren't you telling me?"

Luna looked down at the halfling, face reddening slightly. "What—What do you mean?"

"Rualibrar, you're a terrible liar. You clam up every time the discussion turns to the two maybe survivors of the obsidian flow, and I'd expect you to be one of the more vocal in opposition of that thought. Miranda's absolutely right—it'd take a miracle for them to have survived."

The elf looked at Rhox and Chevron. "Okay, fine. I saved them, okay?"

"Luna! Why?"

"I didn't know what was happening! I saw them fleeing Salamandro's castle at breakneck speed after the other two obviously died. I teleported them back to the Lunar Pyramid, but they knocked themselves out running into a wall. It was only after that that I saw the eruption; they were out basically the whole time we were doing damage control."

Dryad sighed but nodded. "Okay, so they *are* alive. What else haven't you been telling us?"

Luna rubbed her arm. "I kinda might've . . . asked them to help us with this attacker." She motioned to Rhox.

"Wh—Luna! What if they *are* the attacker?"

"Dryad, I don't think they are! Rhox said it himself, he was attacked by one individual."

"Who could've been one of the two!"

Luna shook her head. "Not really. The two who survived were Angelo and Justin. You remember them, right?"

Dryad closed his eyes. "Yeah, I think so. Justin was that elf and Angelo was . . . the swordsman?"

"Exactly. Of the two, only Justin had any magical ability. While I could sense incredible strength in his magic, I'd done a bit of reconnaissance after they left. Justin is of the elven clan of Bailey located in Monsoon City."

"Okay, I don't know what that means."

Luna continued. "They're one of the big families, extremely powerful and extremely wealthy. They keep tabs on all their members. Justin is notorious."

"What? Like wicked?"

"No, like terrible. He's well-known throughout the clan as being perhaps their worst wizard in terms of skill."

Dryad nodded. "Wait, so if —"

"Exactly. If he's so bad with magic, how could he have done so much damage to Rhox? And now Chevron, who by all accounts was attacked by someone on par with Salamandro based on his damage."

"Yeah . . ."

"And Angelo, I did some digging on him, too. You know his last name?"

Dryad shook his head. "What, is he a Bailey too?"

Luna frowned. "Villalobos."

The halfling's eyes went wide. "Wait . . ."

"Yeah. I don't know for sure, but . . ."

"Angelo... Villalobos. Wasn't that—"

"I seem to recall the same, yes."

Dryad slumped back in his seat. "That . . . But that doesn't make any sense."

"It does if he survived. Married an elf, had another kid . . ."

Dryad nodded slowly. "Okay . . . Okay. So what's your plan then?"

Luna crossed her arms. "I hate to say it but 'bait.' I've asked them to help us find our attackers. It's far safer to have those two looking than our own. If they discover the truth, we can swoop in then. And in the event that by some strange trick of nature they *are* our attackers, they'll most likely go after Salamandro again. As far as we know, they don't know where all our locations are but they clearly know where Feuerschloss is."

"Right. But wouldn't Chevron's attack have negated that?"

"Possibly. I'm not sure what to make of that, it's a data point I hadn't expected."

Dryad nodded again. "I hate waiting."

"Yeah, me too."

13

Lead

THE DOOR SLAMMED behind Angelo, and as soon as the sound assured him of its closure, the half-elf stumbled forward, flopping face-first on the bed.

They've laundered the sheets. He was mostly glad for this fact, fairly certain he hadn't been able to make it to the toilet . . . any time at all, really. Some distant part of him cursed that he'd sunk so low, that he needed to be coddled like this. That he couldn't take care of himself.

He twisted his head, removing his face from the fresh-smelling beddings without removing the whole of his head, eyes slowly focusing on the empty decanter on the nightstand. *But there's a reason for that, isn't there?*

He cursed again. He'd been holding a bottle when he'd entered the room. Judging by the considerably lighter weight in that hand, he judged he'd probably inadvertently dumped its contents on the floor. *Not gonna be able to drink it now.* With considerable effort, he lifted that arm up past the threshold of the bed, revealing to himself what was now, indeed, an empty bottle.

As the arm fell and the bottle dropped past his fingers with a loud clink on the floor, he closed his eyes. Alcohol helped numb him, helped him not think about certain unfortunate items, but it was a two-edged blade—it made it considerably more difficult for him to fall asleep, and further made it more difficult to avoid thinking about certain other things.

If Justin were here, he could distract me. Being alone is the worst.

Thoughts of loneliness turned to thoughts of what he'd had before, before all this started: his family. His . . . He screwed his eyes shut and shook his head against the mattress.

His brother.

Angelo's eyes snapped back open. His father had mentioned his having a brother, often off-handedly. Clearly the sort of conversation his father didn't want to have, didn't even like to admit. The sort of thing he'd likely expected his son to forget, it was so infrequent.

But all that had come rushing back when he saw that half-orc in Feuerschloss.

The resemblance was uncanny. He'd looked like what he might expect if his dad had been a half-orc instead of human. His eyes, his cheeks, even his jawline. It all brought back to mind . . .

Angelo pulled an arm underneath himself and rolled on to his side.

Then he gave his name, a name he'd never expected to hear: Diablo Villalobos.

Just like him. Just like his own name. Just like his father's name, Carlos Villalobos.

Diablo wasn't a full brother. He must've been a half-brother through his father. Did that mean . . .

Did that mean his mother was an orc? Angelo blinked and looked up at the ceiling. It was an odd thought for him and he caught himself thinking so. Why was it so odd?

His father had been human. His own mother had been an elf. Orcs are just different that's all. And Carlos clearly didn't care. So why should he?

Angelo pondered his brief experience with the half-orc that had to have been his half-brother. He'd seemed so certain that his own father had died. Why? Something about him being human, which only drove home to him that he shouldn't worry about their differences—nothing was *wrong* with his father having been human. It felt too much like what his mother had said about her family. What he'd experienced any time he went to a town bigger than Springsboro, anywhere he'd been a stranger.

A *half*-elf. That's how everyone saw him. Emphasis on the half. Not a pure elf, not a pure human. Something in between. Mixed.

It felt horrible.

No, even "horrible" wasn't adequate. In his drunken state, he wouldn't have been able to come up with words to describe how it felt. It made him hurt that his own half-brother had fallen into that trap.

He thought about that. Diablo must have been raised by that dragon, Asmodeious. He must have been raised in a house of hatred, of extreme abuse and unrelenting demand.

And why? What purpose did the dragon have for even *having* Diablo, much less raising him like that?

Angelo paused, his eyes closing again. *If I lived in a home of love and support and he lived in a home of hatred and expectation, could we even still be called brothers? Our circumstances were entirely different. I can't exactly blame him entirely for his own misguided views either.*

He rolled onto his back, bleary eyes trying to focus on the ceiling.

Will I have to face him in combat? This . . . thing that Luna has asked of us . . . Will he be there again? Will he try to stop us?

Will he have to?

Angelo lifted the bottle above the edge of the bed again, looking at it with disdain.

I'm gonna have to go back down and get this refilled.

* * *

Manas pulled another book from the shelf and began leafing through its pages, eyes not particularly focusing on any given part, page, or word. He hadn't even looked at the title on the spine, simply pulled it off the shelf as it was.

Behind him, Diablo performed a similar act, brows furrowed, nose buried as he flicked page after page past it. He hadn't looked at the spine either, but for an entirely different reason.

"Manas, why are we doing this?"

"Diablo, I'd say we're on a first-name basis at this point. You can call me Boddyo."

The half-orc slammed his book down on his lap. "Dammit, I don't care! We don't even know where we're looking at this point!"

The gnome sighed and rubbed his eyebrows, setting his own book down on a nearby table, open, facedown on the page he'd stopped at. "Diablo, that's exactly it. We *don't know* what we're looking for."

"Exactly! This . . ." Diablo groaned and chucked his book across the room. "This is frustrating! Why are we even expecting anything useful here? None of these books even mention the Revered!"

"And why should they?" Boddyo motioned to the wall of books behind him. "This is just my personal library. Why would I have anything about the Revered here?"

"Because—" Diablo stood from his seat and paced to one side of the cramped room then spun back around, growling. *"Because, Manas—"*

"Boddyo."

"Boddyo, *fine*, because we're looking up an attack *on* the bloody Revered!"

The gnome side-eyed his companion. "Diablo. Language."

"For fuck's—" Diablo pressed his fingers into his cheeks. "We. Are. Looking. For. Information."

"About the attackers, yes. That doesn't preclude a need for information on the Revered, does it?"

Diablo swiped his chair back into the bookshelf, the furniture colliding with a loud crash.

"Diablo!" Boddyo jumped off his stool. "I get your frustration, I honestly do. But please, could you refrain from destroying my property?"

The half-orc closed his eyes and took a long, deep breath through his nose, sighing it out through his teeth. "Sorry. I just . . . Miranda called it a wild-goose chase and I'm starting to agree with her."

Boddyo nodded. "It's a rough situation, I get that. We're looking for—it's not even a needle in a haystack. It's a needle in a thousand haystacks that each have their own kind of needle but only one's the one we're looking for."

Diablo sat on the edge of the table the gnome had set his book on moments ago, looking up at the ceiling. "I mean, I know next to nothing about you guys as it is. I can see why someone might want you gone I guess . . ."

"Wait, what? Why?"

The half-orc crossed his arms. "Well, for one thing you call yourselves the Revered."

"It was a title! It stuck."

"Okay, but you're all also . . . just . . . ridiculously strong. Maybe someone doesn't feel like all that power should be concentrated like this?"

"Diablo, we gather for the good of the world. We each *accepted* this mantle. That includes you by the way."

"Okay, but . . ." Diablo closed his eyes again. "I mean, has anyone tried to attack a member of the Revered before?"

"Well, I guess. Any individual has their enemies."

"That's not what—" Diablo rubbed a temple. "Can you think of any incidents *like these* where someone was attacked immediately and relentlessly?"

Boddyo tapped his chin. "Well, I guess . . ." He shook his head. "No, that's just silly."

"What?" The half-orc jumped back to his feet. "What is it?"

The gnome sighed and shrugged. "I just . . . I seem to recall there *was* one incident long ago. I don't remember the specifics, but I do seem to remember hearing that a past member of the Revered had been burned to death. A lot like Chevron, I guess."

"Well, why didn't you say anything?"

Boddyo shrugged again. "I honestly didn't think it was relevant. It was such a long time ago, and I'd only been told about it. But now that I think about it, the death might've been kinda similar to Chevron's attack. I don't know."

Diablo sighed. "Well, it's something anyway. A possible direction, no matter how tenuous." He tapped the table with his finger. "You have any books about . . . I don't know, fire cults?"

Boddyo swiveled around on his stool to face the bookshelf, eyes flitting over the rows of texts. "I just might . . . I seem to recall having one or two, maybe off over there?" He pointed down toward one end of the shelf.

Diablo hardly waited for the gnome to finish his words, rushing over to where he'd pointed and immediately scouring spines for any hint as to these books' contents. Boddyo smirked and shook his head, muttering to himself.

"Oh, Diablo. I doubt anyone else has figured it out. They know your name and yet . . ."

* * *

Justin had awoken that morning to much more direct sunlight than he'd had the whole time he'd been here. His eyes snapped open and he practically leapt off his bedspread as though the sunlight had burned itself through his own mired and uncertain thoughts.

It wasn't much of an idea but it had come to him in his sleep, and it was far more of a concept than he'd had to that point. He bolted to the front door of the little burned-out dwelling he'd been using as base camp and peered over the side of the cliff, up the river toward its confluence with the delta. He couldn't quite make it out from here; it was easily an hour walk. He'd found the place purely by accident the first time, and only because he'd decided to spread his searches to the regions outside the city.

The elf quickly gathered a bite to eat, shoving it in a pillowcase he then strapped to his belt before tying the rest of his food in the rafters; he didn't want animals getting into it. He then stepped back outside, strolling north through the unusually thin morning mist toward his destination.

As it had before, the trip took about an hour by foot, the latter half of which was through some incredibly dense undergrowth. He'd used a machete to get through it before, but it seemed this morning as though the plant life was willing to part for him.

Coming back to the banks of the river, he peered through the trees up river. The fog wasn't nearly as strong this far up from the obsidian flow, and just in the distance he could make out the appearance of something unnatural. He hurried up along the sandy banks to the familiar landmark, the item he'd found before that ultimately led him to his destination—an old, decrepit, but still quite discernible water wheel. It couldn't turn anymore, the wooden shaft having rotted out and allowed the wheel to crash into the river, but Justin had no doubt it was turning for quite some time after River City was destroyed.

The wooden water wheel, after all, hadn't been burned. None of it had.

That's what ultimately made it stand out to the elf the first time he saw it. It unintentionally marked an upper bound to the destruction of the city, and further indicated that at least one individual might have escaped with their life.

Justin's ultimate destination this morning, however, was proof positive of this latter assertion. He hurriedly crossed the river at a makeshift set of stepping-stones he'd chucked into the water at one point in an attempt to keep himself dry. Reaching the other side, he ran up and found the trail of black-brown rot that indicated the previous presence of the wooden shaft coming off the water wheel. It pointed into the woods in a clear, obvious direction. He stood up and smiled, beginning to trace it along.

It wasn't long before he found it—an old clay-built structure that not only had avoided the blazes as well but hadn't even hardly weathered, still largely intact. It was far too far from the bulk of the city for him to have felt secure using it as a base; furthermore, it would've been extremely difficult to find the place once the sun set. Still, it exemplified the perfect scenario, a building that could very easily still be someone's home.

It was deep in this building's basement that he'd found, buried under what must have been over a century of detritus, the very altar he was keeping at his old dwelling outside Flood City.

He didn't know why today's drive directed itself toward this place. By all accounts he was looking for a clue about a destructive force, and this building hadn't been destroyed like everything else. But something about it had made him certain when he'd set off that morning that he'd find something useful here.

The elf pushed open the heavy wooden door. The thing had fallen off one of its hinges, so it dragged across the dirty floor but opened nonetheless. He winced; he'd forgotten how loud it was. Still, he pushed, trying to get as much sunlight into the interior room as possible. He had candles in his robe but they could only do so much.

Inside was another familiar sight for him: a rug, several comfortable places to sit, even a fireplace on the opposite wall. The trappings of a typical domestic life. This initial appearance is why he'd been so surprised to find the trapdoor, the room in the basement. The altar. It just . . . didn't fit. Whoever had lived here must have had an interesting life, at least.

He looked up to the ceiling, at the glass bulbs hanging in familiar fixtures. Electricity was nothing special, and that water wheel out by the river had to be doing something. It only made sense that it'd be part of a generator circuit rendered functionless by time.

It'd sure be helpful if that still worked, Justin thought to himself. Even though this building was so old, housing structures hadn't changed all that much, and it was remarkable how dark a typical home could get. It wasn't something he'd had much occasion to think about save for here.

He stepped forward, his nose instantly assaulted by the musty stink of ancient decay. It wasn't the smell of something that had died; indeed, it wasn't altogether unpleasant even. But so, it was overwhelming in the stale room and he brought his robes up to cover his nose. *I'll never get used to that initial burst.*

He moved across the entry room, feet stirring the layer of dust on the floor and creating little clouds with each step as he made his way to a door to the left. The next room had a single window overlooking an old sink surrounded by open shelving and work space—a kitchen was his most obvious guess. Many of the shelves still held various cooking utensils, from saucepans to skillets. It was as though whoever vacated the place did so in a hurry and had left just about everything behind.

Lucky for me, he pondered. *Means the place might still have some lingering secrets.*

Justin pressed on, kicking up more settled dirt from the now tile floor on his way to the pantry. Or at least he'd assumed it was a pantry. Maybe a butler's pantry? He didn't know really what kind of person had lived here; it could've been anything. But a butler seemed a little too optimistic for such a small dwelling so far removed from the nearby, albeit destitute, city. A small room, not much bigger than a basic walk-in closet in any event. Certainly smaller than the bathrooms in each room at Don Kane's casino. Lined with shelves, devoid of much of anything but more dust. Either whoever fled here had enough sense to take the food or else animals had gotten in and raided the place already.

Justin knelt down just inside the door to this small enclosure, fingers probing the baseboard to his left. Finding a familiar crack, he pressed his fingers down and in. The small disturbance in the baseboard gave way, and in the center of the pantry floor a small handle popped straight up out of the wood. The elf smiled. It was an expected reaction, but even now, seeing it brought him a small bit of joy. He still knew the secret.

He reached forward and grabbed the handle, pulling up on it, disengaging the latching mechanism below the floorboards that kept this trapdoor closed. Uneven floorboards lifted up all at once, revealing the path down, the path into the basement.

Stepping onto the ladder that led down into the darkness, Justin pulled a candle out of his robe. He looked at the wick, biting his lip. "Augh, what's the word . . ." He closed his eyes, trying to remember a spell that he knew most *children* in the Bailey clan learned in their first year of schooling.

Candela.

His eyes snapped open. "Candela!" There was a spark and suddenly the candle's wick was lit. Another smile crossed his face, albeit more strained than the last, and he descended into the dark basement.

The upstairs had been musty but the downstairs smelled . . . humid. *Wet.* The walls, lit now by the dancing flame of his candle, were stone masonry but they glistened in the amber glow, water clearly seeping in through the ground. Though the house was somewhat removed from the river, the water table here must've still been quite high, certainly no deeper than the bottom of this dugout. Even so, as his feet found the floor, it wasn't wet. It wasn't exactly dry, but it was dry enough.

He peered over toward the center of the room to a familiar hexagonal indentation in the ground, still present even after he'd removed the altar from its position. He'd thought at the time that the strange patterns he could make out within that indent were just that— perhaps remnants of an older floor pattern or signs that something else had been kept there at some point. But after witnessing the altar form a seventh side within his own basement abode, he realized that must have happened previously. And after meeting Stephen, Angelo, and John, the final piece fell into place.

The number of sides on the altar corresponded to the number of Revered.

That was part of the mystery he still didn't quite understand. The map even corroborated it, but that just left more questions. Why did this altar exist, especially in a place like this? Why wasn't it in any of the major temples like Monsoon City's?

The elf lifted the candle and looked once more around the room. There was a series of shelves against one wall, but he'd already scavenged most of the books that had been there. Several threadbare frames hung on another wall, their contents having molded beyond recognition in the damp environment. A third wall had a large desk pressed against it, also wholly devoid of anything; he hadn't scavenged that. Rather, he assumed whoever had lived here felt the contents of the desk to be more important than the pots and pans upstairs.

He sighed, turning back toward the ladder. *I don't know why I thought I'd find anything here.* But as he put a hand on the wood he paused.

No, there must be something.

He turned his head to look at the desk again. *Something here.*

He stepped away from the ladder toward the desk. He'd already examined it before; the wood was solid, a dense mahogany that simultaneously made it extremely resistant to rot and truly impossible for him to lift out of here. Whoever had brought it here either had lots of help or else was unbelievably strong. He doubted even an orc could've carried it here on their own.

He waved the candle over the desk, knowing the surface was empty but investigating anyway. He pulled one drawer open, then another, and another, again knowing each was empty. The final drawer opened, he sighed. *I don't know why I . . .*

Justin paused again. He looked at the surface of the desk. *No. There's something . . .*

The elf knelt, his fingers running along the underside of the desk. *No, it's not this close . . .* He pushed further back, past the point where his hand was visible, fingers still probing around. *It has to be . . .*

He didn't know what he was expecting to find or indeed *why* he was expecting to find something, but when he found the knot in the wood he knew to press up into it. The wood gave and he heard a slight clicking sound beneath him. He looked down and saw nothing at first, but as he ducked down under the desk to investigate the knot, he saw the back of the right pedestal had pushed out slightly. A hidden drawer.

The thrill of a new discovery filled Justin with such glee, he initially forgot what he'd been looking for. He dove forward, pulling the revealed drawer open, fingers digging in and pulling out a small book.

SLAM. "F—OW!" Justin held his head with his free hand as he more deliberately moved backward then attempted to stand again. He brought the candle to the book, examining it more closely.

It wasn't much. Its cheap design and obvious binding with a plain leather cover made him initially think it couldn't be terribly important, but then why hide it?

Looking around the basement, he realized it was too dark down here to read even with his candle. He ducked back down and closed the secret compartment in the desk, then made his way back upstairs, up to the entry room.

In spite of the ample seating, Justin simply couldn't bring himself to sit. This was the discovery of a lifetime! Hidden behind a secret trapdoor in a secret drawer of a secret desk in a secret basement, it must have had something truly important to the world within its pages!

He opened to the first page and that optimism fell. Topped with a date—admittedly several hundred years ago—the handwritten text told the story in first person of a woman going about her day.

The big secret he'd stumbled upon was nothing more than a diary.

"But surely . . . Surely there was some reason it was so well-hidden . . . right?" Justin sighed, his eyes scanning the page. "Lovely day . . . Saw a deer . . . Wait. 'I moved out here to practice my craft away from prying eyes. The less they know of my ultimate goal the better.' Who . . . Who's 'they'? What craft?"

The elf flipped a page and read on. "Something about carrots . . . Trying to feed the deer . . . Ah, here we go. The craft is magic. This person is trying to practice magic in peace. I guess I can understand that."

He flipped through a few more pages blithely, halting as he spotted something drawn in pencil. He flipped back to it and was shocked by what he saw.

It was the altar. But instead of seven or even six sides like he'd seen it have, this was a cylinder—effectively just one side. "'Checking out the pawnshop in the city on the delta, I found this ancient-looking stone monolith clearly once used as an altar. Something immediately told me I had to obtain it, and looking over it now, I think my intuition was dead-on. I believe this is related to what I'd been researching.' Wait, they found it at a pawnshop!? What the fuck? What kind of pawnshop . . ."

He began flipping pages again, noticing one page with burned margins. "'A curse upon that dragon. Dead. All of them are dead. Had I insisted on going for food I'd be dead myself. I knew that storm was a bad portent. And now . . . I can hardly believe it.' Dragon . . . ?" Justin put a hand to his forehead. "I mean, we'd postulated Asmodeious might've been involved, but . . . how!? And why? What was his reasoning? We don't even know why he destroyed Springsboro, simply that he'd done it, something he himself confirmed. And I can only guess the reason he'd been so antagonistic toward Stephen and Angelo is because . . . they survived. Oh no."

He turned to the next page. "'I apologize to whoever might be reading this in the future. I'm sorry I felt the need to hide this diary, surely you can see why. I'm sorry I didn't stop the destruction of this city. But I must flee now. If I stick around . . . I'm sure, I'm absolutely certain the dragon has been sweeping the delta for any signs of life. He intends to kill any who survived. And right now my research is too important, the task laid before me too monumental. I need to find others blessed with great intelligence and magical ability that we can come together and help each other keep the world in balance. This is not a task for one woman, no matter how strong I might be. A coterie is necessary, and I cannot allow this dragon to find and kill me before this grand project comes to fruition.'"

Justin's hands fell to his side, the diary still in one of them, and slumped against the wall. Slowly, he looked back at the book, then toward the kitchen. He rapidly shook his head, grabbed the front door, and in one swift motion, moved through it and pulled it closed behind him. He scrambled so fast on the slick grass out front, he slipped and fell face-first, rapidly climbing back to his feet and bolting down the river, back toward his base camp.

He'd known whoever must've lived here had to be at least interesting, if not important.

He didn't presume in a million years that it would've been the very founder of the Revered.

14

Resistance

THE SMALL WHITE marble skipped across the wheel with a characteristic clacking Angelo had grown used to. Around and around the wheel spun, the tiny sphere bouncing against the wells with seemingly increasing energy. The half-elf fiddled with a red chip, eyes quickly glancing at the pile of chips of the same color he'd heaped up on one number, twenty-three. The formation had become something of his signature, found on seemingly random numbers on the table any time Angelo played; those who watched had coined the term "Fortress of Solitude" for the characteristic high bids. They weren't always winners, but Angelo won more than he lost and that's what got the crowds charged.

His eyes returned to the roulette as he heard the wheel's spin start to slow. The marble's skittering had slowed into large, wide arcs above the still spinning wheel until it finally fell into a well. The table grew silent as all watched with bated breath for the spinning to slow enough to read the number.

Twenty-three.

An eruption of cheers resounded through the gambling hall, Angelo raising a fist in triumph. The dealer scraped the losing bets off the table; those that remained were largely on outside bets, either on red or odd, players who had faith in Angelo but not the table. The bets were tallied and winnings were divvied, all amongst a chorus of hurrahs and high fives.

The dealer took the dolly off the board, and as he began to move to push Angelo's wager back to him, the half-elf held up his hand. The dealer raised an eyebrow, but Angelo looked up at him and nodded. The dealer shrugged and stepped back. "Place your bets!"

Angelo put another small pile on top of his Fortress of Solitude. It wasn't anywhere near the max bid, but it was certainly more than anyone else at the table had been willing to wager. Little by little other piles began to form across the board, multicolored chips denoting different players.

Angelo liked playing this game because it wasn't a game so much as random dumb luck. He didn't have to think. He just had to put money on the table. If he lost a bundle, it was never a problem; he could always make it back elsewhere with a little more effort. And yet, in spite of this utter lack of strategy outside betting, it seemed to bring the most energy, the most positive noise.

It was a lot of other people's favorite game too.

The dealer grabbed one of the roulette's spokes and gave it a hearty spin before tossing the marble back into its valley. Once more it jumped and rolled around, that lovely clacking almost music to Angelo's ears. As it slowed and the ball picked its slot, most everyone gathered had some idea where it had landed before they could even read it. In an instant, the dealer dropped the dolly, once more on twenty-three.

Once more, the air was saturated with applause and accolades, the dealer pushing another hefty stack toward the half-elf. Someone on his left grabbed his hand and raised it up into the air, causing him to blush.

"Angelo!"

"Angelo!"
"Angelo!"
"Angelo!"
And the half-elf sputtered as his face suddenly became ice cold.

*   *   *

"Angelo!"
The ice bucket dropped from Justin's hand with a clatter to the ground. The elf raised a hand and struck Angelo across the face.

"Angelo! Wake up, dammit!"
The half-elf wavered on the bed as his eyes slowly focused. He realized his entire front had grown cold too, some distant part of him understanding he was drenched. He honestly wasn't sure if the bulk of that wetness was from the ice water Justin had clearly dumped over his head or his own filth from having not even attempted to make it to the toilet.

Justin sighed and shoved his hands up under Angelo's armpits, hefting the half-elf up onto his feet. "Angelo, for fuck's sake!"

Angelo's head wobbled on his neck like a novelty figure as he lifted one finger into the air. "Jus—" And the attempted vocalization was immediately cut short by a torrent of his stomach's contents rocketing themselves through his throat and out his nose and mouth all over Justin's clothed front. His eyes blinked separately, then together as the room started spinning.

The elf yelped and threw himself under Angelo before he collapsed to the ground. "Damn you, Angelo! You can't keep relapsing like this every time I leave! I can't—" He grunted and pushed Angelo back onto his feet at least for the moment. "I can*not* babysit you! You need to—" He looked out the window, spotting the edge of the moon rising above the horizon. "Fuck. We don't have time for this."

Justin turned around, squatting in front of Angelo; he gave the half-elf's arm a tug and sighed in frustration and exertion as the full weight of his companion fell onto his back. "Holy shit, Angelo. Maybe we need to talk about . . ." He pushed one foot forward and strained, legs shaking as he managed to stand himself back upright. "Your weight too."

"Mmm . . ."

The elf cocked an eyebrow and looked to the side where Angelo's head had slumped over his shoulder. "What's that?"

"I'm a growing boy . . ."

Justin rolled his eyes and lumbered forward, wincing as he heard and felt his shoes peel off the floor with each step. *I'm gonna have to apologize to housekeeping . . .*

He shifted Angelo's body on his back for better leverage, reaching forward to open the door. As soon as it was open, he yelped, thrusting a foot forward to keep it from closing while simultaneously reaching back and grabbing whatever he could of the drunken half-elf. He took a few deep breaths, then struggled through the door into the hallway.

"Not that I expect you to . . ." Step. "Understand in your current state, but . . ." Step. "I found something of use. Something . . ." Step. "Important." He sighed, muttering under his breath, "And I don't have to ask if you've upheld your end, practicing your swordsmanship . . ."

*   *   *

"Mickey!" Justin shouted as he kicked the staircase door nearly off its hinges. "Mickey, let me in! I need a favor from Don Kane RIGHT NOW!"

Mickey, taken aback by the incredible volume coming from the skinny elf, stuttered. "L-Look, Justin, you know full well you can't just—"

"Mickey, I swear to the Seven, if you don't get out of my way, I will end you!" The wizard slammed his back against the open door, hefting his half-unconscious half-elf compadre's arm back around his shoulder. "This is—You cannot comprehend how urgent this is!"

"Whoa, geez, is that Angelo? What'd he relapse? Where have you—" Mickey paused, rushing forward to catch Justin before he collapsed on the hall carpet. "Look, you need help with him?"

"Open." Justin righted himself off Mickey's outstretched arms. "That." He took another lumbering step forward. "DOOR!"

Mickey, no longer needed for physical support, bolted to the door to Don's office. "Look, um . . . I'm only doing this because you seem to be in a bad way, and I know Don's been talking of helping you boys out. Never again."

"Whatever, just . . ." Justin lumbered his way toward the open door. "Just move. Please."

"Mickey?" Don Kane's voice rang out into the hallway. "Mickey, is that you? Who else is there? I don't recall having any further appointments this evening."

The stout man peeked his head into the room while doing his best to keep the doorway itself clear. "Uh, look, Don, it's um . . . It's Justin, he—well, Justin and Angelo, but—"

"What does he—they want? I'm tallying up the night's books. Can't it wait until morning?"

Justin, having finally made it to the doorway, braced himself with one arm against the frame and repositioned Angelo. "No, sir, I'm sorry, but it cannot wait. I must speak with you at once." He sighed before hefting Angelo higher onto his back once again. "May I please come in and set this . . . this drunkard down?"

Don Kane closed his ledger and placed it in a drawer. "If it cannot wait, I suppose I can spare some time. Please set Angelo in a chair so you may speak to me unhindered."

"Thank you, Don, that's most generous." The elf lugged the semiconscious Angelo over to a lounge chair in a corner, slumping him down as best he could before walking briskly over to that massive desk. "Look, I've a favor to ask you but it will require some explaining."

Don Kane gestured toward the wizard with a hand. "Well then go on, Justin, explain yourself. Explain what's so desperately urgent that it couldn't wait until your friend there was slightly less inebriated."

Justin sighed again, shaking himself out and collecting his thoughts. "Okay. So here's the thing. The Bailey clan . . . I've been disowned."

"What!? Gracious, Justin, what did you do this time?"

"Well that's just the thing, Don, you see, I didn't do anything!" Justin paused. "Well, certainly not what they cut me out for. They claim—no, they have reason to believe that Angelo and I did something . . . unspeakable. I really don't want to say, but suffice to say it's a very serious accusation and something I would swear to you on the graves of my ancestors I did not do."

It was Don Kane's turn to sigh. "Justin, you're a lot of things. You're a blunderer, you're a delinquent, you have extreme difficulty paying your debts on time." He took off his reading glasses, breathing on a lens before wiping it clean on his vest. "One thing you aren't any longer is a liar. I've known you too long, and I've known of your situation for longer. As much as I may dislike your character, one thing I must stress is not once during your tenure here have you ever lied to myself or Mickey. I believe you." He perched his glasses back on his nose. "Now, mind you, I don't have the kind of sway with the Bailey clan to get you reinstated—"

Justin waved his hands in negation. "No need, sir. I no longer feel any loyalty to . . . to my family. No, the favor I must ask of you is much simpler. You see, this . . . this event the Bailey Clan has accused me of, I must right it. Angelo and I, we're . . . well, we've been tasked with it by a higher authority. I've spent the better part of the last month sequestered elsewhere performing necessary research to fulfill this task. This is why Angelo's state has deteriorated to what you see before you."

Don nodded, his eyes darting briefly to the groaning half-elf in the corner. "Is he going to be . . . okay? Can you bring him out of this?"

Justin turned his head back to look more deliberately at his companion. "Honestly, I don't know. I can't say for certain. He's . . ."—he closed his eyes, turning back to face Kane—"he's lost a lot actually as a direct result of this thing. He may not snap out of it, he may not *want* to snap out of it. But I can assure you that I will try."

Don Kane nodded, making eye contact with the now winded elf before him. "What exactly is the favor you require?"

Justin responded without missing a beat. "This will be a dangerous trek the two of us must undertake. I don't know how long we'll be gone or if we'll ever be able to return. I hesitate to ask, knowing I might never be able to return the favor but I must: we require supplies. Provisions for such a journey. Anything you might be able to provide us toward that end would be useful."

Don Kane drummed his fingers against his desk, biting his lip in thought. "Angelo's—I mean, he used to be a swordsman, correct?"

"Yessir, that is correct."

"Very well. Here's what I'm prepared to do. Angelo's been good for the casino, and you—well, save this last month, you've been a magnificent positive influence and wrangler for him. If not for you, he wouldn't have maintained his health as long as he has, and therefore would not have been able to help us as much as he has. I have both of you to thank, and I've been thinking on this fact for a while now. Here's what I'm putting on the table: all your debts to me, past and present, are null and void as of this moment. I'm not taking 'no' for an answer there."

Justin blinked, taken aback by this strange proposition. "Wh— Thank you, sir."

Don Kane held his palm toward Justin. "I'm not finished. I agree to provide you with the basic necessities: a tarp and a rope for minimal shelter, and a pair of sleeping bags to keep yourselves safe from the elements. With the understanding that you may not return, consider them gifts from the Kane family."

"Y-Yes! That's—I mean, that's precisely what we needed! Thank you so—"

"Still not finished. There's one more thing I wish to impart, again as something of a parting gift. Mickey!" He called out to the still open door. "Mickey, get in here!"

The wall of a man stepped into the room, looking as sheepish as a man of his build possibly could. "What is it, boss?"

"Mickey, go down to the storeroom. I want you to grab the tarp, rope, and bags I promised Justin. And while you're down there, there's a sword propped up against the back wall. Bring it as well."

Justin paused, processing what he'd just heard. "Are you—Are you . . . giving Angelo a sword?"

"That is correct. As I said before, I'd thought long and hard about his—and your—contributions to this establishment, and I believe the value of that sword should just about cover my debt to the two of you. It's ceremonial, but it does hold a sharp blade and has a nice weight and balance to it. I suspect after he's been weaned off the booze that he'd be more than capable of wielding it on this quest of yours. If nothing else, it's minimal protection from the wildlife you may encounter."

Justin nodded, his eyes growing misty. "Thank you so much, sir. You have no idea what this means to me. I'm sure it will mean a lot to Angelo as well once he . . . y'know, comes to."

"Think nothing of it, it's the least I could do. Just promise me one thing."

The elf cocked an eyebrow. "Hmm?"

"Promise me you won't get into any more trouble."

Justin grinned. "Alas, I cannot promise that, but I can promise to try."

* * *

Angelo shuddered, the ocean water saturating every fiber of his clothing practically freezing in spite of the beating sun on the scorching beach. The last thing he wanted to do was go into one of these establishments: shaded, probably great big fans to keep their patrons nice and cool in the heat. The sort of thing that would make his current chill even worse. But as he looked back at the shoreline, the wet white sand where they'd come to just moments before, he knew they had to. They had to know where they were. And merchants of these establishments had every reason to accommodate their clientele's questions, no matter how strange. Someone here could tell them where they are, how far they'd been knocked off course by that sudden microburst.

Stephen pushed the swinging double doors open on a building cheerfully labeled "Copo Cabana." The name didn't seem to make any sense; Angelo silently hoped that was simply the truth and not that he'd been concussed by the crash.

Inside, one particular patron drew everyone's eyes. Dressed head to toe in black robes, he would've been roasting outside, the sort of person who'd really appreciate the damning cool that was indeed found beyond the threshold. An elf, or at least a man of elf descent, from the back, but as he turned, it was clear that descent was full. Long, pointed ears; a gaunt, pale face; and graying eyes with a hint of green. A face Angelo had gotten to know but at the time was a total stranger.

He stood, setting a meager tip on the bar, and passed between the gathered crash victims just as any other stranger would have. There'd been no reason for him to pause, to turn around, to whip Stephen around to look at him more closely.

"It's YOU."

And Stephen reacted as anyone might, as anyone would have expected him to: instant bewilderment. "What do you mean it's me? I've never met you before in my life, I don't think."

"No, you haven't. We've not seen each other before this moment but were destined to meet one day."

Angelo looked at his childhood friend and instantly his own confusion melted into concern. Stephen's expression was certainly one of confusion, but there was something behind his eyes: recognition.

Stephen knew who this person was even though they'd never met before.

"Okay, pal, I think you've had one too many drinks." John stepped between the two, but Angelo's eyes never left Stephen's face. He hardly registered much of anything else that was being said.

The expression he'd seen was like what he'd seen on Stephen's face when they met up with John. An old recollection. Like you almost didn't recognize the person in front of you but then you did.

Why did he recognize this elf?

"My name's Justin. I am a wizard of the clan of Bailey but only by blood relation."

Justin Bailey. He knew Stephen and Stephen knew him.

Before he knew it, he felt the heat of the sun on his sopping skin once more as the conversation moved outside. "I'm not strong enough to keep my name from being permanently tarnished in their eyes. That's where you come in, Stephen. You need to help me learn to focus my magic so it can be stronger."

He . . . thinks Stephen can help him with magic? Why?

"I know of you by your dreams. They are so strong, they broadcast to those in them if they know how to receive them."

Angelo shook his head. This made no sense! "I've never known any of his dreams."

"Well, I did say you had to be in them and that you had to be open to reception."

The half-elf furrowed his brows. He already didn't like this guy.

The conversation continued and Angelo felt himself moving farther and farther away from it, the edges of his memory darkening.

This was the moment they'd met Justin. And the only reason he deigned to help us was this . . . link, this strange, unbelievable link he apparently had with Stephen. He and Stephen were the only reason he'd . . .

Angelo's eyes welled up.

Justin's connection to magic is what brought them to Feuerschloss. His knowledge of the magical world is what linked them to these current dramatics, to the desperate request of that elven Revered Luna. True, they likely would still be looking for any clue as to the loss of Springsboro or perhaps they would have been snuffed out in their sleep, but the only reason things were going as they were now was because of the shared link between Justin and Stephen.

Angelo had no link. He had nothing to tie himself to these dramatics.

The half-elf wept.

15

Feeble

THE SUN PEEKED over the mountains in the distance, throwing its light on the scorched earth, initially giving the shattered black glass field a warm orange glow, which rapidly grew into a searing heat. Within minutes those same mountains began to shimmer as the very air above the obsidian flow rose as if trying to remove itself from the increasingly hot surface for fear of burning.

Justin paused, bracing himself against the base of the southern Cliffs of Chevron, panting as he squinted ahead. He shook his head, watching as Angelo scrambled along the broken land as though he were simply bouldering. *How on earth is he doing that?* He wasn't even showing any signs of a hangover, which astounded the elf almost as much as it concerned him. Angelo had been blackout drunk not two hours prior, yet here he was, clambering over these rocks like a seasoned expert. Either the hangover hadn't kicked in yet—it certainly would soon, with that sunlight piercing the skies—or he still hid some quantity of alcohol on his person.

Or else he's fighting through the pain. That possibility frightened Justin the most. He knew the pain Angelo had been going through and also was familiar with the pain of a hangover. He wasn't sure which was worse, but he had to assume the latter was more tolerable to the half-elf. Otherwise, why would he have kept himself in such a state for so long?

Because you can drink a hangover away, he realized as he shook his head again.

"Angelo! Holy crap, wait up!"

The half-elf gave a cursory glance over his shoulder, visibly rolled his eyes, and slowed his pace precisely one iota.

"Angelo, I'm serious!" Justin scrambled forward on his hands and feet, trying to close the gap as quickly as possible with as little damage as possible. He managed to get about ten feet behind the half-elf, pausing and panting once more. "How . . . How on *Earth* are you so fast? Why are you practically running, anyway? This terrain is treacherous! Remember your leg?"

Angelo looked back at Justin, and the elf could see a burning determination behind his eyes that he couldn't see before. "I just want to end this."

Justin sat down on the glossy surface, eyes wide. He never imagined there'd be a day he'd be afraid of Angelo. But those eyes. They'd pierced straight through him, almost as though he hadn't even been there. He shuddered.

"O-Okay, well, wait up please!"

*　　*　　*

He'd been aware of the light for what seemed like hours. Bright, brighter than it had any right being through his closed eyelids. Or at least he was fairly certain his eyes were closed. As cognizance slowly came, he began recognizing the particular red-orange hue of light shining into his closed eyes at the edges. The center was much brighter and not quite the right shade, significantly lighter. As more awareness crept into him, he realized there were several large dark shadows in his field of view as well. Unchanging, unmoving. Unlikely to be people.

His nostrils couldn't help but take in the strange smell. His slipped mind couldn't place it, but it was unpleasant. Unpleasant enough that he began breathing through his mouth when he could manage to move his jaw. His throat rapidly became dry. No part of him could even access thinking about a drink of water.

It started with a subtle, distant, omnipresent ache. As his faculties begrudgingly returned, it became less and less distant, and more and more centralized. His muscles hurt. His chest seared with each breath. His skin felt . . . wet. Cold? Yet strangely warm. It took him what felt like an eternity to be able to even move a finger, and it felt like he'd submerged his whole hand in literal actual magma when he did. He felt chunks of . . . something crackle and crumble off his flesh. He couldn't imagine what it might have been.

Finally, the ringing began to subside, and in the distance he could begin to make out other sounds. It took some time but eventually they began differentiating enough that he could tell they were voices. First one, then two, and slowly, a third, much deeper, emerged from the din. He knew he recognized their timbers, but that part of him didn't seem to want to wake up for quite some time.

He felt the subtle breeze on the bare skin of his head, could hear its gentle call in his ears, could smell the faintest moisture it contained. It too felt wrong. Too strong on the top of his head. But it was pure. For that, some shred of him was grateful.

There was something he was supposed to be doing. Something to do with that very wind. Something he'd been doing . . .

His eyelids fluttered open, and instantly his eyes were too dry as well. A groan rose in his throat, and Dryad and Luna looked up from their conversation to see Chevron looking back at them.

"Holy shit! Chevron!" Dryad jumped from his stool and bolted around Rhox's bed.

"Chevron!" Luna strode the other direction around the bed, arriving at his side about the same time as the halfling. "Are you really back?"

The dwarf's head shuddered as he tried to move his neck to look more directly at them. "C-Can't—"

"Oh man, he must be parched. Luna, get the—" But the elf was already moving back to where she started, producing a large pitcher of water and a smaller narrow-necked bottle.

"Miranda thought we could use these," she explained as she brought both back to Chevron's side, already pouring a measure of water into the bottle. "Dryad, try to tilt his head."

The halfling nodded and gently put his hands behind Chevron's head, to which the dwarf's eyes screwed shut.

"Chevron, I know it's painful, but I need you to try to swallow, okay?" She carefully placed the bottle's neck on Chevron's lips, slowly tilting it up until a slow trickle of water poured into his mouth. The dwarf swallowed, groaned, swallowed, groaned. In what felt like no time at all to him and an eternity to the others, the bottle was emptied.

Luna pulled the bottle back and began filling it again. Chevron opened his eyes again, swiveling them to look at her. "E-Eyes . . ."

"Eyes?"

"Shit, his eyes are probably dry too." Dryad gently lowered the dwarf's head back onto the pillow. He tried not to groan this time, but any movement was pain. "I wonder if his tear glands were damaged too . . ."

Luna nodded in understanding, and more gingerly than she'd poured it into his mouth, she carefully dropped little droplets out of the bottle into his open eyes. He could feel them rehydrate like a dried-out sponge soaking up what it can. She could see it too, realizing the water wasn't pooling along his lids, and kept drip-dropping it in. As soon as it had gathered enough to run a rivulet out the corner of his eye down his temple, she moved to the other eye until he finally blinked.

"M-much better . . ." The shadows he'd seen before broke loose, and he could feel something popping off his eyelids in much the same way that he'd felt on his hand. "Wh-what is . . . Flaky . . . ?"

Luna and Dryad exchanged glances, and Rhox, behind them, bit his lip. The elf tried to explain. "Chevron, you . . . It's nothing to worry about. It's just your skin is . . ."

Dryad chimed in. "You're in rough shape there, big guy. Those flakes are . . . Well, they're basically charcoal. It's . . ."

"It's what's left of your skin." Rhox leaned toward him. "It was burned off."

"Rhox!" Luna turned back to admonish the half-orc.

"What? He asked! He's gonna find out eventually anyway. Gotta rip the bandage off."

She pressed her fingers into her eyebrows. "Whatever."

"I remember . . ." Chevron's eyes squinted as best as they could.

"You remember? What do you remember?" Dryad pushed himself up onto his toes, trying to bring himself closer to the bedridden wizard.

"Was . . . Was visiting. Rhox was . . . And then I returned . . ." He closed his eyes and tried to remember. "Happened so fast . . . Flung across the chamber in . . . in one blow. And then . . ." He began squirming on the bed. "The heat . . . I was . . . engulfed . . ."

Luna grabbed Chevron's hand, trying to ignore the warm wetness of his charred flesh. "Please, anything else. A description, anything."

Chevron opened his eyes, looking up at the colorful ceiling of the central chamber. "Didn't really get a good look . . . But black. All black. And heavy . . ." He closed his eyes again and his head slumped back.

"Chevron!" Dryad put his hand up in front of the dwarf's nose and mouth, sighing with relief. "He's still breathing. Must've just passed out again."

"Was I like that?" Rhox's eyebrows tilted in concern.

Dryad nodded. "You were real hit-or-miss there for a while. I checked every time you passed out. We weren't sure if you were gonna make it either, though you weren't as bad as . . ."

Luna shrugged. "What do you make of this?"

Dryad rubbed his chin. "I'm not sure. He basically said he was attacked as soon as he appeared in his palace. And if he didn't get a good look, it seems likely the attack happened from the back. Black . . ." The halfling shrugged. "He might've already been passing out at that point. Salamandro had said something about no oxygen too."

"Should we call him here?" Luna leaned on Rhox's bed. "I mean, he saw the scene too. Plus, it can't be argued that he knows more about fire than any of us."

"True." Dryad furrowed his brows. "Salamandro? You there?"

The halfling didn't have to wait long. "Is that Dryad? What's going on?"

"Salamandro, Chevron woke up."

"Oh, that's fantastic! Did he get some water?"

"Yeah, but—Listen, the subject of his attack came up. Could you come up to the Edifice to talk over some things? You're at Manas' place, right?"

"Oh, uh, yeah." There was a pause. "Okay, I'll be right up."

Again, the wait wasn't long; Salamandro appeared from the hall leading to Manas' meditation chamber. "So what did he say?"

Luna crossed her arms. "Salamandro, when you went to retrieve Chevron with Miranda, you used the teleportation pad in his meditation chamber, correct? The method he himself would have used to get back after, for example, visiting Dryad and Rhox here."

The half-orc nodded.

"When you emerged . . . What did you see? Was there damage to the area?"

Salamandro nodded again. "Yeah, the moment I was there, I could see a huge crack in the wall right in front of me, right by where he was."

"Right in front of you? Are you sure?"

"Well . . . Yeah. It was hard to miss."

Both Luna and Dryad nodded, and the halfling continued the questioning. "So that confirms he was likely attacked from behind, at least initially. He said he was flung across the room in one hit."

Salamandro's eyes went wide. "Well, that would certainly explain what we saw, at least in that regard. It must have been quite an impact. But really? Flung across the room in one hit?"

"That's what he said." Dryad paused. "Wait, what do you mean by 'in that regard'?"

"You remember how Miranda and I mentioned the floor?"

Dryad thought. "Vaguely?"

"The floor was indented where his body had been. It makes sense that the wall would be damaged if he hit it hard enough, but the floor doesn't make any sense at all."

Luna's eyes lit up. "Wait, he said something else! He said that when he'd seen the figure that attacked them he saw them as all black and that they were . . . 'heavy.' I didn't know what to make of that."

"Heavy . . . All black?" Salamandro shook his head.

"Yeah, I assumed he just saw whoever it was as a shadow." Dryad shrugged. "You know, on account of being about ready to pass out from the damage he'd taken and the lack of oxygen you'd mentioned might've happened."

"Attacked from behind, one swift motion, then lit on fire . . . black, heavy . . ." Salamandro looked at Chevron's now still body. "It *can't* be . . ." He shook his head again, then turned back to the hall, bolting away from the bed.

"What? Where are you going?"

He paused and looked back over his shoulder. "I have to ask Manas something." He then returned to running.

He knew someone who'd attack an adversary from behind, who'd light his enemies on fire, who was indeed black and heavy, and who'd have a reason to attack the Revered if he ever found out about them. His own master.

* * *

The Cliffs of Chevron had finally shrunk into the twenty-foot cliff face that ran the remaining length of the obsidian flow. It had been a grueling day of travel across the jagged landscape, but at this point of minimal resistance, Angelo had already begun climbing up, Justin bracing himself against the rock face to catch his breath and inspect for bleeding he might not have felt. Behind them, the sun shimmered red-orange above the distant Sapphire Ocean, slowly approaching the horizon.

"Angelo, please! Please, let's stop for the night. I can barely feel my legs."

Above, the half-elf lunged for another handhold. "But we're only halfway there."

"Exactly! We've still got a full day's journey ahead of us."

"But if we get above the cliffs here we won't be struggling against the very land. Our passing will be much swifter."

Justin turned around and slammed his back against the wall. "Angelo, I'm begging you. I need rest. *You* need rest. You don't want to go up against that dragon running on fumes, do you?"

Angelo paused. "Alright, fine. But at the top."

Justin sighed and looked up, the top of his head against the cliff, seeing it rise above his back. In that moment, it felt a million miles tall. "Angelo, I don't know if I can—"

"Nonsense. You'd told me the cliffs around River City are taller than this."

"Angelo, I—I'm *exhausted!* What do you want from me?"

"I want you to climb this cliff. I'm the one carrying the tarp, remember?"

Justin sighed an exasperated groan. "For fuck's sake . . ."

The sun's edge lapped at the ocean, and the elf pushed himself back onto his feet, turning to face his next obstacle. It truly felt like an insurmountable task in that moment, but he reached forward, grabbing onto the rock face and pushing up with his feet.

It felt like hours. His arms shook with each new grasp. His limbs burned. His lungs felt full of molten steel. He could taste copper. He didn't dare look up. But with the sun still shining over the horizon, a familiar hand pushed into his field of vision. He grabbed it and the two of them strained to pull him up over the edge.

Justin lay facedown on the ground, eyes open as he panted. As his vision returned, he saw Angelo pacing in front of him. In the distance, he could make out the makeshift shelter Don Kane's provisions promised, a rope tied between two trees, the tarp draped over it and staked to the ground. A pair of sleeping bags were spread out inside, and in that moment he realized Angelo had removed them from his own load, his back considerably lighter. He put his hands beneath himself and slowly, shakily, began pushing himself up off the ground.

"It's about bloody time."

Justin looked up at Angelo, eyes refocusing again. Had it been this dark before? He looked toward the west, but the sun would've been below the Cliffs of Chevron even when he started climbing.

He looked back to Angelo, then down at the floor of this, the Enchanted Rainforest. A straight line had been formed under the half-elf's feet. *He's been pacing for a while . . .*

"Alright, look, I don't care what you do but I'm . . ." Justin crawled forward on his hands and knees past Angelo into the tent. He unzipped one of the sleeping bags and collapsed on top of it, barely managing to zip it closed again before he passed out.

Angelo rolled his eyes. He looked up in the distance to the east, the shadow of the planet just crossing over the black speck that must have been their destination. Feuerschloss. He tried to think; he hadn't seen it from this far out before. The last time, Luna must have deposited them closer than this. Or perhaps it was the different viewpoint; they hadn't gone up the cliff before. Whatever it was, the point in the distance looked unfamiliar, foreboding.

Or maybe it was his own nerves. The half-elf shuddered as the last light of the sun disappeared behind the horizon, stars beginning to peer through the veil of twilight. He wasn't sure if that was due to his nerves as well or just the coming chill of night.

Angelo turned back to the makeshift shelter within which Justin was already completely passed out. He crawled in beside him, unzipped the other sleeping bag and shimmied into it. Lying flat on his back now, he looked up at the nondescript dark surface that was the tarpaulin. In seconds, his eyes slammed shut, the day's exhaustion immediately catching up with him. He was out in seconds.

*   *   *

That deep, black shadow. The incredible, intense gale as it sweeps over us. Stephen, he's wearing his familiar scaled armor and I-I'm wielding my longsword. It was brand new then, I remember. We've gotten so close to that buck, ready to christen the blade, when—when that shadow hurled past overhead. That harbinger. That devastating shadow. The form of the dragon.

A sycamore. Was it a sycamore? It had to have been, it was so large and tall and spacious on the inside. Besides, sycamores can do that, right? Be alive while their core is rotten out, consumed by ants and termites and bees and whatever else might chew wood pulp for sustenance. So much decay. So much death. So black save for that occasional blinding flash of lightning across the congested sky. The first drops were sparse but swiftly joined by their watery brethren, cascading down in sheets, wave after wave of torrential bombardment like regiments, like rank-and-file, diving to the moistening earth below, the weakening firmament holding up the shelter, that sycamore. If it had fallen, we would have hardly noticed. Stephen and I, cowering like rabbits, fearful of the sudden squall, fretful of the roaring thunder threatening to shred our ears asunder. I know what this is. I know where I am.

I don't want to be here.

I should run.

NOW.

But I can't. My legs are like cement, like stout oaks rooted to the ground. Hours we were like this it had seemed, the two of us waiting for the storm to just end.

Please don't let the storm end. I don't want the storm to end.

But even as I hope, as I pray to whoever might listen and heed, that bastardly sun peeks out from behind those dispersing clouds, and just as quickly as it had started, the storm has ceased to be. That damnable shadow has played its part and we're damnably free.

Don't make me leave this tree. I don't want to leave this tree. I know what I'm going to find when I leave this tree.

But Stephen, he's so innocent. So naïve. He doesn't know. He hasn't seen.

I can't feel my legs as we trudge through the miresome slop that remains of the soft, inviting woodland soil. I want to turn back. I know what this is. I know where we are, where we're going. I don't want to go back.

Don't make me go back.

Please don't make me join Stephen at the top of this ridge.

It's clear as day. Smoke clouds billowing off the charred remains of half-timbered houses. The complex alligator-scale black sheen omnipresent where structure remains. That unholy fetidness, acrid pine-wood burn mingling with the rank, festering stink of charred cadavers as though they might be ill-conceived but happenstance compatriots. It's the silence though, that ringing echoing nothingness, that's the most disconcerting. It wasn't a large town but it was a town nonetheless; it had noises, regular sounds one doesn't realize they take for granted until you're met with that sudden, uneasy wall of silence.

I can't stop the tears. I can't stop my legs. I can't stop running toward it.

No.

I don't want to see.

No.

NO.

NO!

"NOOOO!"

Angelo's eyes shot wide open. The dark of the Enchanted Rainforest loomed over him.

Like that shadow.

The silence was disheartening.

16

Confrontations

JUSTIN LEAPT OUT of his bag more rapidly than he'd ever moved in his life. Angelo's sudden, piercing cry rang out into the otherwise silent rainforest border. He scrambled out from under the tarp, panting and looking around in fear. "Angelo, what? What is it?"

The half-elf groaned and rubbed his temples. "Cause enough for a drink, thanks for bringing it up."

"For the love of . . ."

The sky to the east above the mountains had been kissed with the slightest tinge of orange, clouds in the distance reflecting the bright light of the sun more readily than the sky was willing to diffuse it. It wasn't quite sunrise. Justin shrugged and made to crawl back into the sleeping bag, and Angelo perfectly mirrored his movements in reverse.

"Angelo, what are you doing?"

"I want to get an early start."

Justin ground his finger and thumb into his eyebrows. "Angelo, just because you had a bad dream—"

Angelo motioned behind him with his head. "Sun's coming up. Might as well hit the trail. We've got another full day ahead of us."

Justin groaned. He rolled onto his side, and Angelo began rolling up his bedroll.

"Justin, I'm serious. We don't want to spend the night in clear view of the keep, do we?"

The elf sighed, rolling onto his back. "Fucking . . . Fine. But seriously, give me like five minutes, okay?"

"Sure, but I'm gonna be tearing down the tent in that time."

Justin rolled his eyes, then closed them. Any excuse to catch an extra little bit of shuteye. The sudden cool breeze on his face as the tarp was pulled out from over him caused him to scrunch his nose.

In no time at all, Angelo had torn down the bulk of their "camp" for what it was worth, save for Justin's sleeping bag. "Okay, sleepyhead. Seriously, time to get a move on."

The elf groaned once more. "Can we get some breakfast? Yesterday's exertion has left me with . . . basically nothing. And we're gonna need the energy."

Angelo nodded and tossed the still prone elf a dull-green fruit, the item landing squarely on his chest. "Already got it."

"And what is this supposed to be?"

"Food. Breakfast."

Justin began shimmying out of the bag. "No, I get that, but what is it?"

Angelo shrugged. "Dunno. Some kind of fruit. They're all over around here." He motioned with a hand to the rainforest boundary line, to the immense row of immense trees with these unfamiliar fruits on them.

Justin sat up and picked it up off his bedroll, giving it a test squeeze. "Angelo, it's hard as a rock. How are we supposed to eat this? And how do we know it's even edible?"

Angelo grabbed at a bump on the surface of the fruit, manipulating it with his fingers until it simply pulled away from the remainder of the fruit, leaving a divot that looked straight to the core of the thing. The inside of the chunk he'd pulled off was custard white, with what appeared to be a large black seed within its flesh. "Because I was pretty sure I'd seen them at the local market in Springsboro. Never had 'em myself, but I've heard they're pretty good. Called something like sweetsop."

Justin turned the fruit over in front of his eyes, inspecting it. A hard dull-green exterior shell with numerous similar nodules over its surface, each one bumpy in its own right, like the rind of an orange. If he didn't know any better, he might've thought it was an apple at first. He pinched one of the knobs, wiggling it back and forth until he felt it give inside, pulling it free.

The meat of the fruit jiggled, and when he pinched the large black seed out of it, the meat sagged. The elf winced. "Angelo, I'm not sure—"

But Angelo had already brought the piece to his mouth, biting it off the outer rind. He chewed tentatively, then smiled. "These are actually pretty good! Give it a try."

Justin's eyelids fluttered as he sighed at his companion's lack of care. He brought it to his mouth, teeth tearing it off the rind, and his mouth was immediately filled with an incredible sweetness, almost sickeningly sweet. As the color had suggested, the flavor was quite similar to custard. Justin chewed it, letting the juices linger on his tongue. "Actually, that's not half bad."

"See? I told you! Would I steer you wrong?"

The elf rolled his eyes. "Angelo, you spent the better part of the last—what, two weeks?—drunk out of your gourd."

"Now how do you know that?"

Justin glared. "I *asked*. Not that I had to. Housekeeping can only do so much."

"Aww, you didn't yell at any bartenders, did you? I gotta keep a good rep."

"Angelo, you're not to do that again! I don't care. If we get out of this alive, I'm taking you off the stuff entirely. Cold turkey."

The half-elf slumped forward. "Justin! You know what I went through, you were there!"

"I was there for the latter half. I'd heard from you and Stephen about the first half, which I assure you is quite enough. I'd say I couldn't imagine, but the fact is I don't have anyone in the Bailey Clan I'm close to like that."

Angelo bit into another piece of sweetsop. "Exactly. You don't know how I feel. You can't possibly imagine."

Justin sighed, biting into another piece himself. "Whatever. Let's just hurry this up."

The next half hour passed in relative silence, the slightest wind stirred by the rising sun causing the leaves above them to start to shudder. Their fruits consumed, Justin rolled up his bag and the two continued their trek.

Angelo's eyes never left that black speck on the caldera's rim.

* * *

Manas heard the sound of the teleportation pad in the other room, not looking up from his task. "Salamandro? How'd it go? What did they need to ask you?" Before he could react, the gnome was lifted off his seat and spun around in the air to face the half-orc.

"What aren't you telling me?"

Manas cracked a smile. "What do you mean, big guy?"

"I think you know exactly what I mean." Salamandro lifted him higher, closer to eye level. "You told me another Revered fell the same way Chevron did. Consumed by fire. I know you know more about it than that. Otherwise, you wouldn't have said anything."

The gnome shrugged. "Alright, so it happened while I was a member. Is that what you wanted to hear?"

Salamandro brought one hand back, still holding Manas with the other, and formed it into a fist. "I swear . . ."

Manas threw his hands up. "Wait a minute! What's the matter?"

"Give me all the details."

The gnome sighed. "I honestly don't know a whole lot more about it, but she knew it was coming. Told us to hang low for a while. Said it involved something about a bargain she had to uphold."

Salamandro's eyes softened. "A . . . bargain?"

"Yeah. She fell in love with some guy who couldn't use any magic. Never knew what she saw in him. She got pregnant, and around the time she was due she just . . . disappeared."

"Pregnant . . . Wait, disappeared?"

Manas nodded. "Yeah, she left and told us all not to follow or track her. That this was just something she had to do. But of course we kept tabs on her. You don't just up and leave like that without somebody worrying. And one day she was just dead. Burned to a crisp inside a little cave somewhere up in the mountains."

Diablo's eyes darted around, unfocused. His heart pounded in his chest. His mind raced. "Was . . . Was her husband a human?"

"What?"

The half-orc grunted and threatened with his fist again. "Was her husband a human!?"

"Whoa!" Manas squirmed. "Y-Yeah, I think so."

Diablo dropped the gnome straight back onto his ass. "OW! Dammit, what's going on with you!?"

The half-orc had already cleared half the distance back to the teleportation pad. "You just told me a story I know all too well. I know who the attacker is and why."

Boddyo rubbed at his backside. "What do you mean? Story?"

Salamandro paused, looking back. "You've just recounted to me the story of my mother."

*   *   *

Chevron's eyes were open again, bloodshot but remarkably undamaged considering the extent of his burns elsewhere. He looked back and forth between Luna and Dryad, the two now hovering over him. "Thank you both for your help. This would've been unbearable otherwise. I think I'd've died of dehydration long before now."

Dryad shrugged. "Well, we couldn't exactly just leave you."

"Yeah, I know. But still . . . thanks."

Luna bit her lip. His stilted manner of speech was rather different than the usual playful dwarf they'd grown to know. "How are you doing? You know . . . mentally?"

Chevron closed his eyes, the lids now shallow enough that his irises were still visible through them. "It's . . . weird. I feel alright, but there are a few places . . . some places where I can feel my mind is . . . missing? Like I'm not operating at full capacity."

The halfling nodded. "Salamandro had mentioned something about lack of oxygen, that you might've suffered real and permanent brain damage as a result."

Chevron cracked a smile. "Heh. You wanna know how I survived?"

The pair looked at each other, then back down to him. "What do you mean? What does that have to do—"

"I evacuated the air around myself." He stuck his tongue out. "I knew fire needed oxygen, so I just removed that fuel."

"Chevron! Man . . ." Dryad shook his head. "I mean, I know in the end it was a good thing, but—"

"Yeah, exactly. It was either be unable to breathe for a short bit and only likely die or absolutely die. Wasn't a tough choice in the moment."

"Yeah, I guess . . ." Luna pressed a hand to her forehead.

Rhox propped himself up on one of his arms, his own burns having healed significantly. "You clever bastard. Wish I could've done that, but then again my fire damage was a little less . . . extensive."

Chevron nodded, wincing as a bolt of pain shot up through his back. "Oh, hey, where's Miranda? I wanted to—"

Dryad and Luna exchanged another look, and the elf spoke. "Miranda's still working on the obsidian flow. With your . . . absence she's been working double-time to try and get it eroded."

"Damn." Chevron shook his head. "I wish I could be there helping her."

"She—" Luna caught herself but continued. "She definitely does too. But I don't mean that she wishes you were helping necessarily!

Just she wishes you weren't attacked. She's still kicking herself that she didn't check up on you earlier."

"Oh." The dwarf looked down at himself. "Well, that just means I'll have to recover quickly, doesn't it?"

Dryad rested a hand on the bulge in Chevron's bedsheet that corresponded to his own hand. "Listen, you take all the time you need, okay? You were badly beaten. The burns were one thing but you likely broke your spine and more than one rib. You're probably going to need some serious physical therapy after all is said and done."

Chevron nodded. "Yeah, I can feel that too. Every time I move my neck even I can practically feel the bones grinding on each other. Pretty sure several vertebrae have been dislocated, probably slipped a disk or two."

"Yeah, don't try to move more than that. You were groaning in pain while you were unconscious and we were trying to move you. I can't imagine how bad it'd be if you were aware of it."

"Hey, Luna," Rhox spoke from behind the elf, "you said you'd be checking up on Miranda, right?"

Luna nodded. "Yes, and I have. I guess you've been asleep for most of that too. She's fine, still the same as ever physically. Hasn't been attacked yet." She turned back to Chevron. "And she's thrilled that you're awake. I don't know that . . . any of us thought you'd come out of that."

Chevron grinned. "It takes more than that to take down a bull moose!"

Luna rolled her eyes. "If you're feeling good enough to crack jokes, you'll be back to your normal self in no time."

"Hah! Damn straight!"

*　*　*

Justin ducked under the cover of the copious trees at the edge of the Enchanted Rainforest and violently shook his head trying to fling the collected water out of his hair. Arms outstretched in front of him, he looked down at his robes, sighing in frustration. It seemed that ever since the sun had broken the eastern mountain horizon they'd been getting rained on. In fact, as he looked back over the obsidian flow where they'd come from then forward to where they still needed to go, he could hardly make out any individual speck without so much as a threatening cloud over it.

Angelo, seeing the mage dipping into the relative shelter of the trees, shrugged and joined him. Their paces had been more evenly matched thus far today, owing to the lack of the more extreme landscape they'd had to cross the day before. He lifted his shirt up over his head with some difficulty, the sopping fabric clinging to his waterlogged skin and weighted with what must have been an additional five pounds or so of rainwater. He too shook the water out of his hair, then held the garment in front of his person, wringing it out onto the saturated soil below. "Why, WHY is it raining so damn hard?"

Justin sighed. "It's the Revered. This lava flow wasn't exactly their ideal scenario. It cut off most traffic between Flood City and Monsoon City, even destroyed half of each."

"So? What do they care? Aren't they interested in the general balance and well-being of the world or some nonsense?"

"Well that's—" Justin paused as he processed Angelo's last few words. "Well that's exactly why they're trying to erode it. It represents a gross imbalance. Plant life can't thrive in it. Animals and people can't cross it. Except for birds I guess."

"So they're trying to erode it? Can't they just . . . whisk it away or something?"

Justin rubbed his eyebrows with a thumb and forefinger. "No, they can't 'just whisk it away.' One, that would require an absurd amount of magical ability, and two, that would represent an even larger imbalance. Erosion is just about the safest path."

Angelo looked forward toward the towering volcano still in view, if only just. "But why rain? Aren't there like half a dozen other things they could be using?"

"I don't know what you're imagining but water is the universal solvent. It'll wear this down eventually. Though I'll admit I'm a bit surprised."

"Surprised? By what?"

Justin gazed back over the obsidian again. "I just . . . I would've expected there to be a lot of wind too."

"Wind? Why?"

"Well, one of the Revered, Chevron, specializes in wind. It wouldn't be much against obsidian like this but it would be something. Wind erodes rock pretty well too. But instead . . ." Justin shook his head. "It's almost like Miranda's working overtime."

"Miranda?"

"The Revered of water. Boy, I really need to tell you more about these people. If they knew just how ignorant you are, they'd immediately stop suspecting us of trying to take them out."

"Whatever." Angelo spread his shirt open in front of himself, giving it a few strong whips into the air in an attempt to get more water out of its fibers before wriggling it on over his arms, then his head. "The faster we get to Feuerschloss, the less we have to deal with it, right?"

Justin extended a hand of protest as the half-elf strutted back into the storm. "Ugh . . . I guess you've got a point."

*   *   *

The thunder crashed and shook the very walls of the stone keep. Asmodeious, having taken up near permanent residence in Diablo's chambers, smirked up at the sky he couldn't see past the ceiling. "How truly ironic that it's raining, isn't it?"

He looked back down at the cauldron his apprentice had effectively abandoned. Diablo hadn't returned to the castle since his little attack on the one called Chevron. "They must be frantic at this point. I haven't seen Luna or Dryad since then either. And my less than faithful apprentice simply won't stop playing with them. He'll get his soon enough. But for now . . ."

The surface of the cauldron shimmered and an all too familiar image emerged. A middle-aged elven woman, jet-black hair cascading down her shoulders as she weaved her magic over the very land, trying to remove the blemish on the land.

The blemish he'd caused. His little mark on the world. Asmodeious grinned a wicked grin. "You know, little missy, a less forgiving individual might take offense at your intense desire to wipe out the evidence of their victory. No, I don't hate you for that. I understand even. To an extent. You don't want to do this any more than I want to do this." He ran a finger along the edge of the cauldron. "But the fact that you're capable of it only makes my need to do this more urgent."

He stepped away from the cauldron, rubbing his hands in anticipation, one thing he actually enjoyed about this humanoid form. "Diablo and the one called Manas have been hanging out together. I have to assume Luna and Dryad are too. They've wizened up. But Miranda has to tend to her little task. Either someone would have to stay with her and be bored out of their mind or else check up on her. And I've seen Luna checking up on her, so I know it's the latter."

He stepped back to the cauldron's side, peering in to watch Miranda struggle against her own encroaching exhaustion. "I just have to wait for her to show up and leave. She only appears once an hour or so. Once she leaves, Miranda will be ripe for the taking."

A series of loud bangs broke the dragon out of his reverie. "Is someone seriously knocking on the door?"

"Asmodeious! You great beast!"

I recognize that voice . . .

"Get your scaly black ass out here and fight!"

17

Attack

THE GREAT DOORS parted and out stepped the figure of Angelo's nightmares, the still humanoid form of the dragon Asmodeious. Deep-black robes cascaded down his body, and his walk was such that he almost seemed to float over the ground as he moved through the threshold. His yellow eyes widened as he saw his callers. *How . . . How did they survive THAT?*

Before him stood the two individuals who'd attacked Feuerschloss before, Angelo and Justin. The two he hadn't confirmed as dead like their compatriots, Stephen and John. He couldn't imagine that anyone could have survived the flow he'd sent after them; they had been rapidly losing ground even when they fled here, and it's not like they could have rapidly climbed the cliff to the north that had kept it bound. Not fast enough to escape it. Yet here they both were, totally physically unscathed as far as he could tell.

No matter.

"You know, I have a policy about trespassers."

Justin stepped forward, arms braced in front of himself in both a defensive, and given his admittedly limited but still available magic, offensive position. "Asmodeious. You've been attacking the Revered, haven't you?"

The dragon smirked. "Is that what they're calling themselves? Awfully presumptuous. Can't even survive against a measly dragon like myself."

"What do you mean?" Justin tried to ready a spell but couldn't focus his mind. "Rhox survived. He'd just been assaulted."

"Oh, did they not tell you? I guess it did only happen a few days ago."

"What? What happened?"

Asmodeious shrugged in an exaggerated manner. "Oh, I just killed the one called Chevron is all."

Angelo's face fell and Justin lowered his guard. "W-wait, you killed . . . ?"

"I absolutely did. A lot easier than I'd expected too. Hardly struggled."

"So that's why there wasn't any wind . . ." Justin brought his hands back up. "You . . . You monster! Why? Why are you attacking them?"

"Oh, it's simple really. They seem to think they're better than me." Asmodeious stepped forward without hesitation, and Angelo and Justin both stepped back. "They're powerful, I'll grant. But their decision to enlist my own apprentice was the last straw."

"Your . . ." Angelo's face fell to one of shock. "Diablo?"

"Who else? You think I'd permit anyone else to live here?"

Justin's eyes darted as he pondered what their enemy was saying. "So . . . But that makes sense. That explains the altar, the sudden interest in the Revered. The reason they think we're attacking them."

"Hah! You? You couldn't hurt a fly."

The elf shook his head. "We'll make you change that tune real quick!"

"So it's a fight you want?" Asmodeious chuckled and closed his eyes, his body already starting to expand, head rising toward the top of the castle behind him. His black robes fused to his body; a pair of thick leathery wings sprouted from his back and were quickly joined by a pair of horns from the back of his head. His eyes opened once more—large, draconic—and gazed down at the pair. In one swift motion of his forelimb he swept them into his grasp, then tossed them up into the air behind them.

Justin's limbs flailed wildly as he sailed through the air; Angelo, on the other hand, tucked his arms and legs in against his torso. Both landed on top of the castle; Justin on his back, Angelo on his side.

With a powerful beat of his wings, Asmodeious leapt off the ground, and in a single bound landed on them both, one under each forepaw. The weight was enough to make them both squirm.

"Oh, but this isn't terribly sporting, is it?" Asmodeious grinned down at them. "I could . . . CRUSH"—he swiftly shifted his weight forward onto the two, feeling several ribs on each crack beneath his feet—"both of you rather easily like this. And that's hardly fun!" He rippled his feet on top of them, feeling a strange bit of resistance on the half-elf in particular. He lifted that limb and spotted the source—a sword strapped to his belt.

The dragon smirked and stepped back from both of them, shifting back down into his humanoid form. He thrust his right arm forward, closing his eyes. The air in front of him shimmered, the distortion narrowing into a horizontal line at his hand. With a flash, a claymore materialized in his grip.

"Pick up your weapon, boy. You wanted a fight, now you've got one."

Angelo, still on his side, groaned as the dragon's weight lifted off him. He hardly needed prompting. Asmodeious having lifted his assault, he'd be foolish to not reach for the sword still on his hip. Justin sat up, shaking his head, trying to clear the definite concussion he suffered hitting the stone roof so hard, as the swordsman shakily pushed himself up onto his feet.

The half-elf took a moment to regain his breath; it seemed Asmodeious was willing to give him that much if only to toy with them. He knew that's what this was. He was the proverbial mouse tossed into the air by the cat that was before him, then allowed to run so it can be caught once more.

"I didn't know dragons played with their food."

Asmodeious scoffed. "Food? You aren't fit to be the garnish on my dishes. I don't bother consuming people." He swiped the claymore to his side, holding it in one hand. "Too full of shit."

Justin watched the strange exchange, the gears in his head starting to turn in spite of their concussed limitations. *Food . . . Asmodeious had been eating . . . something, something exotic. What was it . . . ?*

Angelo yanked the ornamental instrument from his belt, drew the blade, and tossed the sheath aside, bringing the sword to his own front. The thing clattered toward the rooftop access door just opening to reveal a face Angelo could hardly forget—his own half-brother. Now officially caught in a pincer, he dared not let his guard down on the dragon.

"You know, it's really too bad you survived," Asmodeious began, eyes flitting to the opening door for the briefest of moments. "I haven't regretted not killing someone since that woman from River City."

Justin was pulled from his train of thought by those words. "Woman from River City?" *Could she be . . . ?*

"Oh yes. A feisty woman that one. Too powerful for her own good. Much the same as you and your friend, I imagine she somehow managed to escape my destruction of that little habitation and followed me to my next target. After a lengthy, arduous fight, she was at death's door but ultimately she made a bargain with me to stop my planned destruction of Flood City." He smirked, motioning with the slightest of nods toward the now open door. "It was frustrating, but the price I extracted from her seems to have been somewhat worth it so far."

Angelo dropped his sword, his eyes darting, unfocused, then up to Asmodeious and back to the half-orc in the doorway. *He's talking about . . . Diablo's mother.* His face twisted to an expression of pain then grief then fury; without any thought, without even realizing he was doing it, he raised his sword and charged, screaming, toward the dragon.

Asmodeious merely stepped to one side and Angelo almost fell off balance as his sword came down through thin air. "Gracious boy, it's almost like it's your first time with a sword." Angelo grunted and slashed his weapon to the side he was being taunted from, only for the dragon to leap up, again evacuating the space. "Didn't your parents ever tell you not to play with them? They're *awfully* dangerous."

"I swear . . ." Angelo panted, eyes still locked on the figure now floating back to the roof. "I swear I'll avenge them. His mother, Springsboro, Stephen . . ."

"You know," Asmodeious rebutted as his feet hit the ground, only to dodge once more out of the way of the blade. "I didn't actually kill him. In fact, *technically*"—and another swift jump out of the way of a swinging sword—"I already avenged his death by killing the man who actually killed him. If anything, you should be more *grateful* . . ." Asmodeious rolled to the left, avoiding another swing, and kicked at Angelo with all his might. "To me."

The half-elf flew several feet backward, his hand involuntarily releasing the sword as he fell to the ground and rolled several times from the force of the blow.

Diablo dared not intervene in this fight. He looked to Asmodeious, then the half-elf on the ground, and over to Justin. If he interfered, his master would surely kill him like he'd done John. And if he didn't, there was the chance . . .

Justin's eyes flashed as he remembered. He'd discovered Asmodeious had been eating unicorn before! *There's a spell for that, isn't there?* He closed his eyes, trying to take advantage of the dragon's distraction in the moment to buy himself a bit more time.

Angelo shook all over as he rose back to his feet, brushing himself off. He limped toward his sword, picking the weapon up off the ground, straightening his back and brandishing it as he had before. "My name is Angelo Villalobos. You killed my father. Prepare to die."

Asmodeious smirked. *He didn't even change the name.* "Oh come now, I kill a lot of people." He brushed off his claymore-wielding sleeve, bringing the weapon to bear. "I probably killed your mother too. Does that not warrant anything?"

Angelo might as well have blacked out. He let out a blood-curdling scream as he raised his sword up over his head and charged straight at Asmodeious.

Justin's eyes flashed open and he swiped his hand in front of him. The spell was complete.

Asmodeious chuckled at the half-elf's form. *He's left himself wide open.* He brought the claymore down to his own midsection, anticipating the final blow.

Angelo brought his own sword down as well, laying it horizontally in front of him; as he got close enough to his adversary, he spun around, deflecting the massive blade. Asmodeious corrected, lifting the hilt of the claymore and pointing the blade down, instinctively blocking.

Angelo howled, and upon finishing his twirl, thrust his sword. The blade glowed with a barely perceptible light, and Asmodeious' eyes grew wide as he watched his own blade shatter in half, the half-elf's sword plunging through and finding its mark—the mark Justin's spell had granted it—through his rib cage and straight into his heart.

Both looked down at the sudden wound with astonishment, the slightest moment of strange peace befalling the scene before it began gushing blood. Asmodeious staggered back, pulling himself off the blade and clutching the gaping hole with a blackening hand. He looked up at Angelo, eyes wide, pupils shaking. His mouth formed words but no sound left his lips as his body grew. He collapsed onto his side, black scales flowing over his form, a pair of wings spasming out of his back. He looked to the elf that had cast the spell, his eyes growing wide. He lifted a forelimb, extending a claw toward Justin.

"You! You're—"

His yellow eyes grew glassy as his body finally stopped moving, slumping where it was, blood still pouring out of his chest.

Diablo shook the shock off himself and ran forward to try to help his master. In that moment, it didn't matter that he'd been trying to kill the rest of the Revered and likely would have killed him too—Asmodeious was his master, the closest thing to a parental figure he'd ever known. But as he checked the dragon's neck, he knew it wasn't necessary—Asmodeious was certainly dead.

Angelo looked down at his bloody blade, chest heaving. He'd done it. He had no idea how but he'd done it. He'd avenged Stephen, John, his parents.

Diablo's mother.

"So why. . ."

Diablo and Justin both looked to the half-elf.

"Why . . . Why don't I feel anything? Why doesn't this feel any different? I've killed him. I've killed him, dammit!" He threw the sword across the roof, metal clanging and sparking against the igneous stone.

Diablo looked back down to Asmodeious' body, squeezing a tear out of his eyes. "Come with me."

"What?"

The half-orc stood up and shook his head. "Come with me. I have something to show you."

Angelo watched as his half-brother strode across the rooftop, back to the door from which he'd emerged mere moments ago. *What . . . Show me? What could he possibly . . . ?* But in that moment, feeling almost numb already, he shrugged. *I want to trust him. I want to see him as my family.*

Justin, still dumbfounded that his spell had worked, watched as Angelo began walking toward the door as well. He shook his head, leapt from his squatted position, and ran to join his companion.

The trio stepped down the staircase with which Diablo was all too familiar, which Angelo and Justin had climbed but one time, but that had burned itself in their memories. Two doors down, on the left, the half-orc led them to his chamber, his meager laboratory.

"Come, look." He motioned to the two to join him beside the cauldron in the center of the room. "This is a Clairvoyance Cauldron."

Justin nodded. He'd tried to create one himself before but hadn't been successful. He felt some amount of jealousy toward the half-orc but quickly reprimanded himself—there'd been a reason he was chosen as a Revered after all. Strangest of all though was a sense of . . . pride? Maybe pride at seeing one finally.

Diablo touched the surface, bringing up a user interface; his fingers moved so quickly, neither Angelo nor Justin could tell what he was doing, but once he'd set it he stepped back, the surface shimmering for a moment before showing a scene that had been extremely familiar to the half-elf—a parlor, sunlight filtering gently through the light, airy window curtains. A human peered out of the door to the kitchen, mouthing something but no sound emerged. In the room, an elf woman reclined, eyes closed and smiling.

The sunlight through the window dimmed and suddenly the scene became dramatically different, intensely dark. The human ran through the room to the front door and threw it open, peering through to the sky. He shook his head, slamming the door and motioning to the elf to join him. Her relaxed face melted to one of concern as she stood and ran to him.

The two hurried through the parlor into the kitchen and the scene flicked to join them, tracking them as the human opened the only door in here, revealing a set of stairs leading down. Both scurried through it, closing it behind them.

Again the screen flicked and they were in a stairwell, both descending rapidly into an old unused root cellar. Angelo's eyes began to water.

Scenes he could only remember. Scenes he would never see again. The room where his mother sang him songs. The home where his father rode him around on his shoulders. The village where he met his best friend.

He knew what was coming. He knew why his parents were cowering in that corner of the cellar. He couldn't erase that vision from his mind. No amount of alcohol could cleanse it from his mental palate.

And in a flash it was realized. The scene was enveloped in bright, blinding light, tongues of fire barely differentiating against the brilliant background. This held for several minutes and Justin looked over, mouth agape, at the half-elf for whom this display was meant.

Angelo's lips were pulled tight from the corners, tugged down, lower teeth bared; his nose ran, his tears flowed down his cheeks.

The rain finally penetrated the flames enough to bring them down out of view. The home had been decimated. Where once had been walls and sturdy beams, now only brittle charcoal remained. And there, in the middle of the scene, two charred corpses clung to each other, embracing even in death.

Angelo dropped to his knees, his head growing dizzy. "Wh-why did you . . ."

Justin knelt down beside him, grabbing his shoulders and shaking him. "Angelo! Angelo, come on! I know, I know this was tragic and traumatic. But you need to snap out of it!"

Diablo motioned to the view, now frozen on the two blackened bodies. "I showed this to you to show you why nothing feels any different. Your parents were, unfortunately, like my own—weak, helpless, unable to survive." He looked back down at the scene. "I was too young to know him, but if what you said before is correct, your father was my father, so that's no surprise. But they're dead. They have ceased to be, and there's nothing that can be done to change that."

Angelo opened his eyes and looked up at his half-brother.

"Your endeavor here was pointless. Nothing of value was gained nor lost by your actions."

Justin yelped as suddenly he was thrown backward onto his back. He watched in almost slow-motion as Angelo sprang to his feet, screaming to the void. The half-elf grabbed the side of the cauldron and yanked as hard as he could, twisting it around onto its side and spilling the contents all over the floor as Diablo scrambled to try to stop it.

Angelo turned toward one of the shelves in the room. He reached out and clutched the side, wrenching it away from the wall and down over the mess, onto his half-brother in the process. As trinkets and baubles skittered across the floor, the half-elf ran for the door, Justin reaching out a hand to try to stop him from his own compromised position.

Still shrieking, Angelo bolted down the hall, back toward the staircase to the roof. Justin scrambled to his feet, hurrying behind his companion.

The half-elf leapt up the stairs three at a time, tears clouding his vision. Justin more cautiously took each step but scrambled up just the same.

Outside, a great rain had begun pelting the keep, already having washed much of the dragon's blood off the stone. Angelo turned and barreled around the corner of the small encroachment on the roof that housed the stairs. Justin threw the door open and lunged forward uselessly.

With no hesitation, no slowing, not even a second thought, Angelo leaped from the side of the roof.

"Angelo!" Justin's eyes followed the half-elf's body as it disappeared below the parapet. "No . . . Dammit, Angelo."

The elf picked himself up off the roof and scurried back down the stairs, down the hall, past the door behind which remained Diablo, still pinned under a bookshelf. Down the grand staircase, through the grand entry hall, and out the massive front door Asmodeious hadn't closed behind himself.

There, in a crumpled heap in front of the castle, was Angelo. Having flung himself off the roof straight forward, he'd landed on his own front, no attempts made to break the fall.

Justin ran forward to his side. He grabbed the half-elf's wrist and felt.

It was weak but he could feel a pulse.

He'd attempted suicide but by some miracle had survived.

"Angelo! Angelo!" Justin dropped the wrist and lifted the half-elf's head with both hands, shaking him around. But he didn't respond. He may have survived the fall but he was out cold. The mage couldn't imagine the sort of damage he'd done to himself. Probably several broken bones at the very least.

He looked around, left and right, trying to think. He spotted a tree, the tree by which they'd left their provisions in the event that, by another miracle, they survived their encounter with Asmodeious.

He carefully set Angelo's head back down and ran to the supplies already growing damp from the rain. He hurriedly tugged Angelo's sleeping bag out of the pile, shaking it open. He ran back to Angelo's side, unzipping the bag on his way. He lay the thing out flat on the ground and carefully, gingerly rolled the unconscious half-elf onto it. He then zipped it closed again.

It wasn't much but it was something. Something to protect him from the elements, to keep his body temperature regulated.

Justin knelt and closed his eyes, sighing. "Okay . . . One, two, three—" He hefted the limp form up onto his shoulder, staggering forward as he struggled to maintain balance even as low as he was. Taking a few more deep breaths, he stood, shaky legs pushing him up off the ground, the half-elf with him.

He looked back to the pile of supplies. "I'm sorry, Don Kane. I don't believe I'll be able to return them." He then turned and gave one final look at the looming castle keep on the rim of the caldera.

"Goodbye, Diablo Villalobos, Revered of Fire."

As the rain battered his robes, Justin turned away from Feuerschloss and trudged down the side of the volcano, down toward the obsidian flow, toward Monsoon City, toward his familiar life, toward some semblance of hope.

EPILOGUE

MIRANDA RELUCTANTLY STEPPED out of her meditation chamber, peering toward the central room of the Edifice. She couldn't rightly believe Salamandro had called a meeting, but considering she and Manas were the only other two who weren't presently staying there full-time anyway . . . she shrugged. It wasn't too far-fetched.

As she emerged from the hallway onto the central dais, she saw the other Revered all turn to look. "Ah, Miranda. Glad you could join us."

"Sorry I'm late. I was dealing with . . . Well, you know." She vaguely motioned down with a hand. "What's going on?"

Dryad shrugged. "Salamandro here wanted us all present for something. He must think it's awfully important because he asked me and Luna what the best method was to get you and Manas here so we could all hear it."

"And you told him—"

"To just ask, yeah." The halfling shrugged. "I know you're busy, but . . ."

"Whatever." Miranda crossed her arms. "Well, it looks like everyone's here now. So what is it? What's so urgent?"

Salamandro's cheeks flushed as he hunched forward. Manas jabbed him in the thigh with an elbow.

"R-Right. So . . ." He looked at the two beds still in the chamber. "I was just attacked. Same as Rhox and Chevron."

"Wh—Attacked!?" Luna's eyes lit up. "Salamandro, you should have said something sooner!"

"Well, I'm saying it now."

"Are you alright? Any injuries?"

The half-orc shook his head. "I got lucky, I'm sure. I managed to evade a direct ambush. I think they were hoping I'd go down like Chevron did, but after having seen that, I was on guard."

"I see . . ." Miranda braced herself on Chevron's bed. "But you're here! What of your attacker?"

"I wasn't able to do much," he shrugged, "but I did manage to deliver a devastating blow to one of them."

"One of them?" Manas cocked an eyebrow as he looked up at the half-orc. "There were two?"

"Aye. The swordsman and the wizard. Our attackers are Angelo and Justin."

Lightning Source UK Ltd.
Milton Keynes UK
UKHW041911090421
381754UK00008B/401/J

9 781664 166356